Lady Catherine's

Accident

A PRIDE AND PREJUDICE VARIATION

LINDA C. THOMPSON

Lady Catherine's Accident - A Pride and Prejudice Variation
First Edition

For information, please contact:
Linda C. Thompson Books
1700 Lynhurst Lane
Denton, TX   76205

Cover Design: Linda Thompson
Cover Photo: Depositphotos.com
Photo By: Montana (Ingrid Perlstrom)
Graphic Flourishes: Lori Whitlock
Flourish By: insima (Indre Simonaviciute)

ISBN-13: 978-1-7332420-4-2

DEDICATION

A little over twenty-four years ago, an extraordinary young man came into my life and stole my heart. My son, Andrew, is a special young man who is loving and caring, particularly to his mom and sisters. He is kind, responsible, and a hard worker. Watching him grow has been a joy, and I am proud of the young man he has grown up to be.

I dedicate this book to "my best beau."

TABLE OF CONTENTS

1. All Because of Cook's Special Tea

Elizabeth Bennet's visit to Hunsford Parsonage was in its third week. At first, she had hesitated to accept the invitation, as she could not imagine spending several weeks with her ridiculous cousin, Mr. William Collins. The previous autumn, Mr. Collins had paid his first visit to Longbourn, Elizabeth's home, and the estate he would inherit when Mr. Bennet passed away. Elizabeth doubted Mr. Collins would be gracious to her or her family after she turned down his marriage proposal. The intelligent young woman desired to marry for love, and Mr. Collins had no affection for her. He proved this when, only two days after Elizabeth's rejection, he proposed to her best friend, Charlotte Lucas, who was now the new Mrs. Collins, However, Elizabeth could not refuse her friend's entreaties to visit. Therefore, she found herself in Kent.

The visit unfolded much as Elizabeth expected. Mr. Collins's thoughtless words, which he had designed to make Elizabeth regret her refusal, instead simply insulted her friend. Fortunately, Lady Catherine demanded much from her parson, which limited Elizabeth's contact with him to meal times. She enjoyed exploring the beautiful grounds of Rosings Park and the time she spent with her dear friend.

The most disconcerting aspect of her visit was not her sycophantic cousin, but the presence of the disagreeable Mr. Darcy, whose acquaintance she had made the previous autumn. When a friend of his had let Netherfield Park, the estate bordering Elizabeth's home at Longbourn, Mr. Darcy had visited to acquaint the man with estate management. Elizabeth's relationship with Mr. Darcy had begun on rocky ground when the man insulted Elizabeth at the local assembly. Subsequent meetings between them often ended in verbal jousting. What cemented her poor opinion of the gentleman was her learning of his dealings with Mr. Wickham.

Seeing him on that first Sunday at church shocked Elizabeth. Mr. Collins explained that Lady Catherine's nephews visited for a fortnight each Easter. He examined his aunt's books and assisted with anything she might need. Though the group from the parsonage had already dined twice at Rosings, Elizabeth hoped that, with her nephews visiting, Lady Catherine would no longer desire their company. In that case, Elizabeth might easily avoid meeting the proud, arrogant Mr. Darcy.

Much to her surprise, the next morning, on her walk through the groves around the estate, she encountered the gentleman whom she hoped to avoid. He greeted her politely, but rather than continue on his way, he remained to walk with her. Elizabeth did not understand why since he spoke not a word. The next afternoon, Darcy visited the parsonage, bringing his charming cousin, Colonel Andrew Fitzwilliam, with him. The colonel was entertaining, witty, and quick to laugh. Elizabeth found him pleasant company, but though Mr. Darcy continued to stare at her, as he had in Hertfordshire, he spoke little. Stopping briefly at the parsonage gate while out riding the following day, the men greeted the ladies, causing Elizabeth's confusion and frustration to mount. This pattern continued into the next week. Though Elizabeth enjoyed the friendly colonel, he made it clear that second sons could not marry where they wished. Mr. Darcy, however, remained staring, grave, and silent with each passing day. Elizabeth could only assume he disapproved of her, but if that were the case, why the continued meetings?

This morning, on her walk through the beautiful grounds, Elizabeth felt the warmth of the bright sunshine on her face. A light breeze gently moved the tendrils of loose hair. Elizabeth could hear the buzz of the bees as they flitted from one fragrant flower to the next. She could almost taste their sweet perfume.

Rounding a curve in the path, Elizabeth encountered Colonel Fitzwilliam, and they exchanged greetings. As they walked, the colonel, suspecting Darcy had feelings for the intelligent, witty, lovely young woman, tried to impress upon Miss Bennet the excellent qualities of his cousin.

"Mr. Darcy did seem uncommonly concerned for Mr. Bingley, often offering his unsolicited opinions," Elizabeth commented.

"Bingley is a young man learning his way around the ton and the behaviors considered acceptable in the first circles. Darcy has saved Bingley from himself on several occasions. He often falls in love at first sight, and the women are usually more interested in his money than in him. My cousin is very protective of those for whom he cares. As we journeyed to Kent, Darcy spoke of rescuing Bingley from a similar situation recently."

"Why does Mr. Darcy think himself better informed of the ladies' feelings than Mr. Bingley is? Is he well acquainted with those women, or does Mr. Darcy make assumptions based on his prejudices rather than sincere observation of those involved?"

"Women began throwing themselves at Darcy from a young age. When his father died, as Darcy completed his education at Cambridge, the situation became worse. Being the owner, and not just the heir, of an extensive estate was like having a target painted on his back. It forced him to learn to expeditiously judge others' intentions."

"And you feel he possesses the skills to make accurate judgments?"

"Having always been a thoughtful individual, Darcy studies situations from all sides before making the best decision for all involved. In my experience, he is rarely wrong."

"How wonderful for him." Sarcasm leeched from her voice, causing the colonel to look at her. "Being omnipotent must be a heady accomplishment." Elizabeth's harsh tone surprised him further. "In this most recent situation, did Mr. Darcy give the reasons for his interference?"

"From frequent observations, Darcy did not discern any particular regard on the lady's part. However, her mother's loudly voiced opinions on Bingley's fortune and an imminent engagement painted the mother as an inveterate matchmaker."

"Might mitigating circumstances exist of which Mr. Darcy was unaware?"

"I am sure Darcy weighed all the evidence."

"I would hope so. Otherwise, everyone involved would be hurt, perhaps needlessly. Colonel, would you please excuse me. A headache is developing. Perhaps I stayed in the sun too long today." Elizabeth turned toward the parsonage and hurried away. She did not want the gentleman to see the angry tears filling her eyes, nor did she wish to say something she would later regret. Outrage coursed through Elizabeth at hearing her dearest sister, Jane, described as an uncaring fortune hunter. Upon reaching the parsonage, she rushed to her room and locked the door behind her. Charlotte allowed Elizabeth some space, but as the time drew near to depart for dinner at Rosings, she tentatively knocked at the door. Elizabeth's eyes were red and dull from crying, so Charlotte convinced her husband that Elizabeth was not well enough to attend the dinner with them.

All the way to the manor house, Mr. Collins worried that his patroness, Lady Catherine de Bourgh, would take offense at Elizabeth's absence. If he knew the great lady would be relieved at his cousin's failure to attend, Mr. Collins would suffer agony. Lady Catherine worried her nephew, Fitzwilliam Darcy of Pemberley in Derbyshire, was entirely too drawn to the impertinent young woman from Hertfordshire. She did not wish anything to upset her plans to marry her daughter to Darcy. However, her worries grew when, after learning Miss Elizabeth would not be joining them for dinner, Darcy rushed from the room, claiming urgent business.

After gathering his hat and gloves, the gentleman exited the back of the house, then rushed to the stables. He paced, patting his crop against his thigh as he waited for the horse to be readied. Vaulting into the saddle, Darcy kicked his mount and galloped in the direction of the parsonage.

Hours later, Elizabeth's fury and headache had both begun to subside, though not enough that she wished to spend the evening in Mr. Darcy's company. Consequently, shortly after the Collinses's departure, Elizabeth descended the stairs with a request for tea and a bit to eat. She missed luncheon and would not partake in the dinner at Rosings Park.

"Is your headache improved, miss?" asked the maid, Sally.

"Somewhat. Thank you for your concern."

Elizabeth moved into Charlotte's small back parlor and curled up in the chair close to the fire. Though spring had arrived, the evenings remained cool. The fire's warmth helped ease the tension in her body, and Elizabeth took comfort in the crackling sound it made. Soon, the maid returned, carrying the tea tray, a sandwich, and biscuits. She prepared a cup for Miss Bennet and stood to wait for further instructions. With her head resting against the wing of the chair, Elizabeth enjoyed the flames' flickering light as they cast patterns on the walls.

Taking a sip, she sighed with pleasure. "This is an exceptional blend."

"Cook always makes this when someone suffers from a headache," replied the maid as she bobbed a curtsey and exited the room, leaving Elizabeth to enjoy the silence.

Elizabeth enjoyed her third cup of tea and felt much better. She was extremely relaxed when a knock at the front door sounded. With the family out for the evening, Elizabeth expected the servant to turn away the visitor. However, a moment later, a knock sounded on the sitting room door.

"Mr. Darcy to see you, miss."

With a little wobble, Elizabeth gained her feet. "Mr. Darcy, what are you doing here?" Her speech was slightly slurred, her tone angry.

Startled by this reception, Darcy continued in a halting fashion, "Mr. Collins informed us you were unwell. I was worried about you."

"You do not need to concern yourself with me, Mr. Darcy." The slur to her speech and her cold tone astonished him. "Please be seated." Waving at the chair across from hers, Elizabeth slumped back into her seat and reached for her teacup. She waited for him to speak. Elizabeth would not make the situation easier for the arrogant man by making polite conversation.

Darcy stared at Elizabeth for several moments, then jumped up and began pacing before her chair. Sipping her tea, she watched as he strode back and forth across the small space.

Though she determined not to speak until he did, Elizabeth surprised herself by blurting, "How could you?"

Darcy looked at her, shocked at the tears in her voice and the glittering anger in her eyes. "How could I what?"

"How could you interfere between Jane and Mr. Bingley? You broke my sister's heart and left her vulnerable to my mother's laments as well as the derision of the neighborhood."

Darcy, startled into outspokenness, said, "Do you mean your sister cared for my friend?"

"Of course she did."

"She did not show it. I thought she was only doing as your mother instructed."

"Just because my mother wishes us to marry the first wealthy man who comes along does not mean Jane and I agree. After watching our parents' unequal match, we desired to marry only for the greatest of loves."

"I want the same for both myself and my friend."

"If that is the case, you did not act in your friend's best interest. Did you also keep her presence from him while she was in London this winter?"

Darcy looked at Elizabeth in surprise. "Miss Bennet was in London?"

"Yes, she returned after Christmas with my Aunt and Uncle Gardiner. She will remain until my return from Kent."

"Did she visit Miss Bingley and Mrs. Hurst?"

"Indeed, she did. They pretended to not have received her letters, rushed her out on some flimsy pretense, and waited over a month to return the call, only to stay all of fifteen minutes. Also, there was the letter Miss Bingley sent upon your departure." Elizabeth's tears were increasing.

"What letter?"

"Miss Bingley told Jane they did not plan to return or think they would miss the area. Then she indicated Miss Darcy would soon be her sister."

"That is ridiculous. My sister is just turned ten and six and is not yet out in society. Bingley looks at Georgiana as a little sister."

"Oh, poor Jane." Elizabeth's tears turned into sobs.

Darcy rushed to her side and took one of her hands in his. "Please do not cry. I shall write to Bingley and tell him where your sister is. I am sorry I interfered. I did not think she loved him. She is so serene that determining her emotions is not easy."

On a sob, Elizabeth asked, "Why was it your job to determine her feelings? Why did you not trust Mr. Bingley to understand her affection for him?"

"I am sorry, Miss Elizabeth. I thought I was doing what was best for my friend, particularly when both his sisters also suggested Miss Bennet had no feelings for their brother."

An inelegant sniff was Elizabeth's only reply.

Darcy held her hand until her sobs subsided into hiccups. "I think you are still unwell," he said. "If you will meet me in the glade tomorrow, where we previously walked on several occasions, the letter for Bingley will be ready to send. Once I get the address from you, I will take the letter to the express office, add the address, and send it on its way. Would that be acceptable? I am sorry for any pain I caused you or your sister. It was unintentional. I thought I was protecting my friend from an unequal alliance. My parents were two of the best people I knew. I loved and respected both of them. They shared a tremendous love, and though it is not a common reason for marriage in our society, it is what I want for those close to me."

"If you loved--hic--and respected--hic--your father so much--hic--how could you--hic--ignore his wishes for--hic--Mr. Wickham--hic?"

Darcy dropped her hands and reared back, almost falling to the ground. "Wickham. What does he have to do with anything?"

"If you respected your father so much, why did you deny Mr. Wickham the living promised to him? You forced him into poverty."

"Wickham's poverty is of his own making. He is a compulsive gambler and constantly living above his means. Everywhere he goes, he runs up debts and walks out on them. His behavior with women is even more shameful. I have found homes for two of the women he abused and left with children. There are rumors of him forcing himself on unwilling young women. One, who was only four and ten, died in childbirth. I am grateful he did not want the living. I compensated him with one thousand pounds that my father left him and an additional three thousand in lieu of the living, to which Wickham signed away all his rights."

Elizabeth looked shocked. "What are you saying?"

"There is no easy way for me to say this other than to tell you the truth. Mr. Wickham is a liar, cheat, gambler, and womanizer."

Collapsing back into her chair, Elizabeth sat stunned. Slowly, her eyes closed, and then Darcy heard a soft sound like a snore.

Rushing to the doorway, Darcy called, "Come quickly. Something is wrong with Miss Elizabeth."

The maid came running but paused in the doorway.

"One moment she was talking and the next she is asleep. What could have caused this?"

The maid walked over to the teapot and lifted the lid. "She drank several cups of the cook's special tea for headaches, which probably put her to sleep."

"What makes it good for headaches?"

"Cook laces it with Irish whiskey."

"Good heavens. Did Miss Elizabeth realize what she was drinking?"

"No, sir, only that it was for headaches."

"I have never seen Miss Elizabeth drink so much as a full glass of wine. She will awake tomorrow sick to her stomach and with a far worse headache than she has now. I will have my valet bring something that you should deliver to her room upon her waking. I will carry her to her room for you, and then I must write a note to her. You will speak of this to no one. Do you understand?"

"Yes, sir."

Darcy followed the maid up the stairs, carrying Elizabeth, who was light as a feather. "Please prepare her for bed while I write my note." Darcy exited after a brief look back at the woman asleep on the bed. He entered the parlor and went straight to the writing desk. He pulled out a sheet of paper, prepared a pen, and dipped it in ink. The only sound in the room was the pen scratching across the paper. Darcy was folding the pages when the maid returned downstairs. Sealing the note, he handed her the letter. "Please place this on Miss Elizabeth's bedside table. She must receive this upon waking. Also, no one--not even your master or mistress--is to learn I was here this evening. Do I have your promise?"

"Yes, sir." With the maid's agreement, he dropped a few coins into her hand.

Knowing it was getting late, Darcy rushed from the house and vaulted into the saddle. He kicked his horse, turned away from Rosings, and galloped across the fields to avoid meeting the Collinses returning from dinner. Darcy entered the house and, using the back stairs, made his way to his room, where he locked the door behind him. Then Darcy rang for his valet. When Clarke arrived, Darcy asked him to write out the recipe for the hangover remedy and deliver it to the maid at the parsonage. "Please remind her to give it to Miss Elizabeth as soon as she has awoken."

The valet looked at his master, surprise in his expression, but he refrained from commenting beyond, "Yes, Mr. Darcy. Will there be anything else?"

"No. Well, yes. Please ensure the maid has all the necessary ingredients. If not, gather what she needs from the kitchens here and deliver them to her as well. Please return to me when you have completed your tasks."

"Of course, sir."

Darcy watched Clarke exit before removing his jacket, cravat, and waistcoat and pouring himself a drink. He settled in a chair before the fire and, while watching the wavy light patterns that the flames cast on the walls, thought about his conversation with Elizabeth. *How did she know I interfered in the relationship between Miss Bennet and Bingley? She was so angry with me. All this time, I assumed Elizabeth felt for me as I did for her. I thought she was waiting for my proposal. Obviously, there are some misunderstandings between us. I will need to mend them before I can pay my address to her. If I repair the relationship between Bingley and Miss Bennet, would that be enough to win her favor? What was all that about Wickham? Did she believe Wickham's lies? I thought her more discerning. However, Father was one of the most intelligent men I have ever known, and he never saw through Wickham's roguish charm. Perhaps we can speak more about this tomorrow and maybe Miss Elizabeth will give me a chance to improve her opinion of me.*

A knock came at the door. Andrew called, "Darcy, are you in there? Let me in."

Darcy opened the door and admitted his cousin. He locked the door behind him. "Aunt Catherine is furious. Where did you go?"

"I had something important to which I needed to attend."

"What was so important for you to miss dinner?"

"My concern for Miss Elizabeth. Did you perhaps see her today when you took your walk about the estate?"

"Indeed, I did. We walked together for a time. I spoke about what a good man and caring friend you are?"

"What exactly did you say?"

"She mentioned your solicitude toward Bingley. I told her how you looked out for him through the years."

"Did you speak of anything specific?"

"I told her how you rescued him from mercenary young ladies in London, and one a short while ago."

"I need to know exactly what you said."

Fitzwilliam repeated the conversation to the best of his memory.

"So that is how she knew. No wonder she was so angry with me."

"What are you talking about, Darcy?"

"I went to see Miss Elizabeth to inquire about her health. She spoke rather harshly and demanded an explanation of my interference in the relationship between Bingley and her elder sister."

"The mercenary young woman with the dreadful mother is Miss Elizabeth's relation?"

"Yes, but I learned tonight that I misjudged Miss Bennet. Her serenity is like my mask. Miss Elizabeth accused me of breaking her sister's heart."

"I am sorry, Darcy. If I had known of whom you spoke, I would never have said anything to her."

"Do not worry, Andrew. I am glad for the opportunity to fix my mistake. Bingley has not been the same since we left Hertfordshire. He did not recover from this infatuation as he did the others. His feelings were deeper than I expected. Miss Elizabeth reminded me that simply because a parent is insistent about something does not mean the children agree. After dealing with Aunt Catherine's delusions for so long, I, of all people, should understand this."

"What will you do now?"

"I would like to offer for Miss Elizabeth, but I believe I will have to work hard to gain her affection."

"What woman in her right mind would turn you down? You have been running from the ladies since your first appearance in society. It only got worse when you became the master of Pemberley."

"Those women are not interested in me, but in what I can give them. Miss Elizabeth is more concerned with a person's character than their money. My behavior did not endear me to her, so I must prove myself before she will agree to be my wife."

"How will you do so while here at Rosings? If Aunt Catherine gets wind of your interest, I am sure she will put a stop to it."

"So far, I have managed to court her discreetly. I will continue to meet her on her walks and hope I can improve her opinion of me."

"I wish you luck, cousin. If you need help planning your strategy, I am at your disposal, but for now, I believe I will retire."

"Good night, Andrew."

Darcy moved to his desk, lit two candles, and turned his attention to his letter. For over an hour, the only sound was the scratch of the quill. When he had a missive that satisfied him, Darcy read it one final time before copying it to send.

Rosings Park
Kent
16 April 1811

Dear Bingley,

During my stay in Kent, I again find myself in company with Miss Elizabeth Bennet. I believe you recall the Bennet family, whom we met during our sojourn in Hertfordshire. In renewing our acquaintance, Miss Elizabeth asked after you and your family. She mentioned that her sister, Jane, is visiting family in London and called on your sisters. I gather they were obvious in their desire to discontinue the association.

I know I offered the opinion that Miss Bennet's feelings were not equal to yours. However, as my conversation with Miss Elizabeth progressed, I discovered my mistake. Miss Bennet's invitation to London was to help her over a melancholy, which began in late November.

I believe I may have been wrong about Miss Bennet's feelings for you--an opinion which Miss Elizabeth reluctantly confirmed. I am sorry that my misunderstanding of her feelings caused pain to both of you. I inquired of Miss Elizabeth about Miss Bennet's London address and am providing it below.

Having not been privy to your conversations with the young lady, I should never have presumed to offer an opinion on this matter. Love is rare in our world. If you still have tender feelings, follow your heart no matter what anyone else says.

Again, my apologies for my presumption.

Darcy

P. S. Miss Bennet is staying at the Gardiner residence at

He did not seal the letter so that he could include the address for Miss Bennet. He left the letter and his sealing wax on the desk to take with him in the morning.

2. Embarrassment and Understanding

Concern filled Charlotte when Elizabeth did not appear for breakfast. Now at half-past ten, and still with no sign of her early-rising friend, Charlotte asked the maid to check on her guest. When Sally knocked at Elizabeth's bedchamber door, the sound of retching reached her ears. The maid rushed to the kitchen and mixed up the drink recipe that Mr. Darcy's valet had provided the previous night.

When the maid arrived at the door again, Elizabeth's weak voice called out to her to enter.

"Good morning, miss. How are you feeling?"

"Worse than last evening, but I cannot imagine why. I cannot recall anything at all about last night. Did I eat anything? Is that why I am sick this morning?"

"No, miss. I think if you drink this, you will begin to improve. Also, there is a letter on your bedside table. It will help you understand what occurred last evening." Elizabeth sat staring, so Sally encouraged her. "Drink up, miss. It is guaranteed to settle your stomach and improve your headache, or so I was told."

19

Elizabeth stared at the maid for a moment longer before taking a tentative sip. The flavor was pleasant, though she had no idea what was in the drink. After several more sips, Elizabeth finished the entire glass. As she drank, Sally moved to open the curtains. However, at the young lady's cry, she closed them again. The light caused stabbing pain in Elizabeth's brain and her hands instantly rose to cover her face. When the room was again dark, Sally took the empty glass and moved to the door. Before opening it, she reminded Elizabeth, "I recommend you read the letter before you come downstairs. Would you like me to send you some toast and tea?"

"Have I missed breakfast?"

"Yes, miss."

"Then, if it is not too much trouble, dry toast and tea would be appreciated. Please tell Mrs. Collins I will join her in about an hour."

"Certainly, Miss Bennet."

Elizabeth picked up the letter on the bedside table. The handwriting appeared to be that of a man and was not one she recognized. She hesitated only a moment before breaking the seal. Elizabeth was quite curious as to what had happened last evening and hoped the letter would provide clarification. As far as she remembered, she had remained home alone while the others had dined at Rosings. Opening the curtains only enough to illuminate the paper, she allowed her gaze to focus on the neat, even hand on the page before her.

Monday Evening
Hunsford Parsonage
16 April 1811

Dear Miss Elizabeth,

I hope you will forgive my forwardness in writing to you. You fell asleep during our discussion, and it was then I discovered you unknowingly drank tea laced with Irish whiskey. We spoke of important topics, and I felt sure you would not remember our discussion upon awaking.

Darcy went on to explain his reasons for separating Jane and Bingley, reiterating his offer to immediately repair matters if she would provide him with Miss Bennet's address in London. He also told her about most of his history with his former friend, Mr. Wickham. Darcy further promised to explain the rest and answer any questions she had when they met in the morning.

Elizabeth read through the letter once, then sat staring into the distance as Sally entered with the light breakfast that Elizabeth had requested. "Is your stomach any better, miss?"

Thinking for a moment, Elizabeth answered, "Yes, thank you. It is. What was in the drink you gave me?"

"Too many things to mention. Mr. Darcy's valet provided the recipe and said his master swears by it. He hastened to assure me, though, that Mr. Darcy does not need it often. Can I help you dress?"

"If you would, bring some warm water while I eat. I would appreciate your assistance, Sally."

"Yes, miss."

As Elizabeth nibbled her tea and toast, she reread the letter. *How could I possibly forget that Mr. Darcy was here last evening? Oh, how will I ever face him again after my behavior last night-- even if it was beyond my control?* Elizabeth read the letter for the third time. *I hope I have not missed meeting him this morning. I am grateful he is willing to repair the damage he did to Jane's relationship with Mr. Bingley. I am relieved that my behavior toward him did not worsen the situation. Can I believe what he says of Mr. Wickham and what more he might have to tell me? Why would Mr. Darcy offer his version of events unless proof existed? He knows I have no reason to take his word over that of Mr. Wickham. Could the gentleman indeed be as bad as Mr. Darcy implies? I wonder if he will offer me proof, or does he expect me to believe him because of his position in society?*

She finished her toast as Sally knocked again. Elizabeth rushed to fold the letter and set it on the bedside table before finishing her tea. At her call, Sally entered and then assisted Elizabeth in donning a clean day dress and her walking boots. The maid dressed her hair in a braided bun, leaving soft curls framing her face and neck. Dismissing Sally, Elizabeth placed Mr. Darcy's letter in her pocket, wrote down her uncle's address, and picked up her bonnet and shawl before hurrying down the stairs.

"Elizabeth, how are you this morning?"

"The sleep was exactly what I needed, Charlotte. Some fresh air will put me to rights. If you will excuse me, I will take a short walk to refresh myself. I hope my indisposition did not inconvenience you in any way.

"Not at all, Eliza, but are you sure you feel up to a walk?"

"You know I always feel better after exercise."

"Which direction will you go? I want to know where to look for you, in case you experience a relapse and do not return."

Elizabeth laughed. "I will walk where I always do, and I promise to return."

Charlotte did not look convinced, but she ceased her questioning.

Elizabeth crossed the road before the parsonage and stepped into the woods before heading for the path where she regularly encountered Mr. Darcy. Walking rapidly, she arrived at her destination. Great was her relief upon seeing the gentleman leaning against a tree, waiting for her. He smiled upon seeing Elizabeth and stood straight, taking a step toward her.

Elizabeth blushed. She could not meet his eyes when she came to a stop a few feet in front of him.

"Good morning, Miss Elizabeth."

"Good morning, Mr. Darcy. I am sorry if I kept you waiting."

"Not at all. I hope you are much improved this morning."

"I am better, and I understand my improvement is due to you and your valet. I am so embarrassed, sir. Please forgive me if my behavior was in any way rude or unseemly."

"There is no need for you to apologize. I was very concerned about your well-being. Having never seen you drink more than a single glass of wine, I worried about how you would feel being given such a strong drink without your knowledge."

Still not meeting his gaze, Elizabeth continued, "I must also thank you for the letter recapping the evening, as I had no recollection of it."

Taking in the intense blush covering her cheeks, Darcy thought she had never looked lovelier. "I recall the first time Andrew, uh, Colonel Fitzwilliam, tricked me into imbibing more than I should. The next morning was dreadful. My head and stomach revolted, and I could not recall a thing after arriving at the club. Clarke's drink was a lifesaver."

Upon hearing the upright Mr. Darcy admitting to such weakness, Elizabeth smiled as much as the pain in her head would allow. With pleasure, Darcy saw her smile and returned it with a smile so wide, it revealed a dimple in each cheek.

Elizabeth reached into her reticule and pulled out a slip of paper. "Here is the address for which you asked. I am grateful to you, sir, for writing to Mr. Bingley. I hope his interest has not changed. Though Jane tries to hide it, I perceive her affections are still what they were last autumn."

"No thanks are necessary. I am only repairing a problem I created."

"Mr. Darcy." Elizabeth faltered. She looked down and scuffed the toe of her boot in the dirt.

Darcy placed his crooked forefinger under Elizabeth's chin and lifted it so that he could see her face--though she would not meet his eyes. "You may say or ask me anything you like, Miss Elizabeth."

"I was wondering about Mr. Wickham."

Darcy schooled his features to show no reaction. "Before you say more, let me finish what I was telling you last evening." Elizabeth nodded. Glancing around, Darcy found what he sought. Offering his arm to Elizabeth, who hesitantly accepted, he led her to the edge of the grove and down a narrow path. When they came out at the other end, a small pond was visible. Two downed trees had been carved into benches. Beautiful spring flowers ringed the area. Elizabeth could smell the hyacinth wafting on the light breeze that rustled the curls near her face and dancing about her neck. The song of a lark reached her ears. Darcy seated Elizabeth on the bench and stood before her.

After pacing for a time while taking several deep breaths, he seated himself beside her and reviewed his words from the letter, while Elizabeth closely observed him. At the end of his account, he stood and began pacing again. Elizabeth did not speak, as she felt Mr. Darcy had not yet finished his tale. Stopping, he looked directly at her. "Miss Elizabeth, allow me to explain the reasons for my poor mood at the assembly. Two months earlier, Wickham attempted to seduce my young sister into believing she was in love with him and he encouraged her to elope. Georgiana was but five and ten at the time." Elizabeth's hands flew to her mouth, trying to contain her gasp. "Luckily, I arrived unexpectedly the day before they planned to depart. I have raised Georgiana since the age of ten, and she could not bear to disappoint me. Thus, she told me of the engagement and planned elopement." Elizabeth caught her lower lip between her teeth as she tried to contain her questions. "I had Georgiana send a note requesting Wickham's presence. He entered the parlor with his usual smile, but it faded the moment he noticed me." Darcy vividly recalled the conversation that followed and was able to relate it to Elizabeth almost verbatim.

"Georgiana said, 'George, is it not wonderful that William arrived? Now we can marry in the church, and he can give me away.'

'Wickham sneered and said, 'You little fool. Your brother hates me. He will never allow us to marry.'

'Why do you not tell her why there is animosity between us, Wickham?'

'George told me there had been a misunderstanding about the living in father's will. I know you will do whatever you can to make things right. Will you not, William?'

'There was no misunderstanding, poppet. Wickham refused the living and requested remuneration, which he received. Unfortunately, he gambled all the funds away in less than three years. Wickham comes back at regular intervals looking for another handout. However, I remain steadfast in my refusal to give him additional funds. He attempted this elopement to get his hands on your dowry. Eloping does not give you the protection of a marriage settlement. He would most likely have abandoned you once he had the money.'

'Georgiana looked at Wickham, but he said nothing. 'We are in love, William, I am sure he does not desire my dowry. You may withhold it if you like. I am sure it will not make any difference to George.'

'Without your dowry, what would I want with you? You were just a means to an end to get me what I was due all along. I am sure your brother lied about the bequest from my godfather, but I cannot afford a solicitor to fight him for it.'

'You do not need a solicitor for that; I will happily have mine show you father's will.'

'How could I trust someone who works for you? Mark my words, one day, I will get what I am due.'"

Darcy's gaze refocused on Elizabeth. "After this last threat, George called to Georgiana's companion, and the two departed together. I do not know where he went. The next I saw of him was that day in the street at Meryton."

"What a horrible man." The vehemence in her voice surprised Darcy. Then he noticed the glaze of tears in her eyes. "Is Miss Darcy well? Has she recovered from the experience?"

"She is improving daily. Her new companion is a huge help, but what I think she needs most is a friend. Someone closer to her age in whom she can confide. Might you allow me to introduce her to you when you return to London?"

"You wish your sister to meet me?"

"I do. I cannot think of a better friend for her. You are kind, caring, and confident. I think Georgiana could learn a great deal from you that would help her face her future and better understand those with whom she comes into contact."

At his compliment, Elizabeth's face blushed a bright red. "I would be very pleased to meet Miss Darcy, but I am uncertain how long we will remain in London after my return."

Darcy pulled his pocket watch from his waistcoat. Checking the time, he said, "If I am to get this letter in Bingley's hands by tonight, I should leave for the express office. Might I call on you at the parsonage when I return?

"I would like that, Mr. Darcy."

"Miss Elizabeth, I would very much like to become better acquainted with you. Would you continue to meet me in the grove in the mornings? It would be much easier to talk if the restrictions of the sitting room did not confine us."

"You are correct in that. I fear we would not have an opportunity to speak at all if my cousin were present." A laugh escaped them both at the thought of Mr. Collins's verbosity. "I do walk early each morning, Mr. Darcy. There could be no impropriety if we accidentally encounter each other." A broad smile accompanied Elizabeth's words.

"Then I pray we have sunshine for the remainder of your visit. When do you plan to return to town, Miss Elizabeth?"

"More than two weeks are remaining in my visit, sir. I plan to return to London on the fourth of May."

"Perhaps you might permit me to return you to your relations, when the time comes."

"Though I appreciate your offer, Mr. Darcy, I am not sure it would be proper."

"I will find a companion for you so that there will be no impropriety."

"Let us see how the intervening days go before you make such a determination, sir. You may decide you do not like my company. I know you found me only tolerable at the Meryton assembly." Again, Elizabeth's cheeks bore a flush of color.

Darcy's face turned deep red with embarrassment. "I did not know anyone other than Bingley heard my words. Truthfully, I did not even look to see whom he indicated. I was still troubled by my sister's situation and not at all in the mood to dance. Please forgive my boorish behavior and thoughtless words. Not long after our first meeting, I thought of you as the loveliest woman of my acquaintance."

Elizabeth studied his face, trying to determine his truthfulness. What she saw convinced her of his sincerity. "I thank you very much for the compliment, Mr. Darcy."

Darcy offered Elizabeth his arm. They returned to the grove and the point where she had crossed the road to the parsonage.

After traveling a little farther in the woods, to where he had left his horse, Darcy mounted and kicked the animal into a canter. He was headed for the village of Hunsford and the express office. Upon arrival, Darcy noted two rested horses and a lathered one tied to the rail before the office. The animals' tails swished at the buzzing flies as they lapped water from the trough. Upon entering, Darcy requested pen and ink. He added the Gardiners's address before folding and sealing the letter which was already addressed to Bingley. Giving it to the summoned express rider, Darcy said, "This must be put into the hands of Mr. Bingley only. If he is not at home, ask for his direction. If not, please return in the morning and make another attempt to deliver it. Please do not give it to one of his sisters under any circumstances. Do you understand?"

"Yes, sir, I will give it only to the gent." After tucking the letter in the satchel slung over his shoulder, the rider vaulted into the saddle. He then kicked the horse into a gallop and leaned low over the animal's neck to avoid the drag of the wind.

Darcy mounted his horse and returned to Rosings. He slipped into the study unnoticed and continued his review of the estate books. He would need to authorize the steward to begin some of the repairs. *I hope the majority of the work can be completed before I depart. Then Aunt will not be able to discontinue the repairs the minute I leave. Extending my stay to match Elizabeth's should allow time for most of the repairs to be made.*

"Darcy, Darcy!" His aunt's harsh voice rang through the house, but he ignored it and continued his work. The neat stacks of papers on the desk sat bathed in the sunlight streaming through the tall windows.

Suddenly, the study door flew open, almost knocking the lady off her feet when it bounced off the wall behind it. "I was calling for you, Darcy. Why did you not answer?"

"I was busy working for your estate. Also, I do not approve of shouting within the house."

Lady Catherine gave him a look of annoyance. "You have not been spending any time with Anne. She is quite out of sorts because you are ignoring her."

"Are the melodramatics necessary, Aunt? I speak with Anne each day, and she realizes I have an incredible amount of work to do while I am here-- for both your estate and my own."

"I expect you to spend the afternoon with Anne."

"She is welcome to join me if she wishes to visit the parsonage. Andrew and I plan on calling there this afternoon."

"There is no reason for you to visit my parson. I am sure you find his behavior utterly annoying."

"That may be true, but his wife and cousin are both pleasant ladies, with whom I share a previous acquaintance. They are also delightful company."

"I forbid it, Darcy. You are to avoid that Bennet woman. I will not allow her to take your attention from Anne."

"You, Aunt, have no say over whom I can or cannot befriend. I do not answer to you. However, as I said, Anne is welcome to join me."

Lady Catherine stormed out of the room and slammed the door. She marched up the stairs to her daughter's room. After flinging open the door, she stomped inside. Her sudden and aggressive entrance caused Anne's Scottish terrier, a recent gift from Darcy, to rush forward, barking at the intruder while keeping herself between the newcomer and her mistress.

Anne's book slipped from nerveless fingers and her hand flew to her heart. "Good grief, Mother, you nearly frightened me to death! Was such a dramatic entry really necessary?"

Yes, it was. We have a dreadful problem. Anne, please control that ridiculous mutt," demanded an irritated Lady Catherine.

"It's all right, Fiona. Come," said Anne, patting the place beside her on the chaise on which she rested. The dog quickly obeyed, settling into place beside her mistress. "Fiona is not a mutt, Mother. Darcy ensures me she possesses an impressive pedigree. Now, what is this of a problem?"

"Your cousin, Darcy, is being snatched away from you right under our noses."

Anne looked down and rolled her eyes as she scratched the dog's ears. "Whatever are you talking about, Mother?"

"Darcy is infatuated with that obstinate, headstrong Bennet girl. If you are not careful, he will be proposing to her instead of you."

"That would suit me fine, Mother. Darcy and I have both told you we do not wish to marry."

"Neither of you knows what is best for you. You two were formed for each other from birth. It was my sister's and my dearest wish that you marry and combine two of the greatest estates in England. It will make the Fitzwilliams the most powerful and richest family in the country next to the royal family."

"That is your wish, Mother. Neither Darcy nor I want the notoriety of such a thing. I am happiest here at Rosings, and Darcy prefers the quiet life at Pemberley."

"You will do as I say if you know what is good for you." Anne meekly lowered her head so her mother would not recognize the mutinous glare in her eyes. "Now Darcy plans to go to the parsonage this afternoon. You will accompany him and ensure that he focuses his attention on you and not on Miss Elizabeth Bennet."

Swallowing her anger and irritation, Anne acquiesced. "Yes, Mother." However, despite her mother's wishes, she would do everything in her power to encourage the relationship between her cousin, William, and Miss Bennet.

At the call to dinner, Darcy entered the dining room to the scent of warm, freshly-baked bread and roasted chicken. For a time, the only sound was that of cutlery against the china plates. Soon, Andrew and Anne, seated beside each other, engaged in quiet conversation, with occasional comments from Darcy. Everyone ignored any attempt by Lady Catherine to interrupt or steer the conversation to more personal topics. At length, Darcy asked, "Anne, would you care to accompany me to the parsonage this afternoon? Andrew and I plan on calling on Mrs. Collins and her guests."

"That would be lovely, Darcy. What time do you wish to leave?"

"That depends on whether you would like to walk or prefer to take a carriage."

"It is a lovely day. Why do we not walk?"

"It is too cold for you to walk, Anne. You will need to go by carriage."

"I prefer to walk, Mother. If I cannot do so, I will stay here."

Lady Catherine clenched her teeth to contain her mounting anger. "Very well, walk, but be sure you bundle up before you leave. It would not do for you to become sick."

"Of course, Mother." Anne looked at Darcy and rolled her eyes.

At approximately half-past three that afternoon, the party from Rosings arrived at the parsonage. Delight filled them to discover that Mr. Collins was out visiting a parishioner. The sunny parlor, decorated in light colors, was redolent with the scent of cinnamon, nutmeg, and almond. The maid delivered a tea tray just moments before they knocked on the door.

The ladies rose to greet their guests before Anne seated herself between Elizabeth and Charlotte. The colonel sat on Charlotte's other side, while Darcy sat as near Elizabeth as possible.

The splash of milk and the clatter of spoons as they stirred the prepared cups were the only sounds. Assisting her hostess, Elizabeth offered plates to the guests with a choice of spiced biscuits with raisins or almond shortbread, from whence emanated the pleasant smells. After Mrs. Collins poured tea for everyone, Anne and Andrew engaged the woman in conversation. Excluding Darcy and Elizabeth allowed the other couple a chance for a private discussion. Charlotte, however, kept an eye on Elizabeth and noted with pleasure that her friend was paying attention to the gentleman from Derbyshire. Having always suspected a partiality for her friend by the reserved gentleman, Charlotte noted their interactions with satisfaction. *I hope Lizzy has enough sense to accept such a worthy man.*

"Were you able to send your letter, Mr. Darcy?"

"I was, and I was able to give the rider specific instructions to put the letter only in Mr. Bingley's hands. He often wonders if Miss Bingley looks at his mail. I did not want to risk her seeing this letter before Bingley. If that were to happen, he might never see it."

"I tried to tell Jane that Miss Bingley's friendship was not true, but my sweet sister sees only the best in people--at least until they prove her wrong. I do not think Miss Bingley will be able to fool her in the future. Jane is also much stronger than people think. She will not let Miss Bingley run her home should things come to the ending I hope."

"You need not be concerned about that. I doubt Miss Bingley will be welcome in Bingley's home much longer. He will either send her to a relative or make her set up a home of her own. He will not take kindly to the fact that she kept Jane's presence from him."

"I cannot say I am sorry to hear it. I would not wish such a difficult relation to be living in Jane's future home. She and Mr. Bingley deserve to be happy."

"What do you hope for your future, Miss Elizabeth?"

"I have always hoped to marry for love. However, if I cannot find that, I hope to find someone whom I can respect and who will respect me in return. Daily, I observe the unhappiness that results from an unequal marriage. I could not be happy in such a situation. It is why I refused

Mr. Collins, despite the pressure and threats from my mother."

Darcy tried to keep his voice low, but it was hard to hide his shock. "Mr. Collins! Did that ridiculous fool propose to you?"

"Am I not worthy of a proposal?" Elizabeth asked with a raised brow, a challenging expression on her face.

"Indeed, you are, but you are deserving of much better than that buffoon. I would lay the world at your feet if you would let me." The intensity of Darcy's voice and look sent a shiver down Elizabeth's spine.

"I am seeing a Mr. Darcy that I could not have imagined existing in Hertfordshire. However, I am afraid I will need to be sure this is not an aberration before I can accept such an offer."

"I hope that you will allow me to prove myself to you while you remain at Hunsford and upon our return to London."

"I believe I would like that very much, Mr. Darcy." At her words, his dimpled smile made another appearance.

When Mr. Collins returned, the party broke up. As the colonel helped Anne with her outerwear, she said, "Miss Elizabeth, would you please join me for tea soon? We can take it in my sitting room, where William and Andrew can join us."

"That would be delightful. I would enjoy the opportunity to know you better, Miss de Bourgh."

"I will send a note with the day and time after making all the arrangements."

Upon the party's departure, Mr. Collins praised Miss de Bourgh's greatness in inviting his lowly cousin. Then he spent almost half an hour reminding her of how to behave with such a noble lady. Elizabeth and Charlotte had a difficult time not laughing at the ridiculous man.

3. Mischief and Mishaps

The morning was overcast, the air heavy, with no sound of songbirds. None of this dimmed the militiaman's smirk. The information from his source in Kent proved most enlightening, and with luck would also be most useful. Mr. Wickham strolled into the inn and asked if any letters awaited him. The innkeeper, who also served as postmaster, turned to the open cupboard divided into small sections behind him and searched for the one that held mail for the militia members. Pulling out the letters, he scanned for the name of the gentleman before him. Then, turning back to the visitor, he smiled and handed him a missive that appeared to be from a woman. "I imagine a man in a red coat gains many admirers."

Wickham grinned. "It does draw women like bees to honey."

Before Wickham could exit, someone else entered and approached. "Good morning, Mr. Pike," the woman said. "I had errands in town this morning and thought I would pick up the mail and save the post boy a trip."

"Good morning, Lady Lucas." Realizing who had entered the shop, Wickham hurried to tuck his letter into his pocket. Doffing his hat to the lady, he exited the shop to avoid engaging in conversation.

The innkeeper turned back with several letters in hand. With a quizzical glance at the writing on the top item in the stack, he turned to discover Mr. Wickham had slipped away. He handed the stack to Lady Lucas. "It looks like a letter from Miss Lucas." Though the innkeeper knew better than to speak of the letters he delivered, he wondered if Mr. Wickham's message had come from the Lucases's youngest daughter. He sincerely hoped not, as he had plenty of occasions to observe that the soldier's behavior with tavern maids was less than gentlemanly.

Turning down the alley near the inn, Wickham broke the seal and quickly perused his letter. Upon learning his nemesis visited the parsonage regularly, he requested a fortnight's leave to attend to a dying relative. No one in the regiment knew Wickham was alone in the world, so his colonel approved his leave.

For the next several mornings, Elizabeth met Mr. Darcy in the grove. They walked for a while, enjoying the birds' song and the bright green of new life all about them. Then Darcy led her to the glade, where they sat on the bench and talked about many topics ranging from books, literature, and the theater, to their families, to the state of the war, and concerns of parliament. One morning they even discussed estate management. Often so engrossed were they in their conversations that they barely returned to their respective homes in time to partake of the morning meal.

Due to the earliness of the church service, Elizabeth and Darcy could not meet on Sunday mornings. As a result, Darcy and the colonel planned to call on the parsonage in the afternoon. Upon returning from church, Elizabeth received an express from Jane. She took a seat in Charlotte's sunny parlor and broke the seal, her breath held in anticipation.

Gracechurch Street
London
21 April 1811

Dear Lizzy,

    Oh, my dear sister, you will not believe what occurred. Mr. Bingley came to call. He apologized for the delay in his arrival but said he was unaware of my presence in town until he received a letter from Mr. Darcy. Shocked at his words, I blurted out my surprise that Miss Bingley had not mentioned my visit to his home. It was his turn to appear surprised, but his expression soon became one of anger. I must believe you now; Miss Bingley is not a true friend, for it seems she purposely kept my presence from her brother. I do hope he will not be too harsh with her, for I would not wish to cause disharmony in his family.

    Mr. Bingley calls daily since learning of my visit with the Gardiners. In fact, he attended church with us this morning and remained to dine. I must end here, for the time grows late. Tomorrow, Aunt wishes to purchase a new gown for me, as Mr. Bingley mentioned an evening at the theater.

I hope you are enjoying your visit with Charlotte, and I await your return to catch up on all the news. Till then, dear sister.

Love,

Jane

P. S. You must explain how Mr. Darcy learned of my presence in London since he is in Kent.

The maid announced the gentleman while Elizabeth read her letter. Standing in the doorway, Darcy was so mesmerized by the sunlight glinting off her hair and the play of emotions across Elizabeth's expressive face that he could not move. When she looked up and smiled brilliantly, he briskly crossed the room to take a seat beside her. Once seated, he leaned close and said, "I hope your letter brought good news?"

"It did indeed. Jane writes that Mr. Bingley sent a note requesting permission to call on her the same day he received your letter. She reports he continues to call daily."

"I am pleased to learn everything worked out well. Again, I would ask your forgiveness for my interference."

"If you need it, you have it, but may I suggest you learn a little of my philosophy."

"What is this philosophy of yours?"

"I firmly believe you should remember the past only as it gives you pleasure."

Darcy chuckled. "I shall endeavor to do as you suggest. Is that what you choose to do when thinking of our past interactions?"

"As there was little in our past that was pleasant, I choose to forget the past and look to the future instead."

"I hope I will play a part in your future." Darcy looked intensely at Elizabeth as he spoke. Something in his voice caused a *frisson* along her spine.

"I believe you may, sir," she teased, but his only response was a dimpled smile, which left her bemused and breathless.

The next morning, as they said farewell following their walk, Darcy took the gloved hand resting on his arm. Lifting it to his lips, he kissed it. "I anticipate you joining us at three for tea." Elizabeth was surprised at the feelings that his warm breath engendered. Again, a shiver traveled down her spine.

When Elizabeth arrived at Rosings later in the afternoon, she found the house in a state of controlled chaos. Servants rushed up and down the stairs, and from somewhere came the bark of a small dog. "Is Miss de Bourgh well?" asked Elizabeth with concern. "Would it be better if I returned another day?"

"No, miss," said the butler. "Miss de Bourgh is expecting you." The butler showed Elizabeth into a small but attractive parlor at the back of the house, overlooking the garden. The décor was unlike any of the other rooms at Rosings that Elizabeth had visited previously. It was bright, the colors light, and it possessed the feel of a garden, unlike the ostentation of the rest of the house.

"Good afternoon, Miss de Bourgh. I know you extended an invitation, but it appears I arrived at an inauspicious time."

"Not at all, Miss Bennet. Please be seated." Anne patted the settee next to her. Elizabeth had just settled herself when a maid arrived with the tea tray, followed by the gentlemen.

"You missed the performance, Miss Elizabeth, but it is a blessing in disguise," said the colonel with a chuckle.

"And what performance would that be, sir? I did not realize a troupe of players was in the area."

"The star of this performance was my aunt," he continued. "In a foul mood at not getting her way over some matter or another important only to her, Lady Catherine ranted and raved and stomped about the room. Her aggression roused Anne's new pet, gifted to her by Darcy, at the beginning of our visit."

Elizabeth tried not to show surprise that Mr. Darcy was giving gifts to the cousin everyone expected him to marry. She hoped it did not mean anything, considering the words he had spoken to her a few days earlier in Charlotte's parlor.

His thoughts running in the same line as Elizabeth's, Darcy hurried to explain. "I had to visit my estate in Scotland in January because of a problem. One of the terriers had just given birth to a litter of puppies. It was old enough to leave its mother when I was ready to return to Pemberley. Consequently, I brought this one back with me and had it trained. I thought it might provide companionship for Anne during her periods of ill health. I know she is often lonely." Almost as if she understood they were discussing her, the wheaten-colored Scottish terrier trotted across the room from her bed and sat in front of Elizabeth.

"What is the name of this cute lady?" she asked, reaching down to scratch the dog's ears.

"This is Fiona," said Anne. "I am afraid it may be necessary for you to take her back to Pemberley, William. Mother was screaming threats about getting rid of the animal after her fall."

"Did Lady Catherine sustain an injury?"

"It was a sight to behold," said Andrew with a chuckle.

"You possess an odd sense of humor, cousin," said Darcy with a roll of his eyes.

Andrew ignored his cousin's words as he continued. "All my aunt's theatrics aroused the puppy, who rushed her and ran about at her feet. Lady Catherine backed away from the puppy and tripped over a footstool. They say she went head over heels, her skirts tangled about her. With arms flailing, she fell, slamming her left side against the hard floor. The physician came and went before your arrival. His diagnosis is that Lady Catherine broke her hip."

"I hope she is not suffering too greatly."

"No, Dr. Walker gave her some laudanum for the pain," Anne said. "He said she will need it for several days and will be laid up for at least two months, more likely three. Though I am sorry for Mother's suffering, I must admit to a sense of freedom. She will not be able to control every moment of my life for several weeks. Perhaps I should travel with you to London, cousins. The staff can care for Mother. Do you think Aunt Ellen would enjoy helping me update my wardrobe?"

"Undoubtedly. That is why I called it a blessing in disguise," replied Andrew. "Mother would love to spend time with you without your mother's interference."

"Do you think we might see some of the sights of the city while I am there?"

"I hope to show them to Miss Elizabeth before she returns home. Perhaps, if she does not mind, you and Andrew could join us."

"I would be delighted to join you."

"This will be so exciting!" exclaimed Anne.

Turning to Elizabeth, Darcy said, "Now, you will be able to accept my offer of transportation. If Anne accompanies us to London, there will be no need for a chaperone for you."

"Then, I gladly accept your offer to return me to town." Darcy's dimpled smile again appeared.

The conversation turned to other subjects and the group enjoyed their time together very much. When they finally realized the time, Anne suggested that Elizabeth stay to supper. "We can have a carriage return you when the meal is over."

"Thank you. I would like that exceedingly. A meal without Mr. Collins's unending commentary will be a true pleasure." Everyone laughed at Elizabeth's remark.

The four young people had a delightful evening. Laughter and conversation flowed without interruption from either Lady Catherine or Mr. Collins.

When the letter arrived at the parsonage announcing Elizabeth would remain to dine at Rosings, Mr. Collins appeared conspicuously flustered. "Why would Lady Catherine invite Cousin Elizabeth without inviting me, uh, us? I wonder if she caused some difficulty for my noble patroness? Do you think I should go to the manor house and attempt to resolve whatever problem my cousin created?"

"I believe your worries are for nothing, husband. Do you think Lady Catherine would invite Lizzy to remain if she were upset with her? I think not. Besides, Mr. Collins, it would be the height of bad manners to arrive at a dinner party uninvited. You would certainly anger Lady Catherine if you did such a thing."

Mr. Collins looked relieved that his cousin had not imposed herself upon his esteemed patroness, but there was also, about him, the air of a pouting child who had lost his favorite toy. Charlotte was trying to think of a way to distract him when, helpfully, the maid arrived to announce supper. Throughout the meal, the expression of discontent gave away Mr. Collins's pique at being excluded from dining with his patroness. Therefore, distracting him from any plans to interrupt became essential. Because it was the first day of a new week, Charlotte asked, "Did you decide on a theme for this week's sermon?"

"Indeed, Lady Catherine suggested reminding the congregation of the pitfalls of attempting to rise above your station." Mr. Collins launched into a soliloquy on the point his patroness felt he should address. Charlotte looked down and rolled her eyes at Lady Catherine's choice for the sermon. She wondered if the lady discerned her nephew's interest in Elizabeth, thus her chosen topic. Charlotte allowed her mind to wander as she reviewed the interactions between her friend and the estimable, but reserved, Mr. Darcy. Charlotte also recalled the way Mr. Darcy had always stared at Elizabeth in Hertfordshire and listened in on her conversations. Since his arrival at Rosings Park, he had visited the parsonage almost daily. Charlotte wondered if they were meeting on Elizabeth's morning walks as well. If so, she prayed Lady Catherine would not learn of it. When Charlotte returned from her mental meanderings, Mr. Collins was still waxing on about the evils of the topic his patroness suggested. Upon the meal's end, Charlotte said, "Perhaps you should continue working on your sermon. Then you will be able to visit Lady Catherine tomorrow with the first draft for her review."

"An excellent idea, my dear Charlotte. You need not wait up for me, as I do not know how long it will take me to finish." Mrs. Collins heaved a sigh of relief as the door to his study closed behind him. After giving her staff final instructions for the night, Charlotte retired to her private parlor at the back of the house to await Elizabeth's return. She picked up an item from her mending basket and set about her task. When the clock struck ten and her friend had still not returned,

Charlotte checked on her husband and then retired for the night.

Just before midnight, Elizabeth and Darcy approached the door of the parsonage. Having noted the light coming from Mr. Collins's study, they halted the carriage at some distance. Darcy handed Elizabeth down and offered his arm. They stayed in the shadows across the road as they approached the door of the parsonage. Once out of Mr. Collins's line of sight, they crossed over and made their way to the door. They stood just out of range of the candlelight emanating from the study. Though no moon showed, the stars in the sky were numerous. As the evenings tended to be chilly, the smell of wood-smoke filled the air. Somewhere nearby, a nightingale sang.

"Thank you for a lovely afternoon and evening, Mr. Darcy. Please thank Anne again for me. I truly enjoyed making her acquaintance. She is quite delightful company without her mother's overwhelming presence."

"Indeed, she is. We always enjoy each other's company but are not often able to spend as much time together as we would like because of my aunt's wishes for the future. When I marry, I will hope to ask Anne to visit quite often, without her mother, of course."

"As pleasant as Anne is, I am sure no one would object to her company for any length of time, but do you believe your aunt would allow such a thing?"

"I am sure my uncle's assistance can bring it to pass."

"Is your uncle, the earl, anything like his sister?" Elizabeth's voice contained a note of trepidation.

Darcy responded with a low chuckle. "He is much more like Andrew, but as he is the head of the family, Lady Catherine is subject to his dictates."

At his reply, Elizabeth emitted a giggle. "I doubt your aunt submits very graciously."

"You would be correct."

"Well, I should say goodnight. I do not wish to draw Mr. Collins's attention."

Darcy placed a hand on her arm as she turned to the door. "Will you be walking in the grove in the morning?" His expression of vulnerability as he awaited her answer made his attentions all the more endearing to Elizabeth.

"I will try to be there by seven." A smile accompanied her reply.

Darcy took her hand in his and briefly brushed the back of it with his lips. "Until tomorrow," he said before releasing her hand. He stood watching as Elizabeth lifted the latch on the door and hesitantly opened it, praying it would not squeak. Once across the threshold, she turned and smiled at Darcy before silently closing the door. Elizabeth tiptoed across the hall and climbed the stairs to her room, making sure to bypass the creaky ones. When she reached her room, she breathed a sigh of relief at the fact that no one had discovered her return.

Upon Darcy's return to his room, his valet assisted him in preparing for bed. Then Darcy poured himself a brandy and took a seat before the fire. Staring into the flames, he instead saw the sparkling eyes of Elizabeth Bennet. They had enjoyed a pleasant day and, again, managed to converse without any misunderstandings or harsh words. He could only be pleased with the progress he had made in improving her opinion of him. Darcy also took the fact that she had agreed to allow him to transport her to London as further proof of her softening attitude. With such pleasant thoughts, he retired to bed and slept well for the first time since arriving at Rosings Park.

While Darcy and Elizabeth met in the grove for their usual walk, Mr. Collins rushed through his breakfast, then departed for his regular morning meeting with his patroness. Unlike the young couple, he failed to note the beauty of spring bursting forth around him. He desperately hoped to find a way to introduce his cousin's invitation the previous night into the conversation and discover the reason for his exclusion.

"I am here to meet with Lady Catherine," said Mr. Collins to the butler. The august gentleman bowed slightly while rolling his eyes, though he did not open the door further. The parson was not particularly popular with the servants at Rosings. They laughed at the way the man venerated his patroness with flowery compliments and ridiculous bows. However, his dismissive treatment of the servants made them resentful, and they treated him only negligibly better than he treated them. This morning, Jackson, the butler, teased him for not knowing of

Lady Catherine's injury, yet had he known the result of his words, he would not have done so.

"I am sorry, Mr. Collins, but Lady Catherine is not receiving visitors today. In fact, the doctor believes it will be several days before she is prepared to receive company."

"The doctor? Of what are you speaking?" asked the parson.

"Lady Catherine tripped and fell yesterday, breaking her hip. She will be laid up for at least two months, likely longer, according to Dr. Walker."

"Why was I not notified? I am sure Lady Catherine required my presence and words of comfort and encouragement."

"I saw no need to notify you, as Miss Bennet was aware of the situation. Lady Catherine needed no company, as the doctor sedated her with laudanum."

"My cousin was aware of Lady Catherine's injury?"

"Yes, sir, as I said."

"Take me to Lady Catherine. I demand to confirm for myself that she does not need anything from me."

With a smirk, the butler retorted, "As I said, the doctor indicated she is not to receive visitors."

"Then I demand to speak to the doctor. He must understand how much Lady Catherine depends upon my counsel and comfort."

"The doctor is not here at present, as he is attending to an emergency elsewhere. You can wait in the parlor for the doctor or check back later. I do not know when he will return."

"I will attend to some matters and return soon. Please ask the doctor to wait or stop by the parsonage so that we might speak," said Mr. Collins as he stomped down the front steps and continued down the drive with forceful purpose. *He looks angrier than ever before,* thought the butler.

Mr. Collins entered the parsonage and slammed the door behind him with enough force to rattle the windows. Shocked at the unexpected noise, Charlotte came from her parlor with her hand over her heart. "Whatever is the matter, Mr. Collins?"

"Where is Cousin Elizabeth?"

"She is out for her morning walk, as usual."

"When did she come in last evening?

"I am not sure. Eliza had not arrived when I retired at ten."

"Then I was still up when she returned home?"

"I would assume so, unless you left to attend to parish duties without my knowledge."

"I did not."

Charlotte could not imagine what the problem was, but she was growing more concerned by the moment. Though Mr. Collins occasionally possessed a quick temper, it did not happen often, and his wife had never before seen him this angry.

It was unfortunate that Elizabeth entered the house at just that moment. Mr. Collins swung around with a glare. He reached out and grabbed Elizabeth's arm, his grip firm enough to leave a bruise.

"Mr. Collins, you are hurting me!"

"Mr. Collins, let go of Elizabeth this instant. What do you think you are doing?" cried his wife. The parson maintained his crushing grip on Elizabeth's upper arm.

"Stop! You are hurting me!" Elizabeth shouted this time. A moment later, the front door crashed in and Mr. Darcy stared at the others before him. Darcy had walked Elizabeth back to the parsonage and watched her enter. He had stood watching afterward, thinking of their morning together. When he heard Elizabeth's shout, he had rushed to her assistance.

"Mr. Collins, let go of Miss Elizabeth's arm."

"This does not concern you, Mr. Darcy. Get out!"

"Witnessing the assault of any woman must concern anyone who considers himself a gentleman."

"You should be concerned with your betrothed, not my cousin. Now, please leave my house."

"If you do not release Miss Elizabeth now, I shall remove your hand for you." Darcy's cold expression and implacable tone would have quailed a lesser man, but Mr. Collins was too far gone in rage to recognize the danger to himself.

"Mr. Collins, please," implored his wife. "Is this any way for the parson of Lady Catherine to behave?"

"I am doing this for Lady Catherine."

Darcy's patience was at an end. With a crushing grip, he grabbed Mr. Collins's thick wrist in one hand. With the other, he pried the man's pudgy fingers from Elizabeth's arm, as gently as possible. Then he pushed the man toward the parlor and into a chair as he stood over him. "Now, apologize to Miss Elizabeth and explain your behavior," demanded Darcy.

As Darcy pulled away Mr. Collins, Charlotte put her arm around Elizabeth and led her to a seat in the parlor.

Mr. Collins glared at his cousin, but no apology was forthcoming. "What excuse can you give for not informing me of Lady Catherine's injury?" he snarled.

"This is the first I have seen you since early yesterday. I have had no opportunity to tell you about it."

"What time did you come home last evening?"

"It was late when the carriage from Rosings returned me here."

"How late?" he challenged.

"It was near midnight."

"I was in my study until nearly half-past twelve. Obviously, I was awake. Why did you not tell me what happened to Lady Catherine?"

"Mr. Collins," said his wife, her tone firm, "you instructed the household to never interrupt you when you are working in your study."

"That is only for unimportant matters. Anything to do with my patroness is always worthy of my time and attention."

Thus far, Elizabeth had remained quiet, listening to the discussion and rubbing her sore arm. Now she asked, "How was I to know?"

Darcy noted Elizabeth's action and beckoned to Sally, the maid, who was hovering in the hallway. "Please bring a cool cloth for Miss Elizabeth's arm."

"Yes, sir."

Mr. Collins glared at Darcy and the maid for a moment before answering Elizabeth's question. "Anyone with an ounce of sense would know the concerns of my patroness are always important to me."

At hearing her ridiculous cousin speak of having sense, Elizabeth caught Darcy's eye and gave him a weak smile. Darcy's lips barely quirked upward, but the anger in his eyes was visible.

"Your actions put me in an unfavorable position with my patroness, cousin. I should have been by her side, providing her with words of comfort, but your thoughtlessness has made me look bad and uncaring. What will Lady Catherine think of me?"

"That is the reason you felt it appropriate to abuse Miss Elizabeth?"

"As I said, this is no concern of yours, Mr. Darcy." Then, turning to Elizabeth, Mr. Collins said, "I should have refused when Mrs. Collins asked to invite you to visit. Anyone as ungrateful as you could never deserve the attention and condescension of someone as gracious and wonderful as Lady Catherine. I thank my lucky stars you refused my proposal, as it is obvious you were not deserving of the lofty position I offered you."

Charlotte blushed at her husband's words, while Elizabeth's irritation was palpable. However, it was only Mr. Darcy who spoke. "I find it amazing you had the temerity to offer for Miss Elizabeth. You are not worthy of cleaning her boots."

If possible, Mr. Collins's face grew redder at the insult. "I offered her a wonderful future and a chance to become the mistress of her family home.

It was the best offer she could expect, and I will take great pleasure in throwing the whole family from the house the minute Mr. Bennet dies!"

"Such Christian charity you demonstrate, parson." Darcy's voice dripped with sarcasm. The maid had already provided Elizabeth with the cool cloth that was currently wrapped around her arm. "How is your arm, Miss Elizabeth?" He examined the injured area and quickly returned to her face, staring intensely into her eyes to determine how much pain she suffered.

"It is quite sore, but I am sure it will cause no lasting harm."

"I think it would be best to remove you from here. I am sure Anne would be pleased if you would join us at the manor. It is not safe for you to remain here." Darcy cast a disparaging glare at the red-faced parson.

"Yes, she must leave forthwith, but Charlotte can take her to meet the next post coach. She does not deserve to stay in comfort after what she did. I will not allow her to impose herself on Lady Catherine at such a time."

"You have no say in the matter," said Mr. Darcy coldly. "My cousin, Miss de Bourgh, is very fond of Miss Elizabeth, and she is acting mistress during her mother's illness."

Standing, Charlotte said, "I will help you pack, Elizabeth."

Darcy put his hand under Elizabeth's uninjured elbow and helped her to her feet. Without another word, she followed her friend from the room. After the ladies' exit, Mr. Darcy closed the parlor doors before turning to face the other occupant. "For now, I will not say anything about your disgraceful treatment of Miss

Elizabeth. However, if I ever hear of you abusing another woman, you will answer to me. You should know that my godfather is a bishop. I wonder how long you would retain your position if I reported your behavior to him. And should the church fail to take action, I will call you out. As I am an expert with both sword and pistol, what do you think your chances would be?"

Darcy said no more but continued to glare at the little man before him. Mr. Collins's eyes showed that his anger remained, but the beads of perspiration on his brow confirmed his understanding that Darcy meant what he said. The gentlemen's standoff continued until a knock at the door announced the ladies' return.

Darcy exited the parlor and closed the door behind him so Mr. Collins would not overhear his words. "I hope my behavior did not upset you, Mrs. Collins."

"Not at all, Mr. Darcy. I appreciate your rescue of my dear friend."

Darcy relayed his conversation with Mr. Collins to the ladies. "Please promise me should your husband ever repeat such behavior, you will contact either Anne or myself. I will not allow a man who holds such a position of trust to retain it if he cannot control himself."

"I have seen signs of his temper before, but he has never harmed anyone, to my knowledge. However, you have my promise. I will report it should it ever occur again."

"Thank you, ma'am. I walked out this morning, so I will walk Miss Elizabeth to Rosings. However, I will send some men to collect her luggage." Charlotte nodded. Turning, Darcy extended his arm to Elizabeth. "Shall we go?" He smiled brightly at his companion. He could not deny that, on one level, he was pleased with this turn of events, as he could spend more time in Elizabeth's company. Darcy stopped at the door and looked back at Charlotte. "Please feel free to visit Miss Elizabeth at Rosings whenever you wish."

"I will be happy to do so should the occasion arise," said Charlotte with a glance at the closed parlor door. She followed the couple from the house and watched until they turned into the gates of Rosings Park. Not wishing to see her husband, Charlotte retreated to her private parlor and returned to her mending.

4. The Many Frustrations of Mr. Collins

Mr. Collins stood staring at the closed door before he began to pace the room, uttering imprecations upon Elizabeth. He was furious with his cousin, and it appeared she had compounded her dreadful behavior by distracting Mr. Darcy from his cousin and betrothed, Miss de Bourgh. *I must find a way to see Lady Catherine. If I remove the danger to her nephew, perhaps she might forgive me for failing her in her time of need.* As an idea popped into his head, he strode to the door and threw it open. Thankfully, no one remained in the hall, for his control of his temper was shaky at best. He crossed to his study, where he pulled out some parchment and began writing furiously. When he finished, he marched from the parsonage, slamming the door behind him.

As they approached the main house, Mr. Darcy spied the appearance of bruising on Elizabeth's arm, which appeared to be swelling. "I believe we should call the doctor for you when we reach the house."

"That will not be necessary, sir. I am sure I shall be fine in the morning."

"But I am concerned at the swelling, which continues to increase."

"I thank you for your consideration for my well-being, Mr. Darcy, but it would be complicated to explain my injury. The imprint of Mr. Collins's fingers is obvious. If it were only Mr. Collins who would suffer, I would not hesitate to allow you your wishes. However, I cannot embarrass my friend in such a manner." Elizabeth stopped speaking, but Darcy realized something still bothered her.

"What is it that bothers you?" Darcy's tone and words were gentle, but he perceived her hesitation.

"Do you think, well, what I mean is--"

"Just speak, Miss Elizabeth. I will not judge you for your words."

Elizabeth took a deep breath and then spoke, without meeting his eyes. "Do you think it is safe for Charlotte, I mean Mrs. Collins, to remain there? Do you suppose he has ever struck her?"

"From what Mrs. Collins said, I do not think so. However, I did warn him that should word of him abusing another woman ever reach my ears, he would not escape the incident unscathed."

Though it was not a laughing matter, Elizabeth could not help the giggle that escaped her. Darcy could understand the stress the situation raised in her. Her response was simply relief at knowing her friend was safe.

They arrived at the house to discover both Andrew and Anne had already finished eating and were exiting the dining room, wondering what had become of him.

Andrew spoke before Darcy was through the door. "There you are, Darcy. We could not wait any longer for you to break our fast. What kept--" Andrew broke off when he witnessed Elizabeth entering with Darcy. "Good morning, Miss Elizabeth. What brings you to Rosings so early?"

Elizabeth looked at Darcy, uncertain how to respond. It was then that her shawl slipped from her shoulders and Anne could clearly see the bruises.

"Miss Elizabeth, what happened to your arm?"

Rapidly returning the wrap to its proper place, Elizabeth again did not answer but looked at Mr. Darcy questioningly.

Darcy escorted Elizabeth toward the dining room and pulled out a chair for her. Sunshine filled the room, which retained the redolence of the foods still on the sideboard. "If you will allow me a moment to fix plates for Miss Elizabeth and myself, I will explain the circumstances leading to my late arrival and Miss Elizabeth's need to accompany me here." Elizabeth's face flushed at the thought of her disgrace becoming more widely known. "Oh, and could you request that someone transport her luggage from the parsonage? It is packed and waiting for retrieval."

Anne did as requested as she and Andrew retook their seats at the table. The foursome made desultory conversation while waiting for the delivery of the meal and the servants' departure. Darcy finished the scrambled eggs, potatoes, and sausage on his plate and drank his coffee before settling back in his seat. "I was fortunate to meet Miss Elizabeth as she walked this morning, so we continued together for some time. I returned her to the parsonage and had not yet turned away when I heard her cry out." Darcy continued to relate the events of the morning. "I hope you do not mind me offering her the hospitality and safety of your home, Anne."

"Of course not, Darcy. I would be quite put out with you if you left her there to deal with that abusive dimwit. I am also grateful you made me aware of the situation. I shall keep my eyes and ears open to learn of any further such behavior. I will also be certain to offer Mrs. Collins assistance should I ever note her in need of such. Are you certain we should not remove him from his position for actions so unworthy of a clergyman?"

"I do not expect him to make a repeat performance, as I have threatened him with church action and the risk of being called out should I ever learn of him doing such a thing again."

"I hope you will allow me to help you should that time come," declared a disgusted Andrew.

"Well, if you have finished your breakfast, Miss Elizabeth, allow me to show you to a guestroom."

Elizabeth nodded and started to rise when a sudden thought caused her to slump down again. Turning to Mr. Darcy, she blurted, "What am I to do? Mr. Collins's resentment was clear on his face. Mr. Collins will assuredly write to the Lucases and spin an entirely different tale that will reflect poorly on me."

Darcy and Andrew shared a look of concern, but it was Anne who spoke. "I will send a note to your father, explaining that I desired to know you better and invited you to stay with me until it was time for you to return to town. We need say nothing about Mr. Collins's actions."

"That is a relief, as I do not know how my father would react to such news. He is usually so lackadaisical in his parenting, but I do not think he would take aggression against one of his daughters with his usual calm."

"I doubt Mr. Collins will mention his misdeeds. However, if you think it necessary, I can add some lines of my own to Anne's letter to set his mind at ease about the need for action," added Mr. Darcy.

"That would perhaps be best. If Papa were to overreact and harm came to him, it could be disastrous for my family."

"Why is that?" asked Colonel Fitzwilliam.

"Mr. Collins is a distant cousin of my father's, and he is my father's heir, as Longbourn is entailed on the male line. You see, I have only sisters, and since I turned down Mr. Collins's proposal of marriage, that gentleman would cheerfully throw us all into the hedgerows upon my father's death, as he just stated." Elizabeth blushed profusely, recalling Mr. Darcy's words upon learning of her cousin's proposal.

She started, then forced herself to control the giggle that wanted to escape when she heard his mumbled words: "It is unfathomable that the dunderhead had the impertinence to propose to you! And then to question whether or not you had any sense!"

Anne and Andrew looked at Darcy, surprised by his quiet words, though neither spoke. Elizabeth smiled at him before replying with her usual satirical tone, "Your epithet is well-chosen, sir. For he was too dense to understand the word 'no.'" Elizabeth's words broke the tension and made everyone laugh.

Anne called for her housekeeper, requesting some ice to reduce the swelling of Elizabeth's arm.

"If you do not mind waiting with the others, miss, I will send the ice to you," said Mrs. Creeley. "Then I will notify you when your trunks arrive and your room is ready. A maid will be standing by to assist you in changing."

Then Anne led her guests to the morning room, where she moved to her writing desk and began her note. When she had completed her part, she called to Darcy to add his lines. While her cousin wrote, Anne requested that one of Darcy's grooms saddle a horse to take a message and come to the door to receive it. Within a few minutes, the requested servant arrived. He accepted the letter and instructions from his master. Shortly thereafter, he was riding hard for Longbourn in Hertfordshire.

The same afternoon, Charlotte appeared at Rosings. "My concern for the events of the morning would not allow me to go without checking on your injury. As Mr. Collins was nowhere to be found, he could not object. How is your arm, Eliza?"

"Thanks to some ice, the swelling is gone. When the bruises disappear, I shall be good as new."

"Can you stay for tea, Mrs. Collins?" asked Anne.

"I thank you for the offer, but I should return home before my husband does."

"I shall send a note for another day, then," said Anne.

It was ten in the evening and his family had already retired to their rooms. Mr. Bennet was sitting and enjoying the quiet when he heard a knock at the front door. He listened carefully but did not hear anything further. Then, a moment later, a soft tap sounded on his study door. "Come."

The butler entered. "An express came for you, sir."

"Thank you, Mr. Hill." Noticing the return address, Mr. Bennet quickly broke the seal. He scanned the lines once and then again more slowly. *That imbecile dared to lay hands on my Lizzy! And what has Mr. Darcy to do with all of this? Oh, well. I suppose I can be grateful that he handled the matter for me, and I need not trouble myself to travel when I detest it so. I shall need to bestir myself a little, for I believe I should mention this to Sir William, for Charlotte's sake.*

With that, the gentlemen put the letter in his desk drawer and returned to his book and port.

And so it was that after breaking his fast the next morning, Mr. Bennet mounted his horse and rode to Lucas Lodge. His long-time friend was exiting the dining room as the housekeeper invited Mr. Bennet into the house.

"Ah, Bennet, you are about early this morning."

"Yes, well, there is something I believe I must tell you about."

"Follow me to my study and we shall discuss it. Would you care for coffee or tea?"

"No, thank you, but a small glass of port would not go amiss."

"What problem makes you request port so early in the day?"

"Mr. Collins."

Sir William was pleased his daughter had found what she was looking for, but he did not think much of his son-in-law. "What did the buffoon do now?"

"Well, he put his hands on my Lizzy in anger." Bennet's tone displayed his displeasure with the situation. "I understand this might be the first time the situation occurred, but as he is married to your daughter, I thought you should be aware of the matter."

Sir William's face was a study in thoughtfulness, which gradually turned into displeasure. "I will need to have words with my son when I return to retrieve Maria. Perhaps I should retrieve her early under the circumstances? What think you?"

"Being of weak understanding, he may have an uncontrollable temper, though I saw no sign of such during his visit. However, I would not doubt he holds a grudge against Lizzy for refusing his proposal. That could have made him lose control, though I imagine a stern talking to would not go amiss." Neither gentleman cared for confrontation, but they would not stand by and allow a woman to be abused if they could prevent it.

Mr. Bennet remained to visit with his friend as the gentlemen discussed the status of their estates and the progress with the spring planting. In under an hour, Mr. Bennet was again home and ensconced in his book room, book in hand.

In the next day's mail, Mr. Bennet received the following letter.

Hunsford Parsonage
Kent
23 April 1811

Dear Cousin Bennet,

I demand you remove your daughter and return her to her home. Her thoughtless actions embarrassed me in front of my patroness. If that were not enough, she has thrown herself at Mr. Darcy in the presence of his betrothed, Miss Anne de Bourgh.

I will not tolerate her presence any longer. I expect your immediate arrival to remove her and demand you discuss with her appropriate behavior for a young lady of her standing. Her actions are little better than those of a trollop, and she is reaching far above her station. Lady Catherine would never accept such a lowly creature as Cousin Elizabeth marrying into her family.

I will not tolerate such poor behavior in my home, nor, under the circumstances, do I wish to continue my correspondence with your family. After the indignities I have suffered at the hands of Cousin Elizabeth, your wife and any unmarried daughters should not expect any consideration from me upon your demise.

Respectfully,

William Collins

Mr. Bennet tossed aside the letter. It did not deserve his immediate attention.

During Elizabeth's first week at Rosings, the residents remained mainly at home, though with many outings around the estate. There were a few nearby sights Darcy wished to visit with Elizabeth, but they delayed those trips to allow the bruising on her arm to fade. While the friendships grew between the four young people, Mr. Collins still attempted to see Lady Catherine daily. In his desperation, he asked to see Miss de Bourgh one morning toward the end of the week. When shown into the parlor where the young lady sat, he frowned upon noticing that Cousin Elizabeth sat beside Mr. Darcy on one sofa while Miss de Bourgh and the colonel sat across from them. The gentlemen glared at the intruder. Elizabeth returned his glare with a stare of her own, but it was Miss de Bourgh who spoke.

"You wished to see me, Mr. Collins."

"Indeed, gracious lady. I was hoping you would allow me to see your esteemed mother. I am sure I could offer her words of comfort at this difficult time."

"Mr. Collins, as I am sure Jackson told you, the doctors say Mother should have no visitors. At present, the pain is excruciating and she remains sedated to keep her comfortable. I am not sure when this will change. It would be best if you stopped dropping by. I will ensure that word is sent to you when it is appropriate for Mother to receive visitors. Now, if you will excuse us, my guests and I have plans for the day."

"Might I have an additional word in private, Miss de Bourgh?"

Anne looked at Andrew and rolled her eyes. "I can give you only a brief moment."

Darcy stood and offered his arm to Elizabeth. "We shall retrieve our outerwear and meet you in the hall," said her cousin. They walked toward the door, giving Mr. Collins a wide berth as they passed. The glares that the gentlemen exchanged could have resulted in an angry outburst with little effort. "Trollop," muttered the parson after they passed. Elizabeth and Mr. Darcy heard the man, and Darcy would have addressed his poor behavior, but Elizabeth kept a firm grip on his arm. With a pleading look and a small shake of her head, they continued on their way.

While Mr. Collins glared at the departing couple, the colonel approached him, standing very close. "That is no way to speak of a lady, sir. I am fond of Miss Elizabeth, and you would not enjoy it if I decided to teach you proper manners when speaking to a gentlewoman."

Mr. Collins's face turned a mottled red as he stiffly returned, "That will not be necessary, Colonel."

"Then never let me hear you making such disparaging remarks about Miss Elizabeth ever again." Collins would not meet the colonel's eyes, nor did he make any reply. "I will wait at the door for you, Anne." With a final dark glare at the grouchy little man, the colonel left, closing the door behind him.

Anne returned to her seat but did not invite the parson to sit down. "What is it you want, Mr. Collins?"

"As the spiritual advisor to your mother and, by extension, yourself, I feel it incumbent upon me to warn you that you should not be entertaining a woman possessing the character of my cousin. She withheld the information about your mother's illness, denying me the opportunity to offer my comfort and assistance. And her attempts to steal Mr. Darcy right out from under your nose are quite blatant. You must watch out for your interests with such a harl--disgraceful woman around."

"Enough, Mr. Collins. Your behavior disgusts me, especially as you are a man of the cloth. Even if Miss Elizabeth had an opportunity to mention my mother's accident earlier, you would have been able to do nothing. She is not permitted to have visitors--something you seem incapable of understanding. As for her behavior toward my cousin, there is no betrothal between Mr. Darcy and myself, and there never will be. Mr. Darcy admires Miss Elizabeth. I hope they will both be very happy. If you dare to defame my guests in such a way ever again, I will make my displeasure known, and you will not like it in the least. Do you understand?"

"No betrothal! I had it from your mother myself. She could not be mistaken about such an important matter."

"It may be my mother's wish, but Mr. Darcy and I have no intention of granting her desires. We would each prefer to find someone to love. Now, do not return to Rosings until summoned. And remember what I said about speaking ill of Miss Elizabeth or of a betrothal where none exists."

"But--"

"Out, Mr. Collins, and I mean now!"

The man bowed very low and backed out of the room. However, Anne did not miss the angry expression on his face.

Andrew entered the room almost immediately after the parson exited. "What did the toad want?"

"To complain about his cousin and warn me she was attempting to steal William from me."

"Does the man not listen? Darcy warned him about speaking poorly about Miss Elizabeth, as did I before departing."

"I believe I will have him banned from the house during our visit to London. The last thing I want is him telling Mother about Darcy's affection for Miss Elizabeth. Fortunately, she will not be able to come after us, even if she learns of his interest."

"The man had best not spread further rumors, or Darcy will hand him his head on a platter."

"I would not mind if we had to replace the parson, especially if we could find someone with a modicum of sense. Though I would not wish any harm to come to Mrs. Collins, I can only hope to someday be able to appoint someone worthy of the position and more concerned with the parish's well-being than my mother's." The cousins shared a laugh.

"What could possibly be funny after being forced to deal with that repulsive man?" Darcy's irritation was still evident.

Miss Elizabeth, who was on his arm, wanted to dispel his poor humor. "I find laughter to be the best way to deal with my cousin. I cannot imagine a more ridiculous man, can you?" The colonel and Anne laughed with Elizabeth.

"He does seem suited to Lady Catherine," added Andrew, and the laughter grew.

Looking down into Elizabeth's smiling face and sparkling eyes, Darcy could feel his annoyance slipping away. In a moment, he was laughing along with the rest.

"Shall we depart?" asked Anne.

"I am anxious to visit Ightham Mote.(1) We saw a castle or two on one of my summer tours with my Aunt and Uncle Gardiner, but I have never seen a mote."

"The house dates back to about 1320 and was built in the Tudor style. The house is built of Kentish ragstone and Wealden Oaks. Along with the mote and the house, there are gardens, streams and lakes fed by a natural spring, and an orchard," explained Darcy.

"Are we taking a picnic along with us?" asked Andrew.

"Yes," acknowledged Anne, "I will ask Jackson to bring it out for us."

"Then let us be on our way!" Andrew offered his arm to Anne and led her to the carriage, with Darcy and Elizabeth following.

It was a frustrated and angry Mr. Collins who returned to the parsonage. He stormed into his study and slammed the door behind him. His mood did not improve when he noticed a letter on top of the stack of mail on his desk. The return address was that of his cousin Bennet. Mr. Collins had been expecting the gentleman's arrival before now, and not a letter. Breaking the seal, he opened the message to find the following:

Longbourn
Hertfordshire
23 April 1811

Collins,

> *How dare you lay hands on my daughter in anger. That is not the behavior of a gentleman and certainly not of a clergyman. You disappoint me. I thought better of you, but I see the apple does not fall far from the tree. Your father was a brute who mistreated people. It was that which caused the breach in our relationship.*

I warned your father-in-law of your behavior. I am sure he will be discussing this matter with you when next you meet.

I do not need to retrieve my daughter, as I am aware that Miss de Bourgh has invited Elizabeth to be her guest at Rosings Park until her scheduled departure. Furthermore, Mr. Darcy has written that he will be coming to Longbourn to speak with me upon his return to London. I am grateful to the gentleman for saving my daughter from your villainous behavior. If, as I presume, he wishes to discuss a future with my daughter, I will happily grant him Elizabeth's hand for his heroic actions.

Have a care with your behavior in the future, sir. By law, you must inherit my estate, but that does not mean I must leave you any monies to maintain it. How would you manage Longbourn if its coffers were empty when you take over?

Thomas Bennet

Mr. Collins fumed as he finished the missive. *How could things have spun so out of control?* He had never felt such anger as he knew upon learning Elizabeth did not immediately inform him of the injury to his patroness. However, everyone made it clear he could have done nothing about it, nor could he even see the great lady. *Am I over-reacting to the situation? I have already infuriated Mr. Darcy and received threats of bodily injury or punishment by the church from both him and the colonel. Miss de*

Bourgh refuses to allow me entry to the house until summoned. And now Bennet is threatening to bankrupt the estate before my inheritance. What should I do to rectify this? The man put his head in his hands and closed his eyes, trying to review the matter with more objectivity.

5. Setting a Trap for an Unwelcome Intruder

Several days after the trip to Ightham Mote, the residents of Rosings took a day trip to visit some Roman ruins in the area. This time they traveled to Lullingstone to visit the remains of the Roman estate built on the site. They departed early, arriving at Lullingstone Roman Villa(3) by ten in the morning. As they rode to their destination, Darcy explained that the original building had first appeared between 80-100 AD. One of its most unusual features was a bathing room. There were also ruins of a temple. Around 500 AD, a fire had ravaged it, destroying most of the house. Some of the original mosaics remained intact, and the group was able to view these ancient artworks. In the middle ages, a castle had been built on the site. After seeing the many buildings, the young people enjoyed the picnic lunch they had brought along. In the afternoon, they strolled the grounds, enjoying the gardens and groves. The group departed so as to arrive at Rosings in time to change for dinner.

They also enjoyed lunch on the terrace and a picnic in the pavilion overlooking the gardens. Little did they know, their activities drew the attention of an unwanted, uninvited observer.

Unknown to her family and friends, quiet Maria Lucas had fallen under the spell of George Wickham. Learning that Miss Elizabeth Bennet's visit to Kent would coincide with that of Fitzwilliam Darcy, Wickham desired to know what had occurred between the two. Upon first encountering Darcy in Meryton while standing with Miss Elizabeth, Wickham instantly realized Darcy's interest in the country miss. Wickham had been quick to spin his tale of woe at Darcy's hands and believed he had turned the young lady against the gentleman whose attention she drew.

Upon receiving the letter indicating that Mr. Darcy visited the parsonage almost daily, Wickham requested leave and immediately journeyed into Kent to discover what he could about Darcy and Miss Elizabeth. After a few days of watching the manor house, Wickham's frustration grew, as he could not follow Darcy when he rode out early each morning without being discovered. Perhaps he should instead follow the young lady. And so, Wickham took up a position outside the parsonage, well hidden from view, where he could keep an eye on the comings and goings. On the first day, he did not arrive in time to observe Elizabeth's departure. However, he was there when she returned. With surprise, Wickham watched Darcy walk Elizabeth to the parsonage's door and, after a glance at their surroundings, raise one hand to his lips, placing a lingering kiss on the back of it. Even after the young lady disappeared, Darcy stood staring into space with a smile upon his face.

Assuming Darcy would return to Rosings Park, Wickham turned to depart when he heard the thud of something impacting wood, then a resounding thwack. Turning back, he noted Darcy standing in the parsonage's open doorway as well as his command: "If you do not release Miss Elizabeth now, I shall remove your hand for you."

Wickham moved stealthily among the trees until he was close enough to attend to the rest of what was said. However, the maid closed the front door before he overheard much. Wickham remained hidden and waited for Darcy to emerge. When he did so, Miss Elizabeth held his arm. Wickham remained in hiding as Darcy spoke to Mrs. Collins: "Please feel free to visit Miss Elizabeth at Rosings whenever you wish."

Wo ho! What is this? Is Darcy taking Miss Elizabeth to stay at Rosings? I wonder what he means by such a step. Are they engaged? Is she to be his mistress? No, Miss Elizabeth would never demean herself in such a manner. Is it possible Darcy managed to change her opinion of him? I will just have to return to the main house and try to discover the state of their relationship. Perhaps I can encourage that dolt of a parson to help me separate them. I cannot allow Darcy to achieve any level of happiness when he so cruelly denied me my felicity. Wickham's thoughts turned to all the times when Darcy had refused to help him with his debts. *He tricked me into signing away the living, and then denied me Georgiana and her dowry after all the work I did to convince the simpleton that we were in love.* George shook his head in disgust, and his will hardened. *Darcy will pay for all his mistreatment of me. Indeed, Darcy will pay dearly.* Wickham gave a wicked laugh as he settled in to watch and wait for Mr. Collins to leave the parsonage.

His patience was rewarded momentarily when he heard the door on the parsonage slam. Then he noted the parson striding away toward the village of Hunsford. Keeping to the tree line along the road, Wickham followed. The parson maintained his purposeful stride, and Wickham discerned the anger radiating from the man. Seeing the parson enter the inn, Wickham smiled evilly and soon followed. Glancing about the room, he saw Mr. Collins seated at a table near the fireplace, a mug of cider before him. Wickham cheerfully called out to the barkeep for a pint as he placed a small coin on the bar in front of him.

Stealing a surreptitious glance in the parson's direction, Wickham discerned that his arrival had gone unnoticed. He would have to make the first move. Making a show of it, he glanced around the room and cried in delight at seeing a familiar face. "Ah, Mr. Collins, I believe. Fancy running into you here."

The parson glanced up in surprise as someone called his name. Still angry, he considered the man, but no sign of recognition appeared. He returned his stare to the mug before him. Hiding a frown, George moved toward the parson's table. "It is Mr. Collins, is it not?" The man peered up but did not speak. "My name is George Wickham. We met in Meryton. I believe you accompanied your lovely cousins into the village, and I had just joined the militia."

Recognition flashed in Mr. Collins's eyes. "Beware their beauty, for, in reality, they are vipers waiting to strike, even after the kindness and condescension of myself and my esteemed patroness." The words were no more than an angry mumble, but they reached Wickham's ears.

"I perceived the often unruly behavior of the youngest two sisters and the middle one's predilection to sermonize when given a chance."

"That is all true, but the worst of the bunch is Miss Elizabeth, the second daughter." Mr. Collins consumed the remainder of his drink and set down the mug so hard, the metal rang like the chime of a bell.

"Let me buy you a drink and you can tell me the tale of Miss Elizabeth's betrayal. At the parson's nod, Wickham held up his glass for two more ales. Mr. Collins drank the first one before pausing to realize it was ale, not cider. However, in his anger, he felt he deserved something more potent than usual. While still nursing his first mug, Wickham pushed the second glass toward the parson. Again, Mr. Collins took a long draught before placing it back on the table before him.

"I infer from your earlier words that Miss Elizabeth harmed you in some way. Is there anything I can do to help correct the situation?"

Collins did not answer right away, but eventually he muttered, "I must separate her from Mr. Darcy. When she recovers, Lady Catherine will be distraught to learn of his defection. She might even be angry with me for bringing the young lady into his presence."

In shocked tones, Wickham asked, "Has Miss Elizabeth caused Darcy to break his engagement to Miss Anne?"

"It would seem so, and right under the noses of Miss Anne and Lady Catherine. I desired to send her home, but Mr. Darcy would not permit it. I can only hope Mr. Bennet will respond to my letter by promptly removing his daughter from my home. After she so ungraciously refused my offer of marriage, it was a mistake to allow her to visit."

Wickham struggled to maintain his countenance at the ridiculous parson's words. He could well imagine the set down that Miss Elizabeth had given the man for what Wickham assumed had been an inept proposal. "You did well to write to Mr. Bennet. Is Miss Elizabeth's visit to be much longer?"

"For another fortnight, I believe."

"Perhaps I can be of assistance to you. I am on my way to visit a relation in Ramsgate, but this situation seems far more important than a few days of relaxation with family and friends."

Wickham continued to ply the parson with ale as he learned all the particulars of the events leading up to the parson's arrival at the tavern. Then they attempted to hammer out a plan to separate the two. Wickham had to help a very drunk parson back to his home before the evening ended. Leaning the parson against the door, he knocked briskly and dashed out of sight. The door opened and the inebriated man fell face-first onto the floor of his entryway. After the door closed again, Wickham snickered at the thought of the headache the silly little man would have on the morrow.

Finally, the time came for them to turn their attention to the journey to London. Charlotte managed to visit Elizabeth on the day before their departure.

"I am sorry I could not come sooner. Mr. Collins has forbidden me to visit after receiving your father's letter. He mutters about ungrateful relations and threats of turning out your family the moment your father dies. However, I did not wish you to depart without saying goodbye."

"Thank you, Charlotte, I do hope this small defiance will not cause any problems in your marriage."

"You need not worry. I can handle my husband.

"Can you stay long enough to enjoy tea with us? I am sure the others would like to visit with you."

"As I do not expect Mr. Collins to return for more than an hour, I would be happy to do so."

"How is he these days, Mrs. Collins? I am pleased he took my words to heart and did not return to entreat daily visits with my mother."

"Though he is often distracted and quite out of sorts, he is well. I have attempted to guide Mr. Collins to some kinder sermon topics during Lady Catherine's illness, even offering to read them in her absence. Hopefully, in the coming weeks of her recovery, I can encourage him to be less compliant with her wishes and more concerned for his parishioners."

"That would be a great improvement," concurred Elizabeth. "May you be successful in your endeavor!" The friends glanced at each other and then broke out in giggles, soon joined by the others in the room.

After three-quarters of an hour, Mrs. Collins rose to depart. "I have enjoyed our time together this afternoon. Eliza, I am so glad you came to visit me, but I am sorry for the trouble my husband caused you. Safe travels on your journey to London tomorrow. I do not know when I shall be able to correspond with you again."

"I understand, and as I said, I do not wish to cause more trouble between you and Mr. Collins."

Anne hesitated only a moment before offering, "I would be happy to act as a go-between for you and Lizzy if you wish to continue your correspondence."

Startled, both ladies stared at her. "I would not wish to inconvenience you," said Elizabeth, "though I greatly appreciate your offer."

"It would not be an inconvenience. I was hoping you would agree to write to me after you return to your home. If you include your letters to Mrs. Collins, I will be sure she receives them."

The other ladies exchanged a look. When Charlotte nodded, Elizabeth turned back and accepted her new friend's offer.

"It is very kind of you to assist us in this way, Miss de Bourgh," said Charlotte. "I would be sad to lose touch with my oldest and dearest friend." The woman took Elizabeth's hand and squeezed it as she spoke. Darcy and Anne accompanied the ladies to the door, where the childhood friends hugged in farewell. After Mrs. Collins's departure, Anne went to talk to the housekeeper while Darcy and Elizabeth took one last stroll in the gardens. It was because of this walk that only the colonel was present when a concerned Jackson requested a moment of his time.

Andrew stood and rapidly exited the room.

In the hallway, the head groom spoke quietly to him.

"Several of the undergardeners noted a stranger on the property. It appears to be the same one each time. He is always loitering near a window or outside the border of the formal gardens. He also lingered near the stables. We cannot determine what he hopes to discover, and he always manages to elude capture."

"Do you have a description of the man?"

The groom gave the description, causing a fierce frown to appear on the colonel's face. "Here is what I want you to do," said the colonel as he laid out a plan for their travels the next day. "Let his coachman know I will inform Mr. Darcy of the arrangements I made to ensure our safety."

"Yes, Colonel Fitzwilliam," said the groom as he departed to fulfill his duties. Then Jackson asked, "Will you ensure Miss Anne is safe? No one would wish to be responsible for informing Lady Catherine should harm come to her daughter."

"I will guarantee her safety," rejoined the colonel with great solemnity.

After an early dinner, the group retired for the night, as they planned to depart by nine the next morning. The gentlemen said goodnight to the ladies, but Darcy was surprised when Andrew followed him to his sitting room.

"What can I do for you, Andrew?"

The colonel poured two brandies, then handed one to his cousin as he sat in a chair before the fire. After a quick sip of the smooth liquor, Andrew relayed what he had learned from the head groom and the plans he had made to ensure they journeyed in safety.

"Do you think it is really him?" asked Darcy. "Based on his current employment, how could he be here?"

"I would not put anything past him, would you?" A raised eyebrow accompanied his words.

"I suppose not. I pray we can end this once and for all."

"That is my hope as well, cousin, and you shall not dissuade me from my purpose this time." Andrew smirked, then finished off his brandy and said good night.

Regrettably, for Darcy, sleep did not come easily. He finally managed to distract himself with thoughts of Elizabeth and drifted into a peaceful slumber.

6. An Eventful Trip to London

The next morning, a maid helped Elizabeth dress. She descended to the breakfast room to find Mr. Darcy and the colonel already present.

"Good morning, gentlemen. How are you?"

Both men rose as Miss Bennet entered the room. "Good morning," answered Colonel Fitzwilliam.

"Good morning, Miss Elizabeth. Are you prepared for our journey?"

"Yes, Mr. Darcy. Though I have enjoyed my time in Kent, I look forward to seeing my dearest sister again."

A twinkle in his eyes, Darcy said, "I am certain you two have much you wish to discuss."

"I believe we both have some happy events to share." Elizabeth's eyes held a matching twinkle as she replied.

Elizabeth moved to the sideboard to fill a plate. However, before the gentlemen could retake their seats, Anne entered the room and the greetings were repeated.

Once he finished eating, Colonel Fitzwilliam excused himself from the group. "I wish to check the vehicles before we depart. Darcy, you do not mind waiting for the ladies, do you?"

"Of course not, Andrew. We shall be ready in--." Darcy's voice trailed off as he glanced at the two ladies.

"Fifteen minutes," responded Anne, her brow raised questioningly at Elizabeth, who nodded in agreement.

"You need not rush, ladies, as it will probably take me longer than that to ensure the vehicles are safe for our travels."

"Then we will prepare, Andrew, and await you in the ground floor reception room," said Anne. "Will you please request that one of the grooms walk Fiona, so she is ready when we are? I am grateful to you for allowing me to bring her along, William."

The others finished their meal and separated to attend to last-minute needs before their departure. The three were chatting about the events and sights they wished to visit while in London when Andrew entered.

"I believe we are ready to depart." Though he spoke to the room in general, his eyes connected with Darcy's. Darcy raised a brow and Andrew nodded. The exchange went unnoticed by Anne, but, Elizabeth, her gaze often on Mr. Darcy, noticed and wondered what it could mean. She would consider the matter later. They all stood and gathered the items they would take with them inside the carriage before moving to the door. With surprise, Elizabeth noted a second carriage.

"Are we taking so much that we require two carriages?"

"On our journey here, my valet and Andrew's batman rode in the carriage with us. Now, with the addition of you, Anne, and her maid, we require a second vehicle." Darcy disliked misleading Elizabeth, but he did not want her and Anne to worry as they traveled.

Soon, they were all aboard. The ladies sat in the forward-facing bench. Between them sat a basket containing Fiona. Anne's hand cursorily stroked the dog. Within ten minutes, the carriage had turned out of the gates of Rosings Park. Charlotte stood on the doorstep of the parsonage, waving goodbye as it passed. They skirted the edge of Hunsford village, where they joined the road to London. At that point, Anne let out a long sigh.

"Are you well, Anne?" asked Elizabeth in concern.

"Yes, why?"

"Well, you sighed so heavily I thought something might be wrong."

Anne blushed but a slight smile turned up the corners of her mouth. "I guess I did not realize the extent of my concern that something would happen with Mother that would prevent me from taking this trip. Mother does not care to travel, and because she insists that Darcy and I will wed, she does not feel the need for me to experience the season or any of the events in London. I am relieved to be safely away and beyond my mother's reach for several weeks."

At her friend's words, Elizabeth tried to keep her smile in check but was unsuccessful due to the laughter that the remark evoked in both of Anne's cousins.

"We shall ensure you do all you wish during our time in London," pledged Andrew.

"Indeed, if you can tolerate his company and his general can spare him, we will press him into service as your escort. Then the six of us can plan as many outings as you would like!"

"The six of us?" asked Anne in confusion.

"Yes," explained Elizabeth. "My elder sister, Jane, is also in London for a time, and she has lately reunited with Mr. Charles Bingley, who is a close friend of Mr. Darcy's."

Darcy and Andrew wore almost identical expressions of pleasure and embarrassment, but Elizabeth's warm smile helped alleviate the feelings of guilt in both men.

The carriage was halfway between Rosings and Bromley when three masked riders, each armed, appeared in the roadway. The coachman drew the horses to a halt and gathered the reins in one hand, lowering the other across his lap. The center horseman did not speak but motioned with his arm. The other two men dismounted and approached the carriage. Each held a shotgun before him and also had a pistol tucked into his belt.

As the vehicle began to slow, the men speedily switched places with the women so the latter would not be visible to the men approaching from the front. Andrew leaned down, opened a compartment in the rear-facing seat, and pulled out two weapons, which he thrust into Darcy's hands. Then the colonel tucked a knife in his boot and withdrew two more weapons. As the tension in the carriage mounted, Fiona jumped from her basket and into Anne's arms. She looked out the window beside her mistress, baring her teeth in a snarl.

The ladies' eyes grew wide and Elizabeth felt Anne begin to shake. She put one arm around Anne's shoulder and clasped the other hand tightly with her own. Leaning in, Elizabeth murmured, "It appears the men prepared for emergencies. I am sure all will be well. If you wish, you can lay down across my lap, and you will be unseen." The steadiness in Elizabeth's voice helped calm Anne, who squeezed Elizabeth's hand and gave a small, tremulous smile.

The highwaymen stopped just before the carriage windows, expecting to see two ladies. However, the sight that met their eyes was that of two gentlemen, each pointing two pistols at them. They hesitated but, at a mumbled word from their leader, demanded, "Send the ladies down. They be comin' with us. Pay the ransom an' we'll return 'em, but there be no promise they'll be in the same condition as when they left you." His bawdy laughter left no doubt of the men's intentions, and his cohort was quick to join him.

The colonel studied the man before him. Though large in stature, he did not appear to be overly intelligent. A glance at the man on Darcy's side of the carriage confirmed his opinion.

"I think not," said the colonel.

At that moment, another carriage appeared behind Darcy's. The moment it began to slow, several armed men leaned from both sides of the carriage, their guns also trained on the highwaymen. Even before the carriage stopped, the men were jumping to the ground and advancing toward the offenders.

While the two lone men considered their leader with alarm, Andrew slowly and subtly stepped down from the right side of the carriage. He moved to the edge of the road, still holding both pistols. "It is no use, Wickham," Andrew called out, "you will not escape this time."

The man on the horse made no move. The colonel was close enough to view the widening of his eyes in surprise.

"You may have been able to sneak about Pemberley unobserved because of your familiarity with the property, but Rosings's grooms and groundskeepers have repeatedly seen you, and from close enough to give me an accurate description of the intruder."

"That matters not, as we outnumber you."

"Perhaps you should take another look," taunted Andrew, who had heard the arrival of the other coach.

Trying to make the movement subtle while maintaining his focus on the coachman, Wickham quickly swept his eyes to the sides of the carriage. Dismay filled him when he found at least two men on each side, their weapons trained on his cohorts. When his gaze returned to the front, Wickham noticed the coachman pointing a pistol directly at him.

"As you can see, you have been outmaneuvered," Andrew said. "You will not escape your punishment this time. If you think you can turn and flee, I promise to put a bullet in your back. Because of your actions, I will suffer no punishment for it."

Trying to maintain his bravado, Wickham needled, "I never figured you for a coward, Fitzwilliam. Darcy yes, but you no. Only a coward would shoot a man in the back." The quaver in his voice gave away his fear.

While Wickham focused on Andrew, William whispered, "Get on the floor and stay out of sight." Realizing he meant to put himself in harm's way, Elizabeth widened her eyes in fear, but Darcy squeezed her hand and gave her a reassuring smile before he climbed down.

Though Elizabeth could not espy him, Darcy's voice, loud and clear, came from outside. "I do not know what this man offered to pay you, but I can assure you he does not have the funds to make good on his promise. He is supposed to be in Hertfordshire with his militia regiment. I recently had someone make the rounds of the village near his post and discovered your leader owes over seven hundred pounds in unpaid debt. That is over eight years' salary in the militia. How can a man so deeply in debt pay what he owes you? If you put down your weapons now, I will pay double what he promised you to your families and explain to the magistrate that you cooperated. After all, you have attempted to rob the son of an earl. I doubt the courts will take such an offense lightly."

"It be just us and our mum. You'll see to 'er care if'n we give up?" asked one.

At the same time, the other said, "You'll put in a good word for us?"

"Yes." Darcy's firm and clear gaze affirmed his words.

Despite the epithets that Wickham screamed at the men, both placed their weapons on the ground, then put their hands in the air. The footmen from the back of the Darcy coach tucked their guns into their belts and grabbed rope from the boot of the carriage to tie up Wickham's accomplices.

"Well, now, Wickham, what will it be? Are you going to surrender, or do I get to shoot you?"

Wickham was furious. He had planned everything down to the last detail. Even if someone spotted him in the area, Darcy and

Fitzwilliam could not have known his plans. He saw red that, again, he was to be denied what he wanted and most likely would not escape. However, if that were the case, he would do as much damage as possible rather than giving up without a fight.

Turning his head in Andrew's direction, Wickham appeared to be pondering his choices. With a slight pull of the reins, he caused his horse to dance sideways, giving him a clear shot at Darcy. Wickham lowered his head as if in defeat, his arm lowering infinitesimally.

Andrew knew Wickham would not easily submit, so he kept his gaze trained on the scoundrel.

Then everything happened at once. The ladies heard three shots and could not contain the cries of alarm that escaped them. The commotion caused Fiona to bark wildly. Without a thought for herself, Elizabeth jumped from the coach on Darcy's side, crying, "William, tell me you are not hurt!"

Darcy, bent over someone sitting on the ground, turned and glared at Elizabeth. His tone sharper than he intended, he shouted, "I told you to stay in the carriage!"

Elizabeth's eyes lost their fury, but upon seeing the blood on Darcy's shirt sleeve, she blanched and cried, "William, you are bleeding. Please let me tend to your wound."

"It is not my blood, Elizabeth. I am uninjured." Her relief was extreme, but she checked him over twice to confirm there were no signs of harm. Darcy led her to the carriage and helped Anne from the floor before assisting Elizabeth back in. "We should not be here much longer. The magistrate and constable from Hunsford are in the carriage that followed us. We sent the servants on ahead, as is usually done."

"You knew something was going to happen?" asked Lizzy in confusion.

"Wickham was seen near Rosings. We did not know his plans but suspected he might try something, so Andrew devised a plan of action to protect us."

"It appears the colonel is a skilled strategist." A little chuckle accompanied Elizabeth's words, but the laughter did not reach her eyes. "I shall expect a full explanation when we resume our journey." A crooked brow accompanied this statement.

"Of course. Now, if you will excuse me." Darcy closed the door and turned away toward the front of the carriage. Wickham's body lay in the road. The colonel and Darcy's coachman stood over it. Looking at Wickham, Darcy noted blood on one of his hands and a shot to his forehead. "What happened?" he asked.

It was his cousin who answered. "He pretended to surrender, but I knew he would want to inflict as much damage as possible before doing so. He raised his gun to fire at you. Your coachman shot the hand holding the gun, causing him to miss you, I pray, and I dealt him the lethal blow." By this time, the constable and magistrate had exited the second carriage, and both came forward, guns drawn. They reached the group near the downed body in time to hear the colonel's explanation.

Lord Carstairs, the magistrate, said, "I will send the body and prisoners back to Hunsford with the constable. However, if you will permit me to accompany you to Bromley, I will take your statements before renting a horse to return to my home. If you are needed to testify, I will notify you at Darcy House."

"That is fine. My staff can forward your message should I not be in residence," replied Darcy. "Oh, would you also ask the two who surrendered what Wickham promised to pay them? I promised to double it, give the funds to their families, and recommend leniency because they surrendered. Wickham hired them for their brawn because neither man appears to possess much intelligence. I am sure they agreed to help because whatever amount Wickham offered would assist their family during these difficult times."

"Of course, Mr. Darcy," agreed Lord Carstairs.

Wickham's body was thrown over the saddle of his horse, while the hands of the two accomplices were tied to their mounts. The constable and two others took up the leading-strings and turned toward Hunsford. Over his shoulder, the constable called, "I will investigate if any others plotted with Wickham."

Those from Rosings Park who had assisted returned to the carriage, which found the first road that would allow it to turn about and return to the estate.

Lord Carstairs ascended into the carriage and took his place on the rear-facing seat with Darcy and Colonel Fitzwilliam. Darcy considered the ladies. Anne was pale from the experience and clutched one of Elizabeth's hands, while she cuddled the now-quiet Fiona with the other. Darcy could tell from the look in her eyes that Elizabeth was anxious to learn the full extent of what had happened. He introduced the magistrate and explained to the ladies that they would stop in Bromley for refreshments, at which time the men would explain everything while the magistrate wrote their statements for their signatures. When the reports were complete, they would continue their journey to London, though they might not arrive in time for tea.

"I will send an express when we leave, giving your family an updated estimate on the time of our arrival," said Darcy.

"My thanks, sir. I am sure they will worry should we not arrive as planned."

"It is my pleasure, Miss Elizabeth." Darcy gave Elizabeth a reassuring smile. The group traveled in silence until they reached their destination.

7. A Happy Reunion

When the carriages reached the Bell in Bromley, Colonel Fitzwilliam took charge. He requested writing supplies for their bespoke private room. Miss de Bourgh's maid rushed out to assist her mistress but had to wait for the colonel to help her down. Between the two, they ushered her inside, with the magistrate following. The servants had been sent ahead to await their arrival, knowing the others might encounter trouble on the way. While the colonel spoke to the innkeeper, Darcy assisted Elizabeth from the carriage. She paced beside the vehicle while Darcy addressed his coachman and the others who had helped them on the journey. When he finished his task, Darcy offered Elizabeth his arm and they followed the others into the inn. They paused at the door as Elizabeth reminded Darcy that someone would need to water and walk Fiona while they stopped. Darcy requested the assistance of a footman in this endeavor.

With Anne still somewhat unsettled from the attempted hold-up and kidnapping, Elizabeth requested tea and light refreshments for the group. When the serving girl departed, the others settled themselves around the table. Darcy and Andrew sat next to the magistrate, who sat at the head of the table. Elizabeth took the chair next to Darcy, with Anne beside Andrew. It was the colonel who again took the lead. The magistrate, already knowing about the stranger trespassing on the grounds of Rosings, listened and wrote as swiftly as he could while Andrew outlined the events of the morning, from the time when the three men had stepped into the road to the time when the magistrate and constable had arrived to hear his account of the shooting of Wickham.

"I believe this will serve as your statement, Colonel Fitzwilliam. However, Mr. Darcy, if you could write out your report, as you did not witness everything the colonel did, we should be able to conclude this matter posthaste." At Darcy's nod, Lord Carstairs pushed the paper, quill, and ink in the younger man's direction.

As Darcy began to write what he knew and observed, the young lady returned with tea. As Anne's face was still alarmingly white, the colonel addressed the serving girl. "Could you please bring me a glass of brandy?"

She bobbed her head in agreement and returned promptly with the desired item. The colonel took the glass and poured a small amount into Anne's tea, which Elizabeth put in front of her. "Take small sips, Anne," Andrew said. "The brandy will help you recover from the excitement. I would feel I failed in my responsibilities if you fainted from the shock of this experience." He accompanied the words with a warm smile. Anne blushed at the attention and did as Andrew requested. After a few sips, the color returned to her cheeks, and the tension in her shoulders melted away.

"I pray Mother never learns of this incident, for she would surely keep me locked away at Rosings for the remainder of my days." Anne's smile encouraged chuckles from the others and allowed everyone to recover their equanimity.

When Darcy finished his statement and signed the document, Lord Carstairs spoke. "I thank you for your forethought and planning in the handling of today's events, Colonel, Mr. Darcy. You gentlemen saved these young women from an ordeal that would have been more unpleasant than what they experienced. I believe the world is better off without a scoundrel like Mr. Wickham in it." The magistrate rolled up the statements from the gentlemen and tucked them in a pocket inside his greatcoat. Then, standing, he said, "I must take my leave, but I pray the remainder of your journey is uneventful." With a bow to those present, he turned and departed.

Darcy took a swallow of the brandy before him, then grabbed a pastry from the plate. He turned to write his note to Mr. Gardiner, providing their new arrival time. "Ladies," said Darcy, "I believe it is time to be on our way. While you attend to last-minute needs, I will send my express to Elizabeth's uncle." As Darcy exited the room, the ladies finished their tea and excused themselves to visit the necessary. That completed, they found the gentlemen waiting for them in the entry to the inn. Andrew offered his arm to Anne, while Darcy offered his to Elizabeth. They escorted the ladies from the building and assisted them into the carriage.

They were soon underway. The remainder of the ride passed pleasantly as the conversation flowed effortlessly between the friends. They all looked around in amazement when the carriage wheels began clattering over the cobblestone streets signaling their arrival on the outskirts of London. Only a short while later, the vehicle pulled up before Sixteen Gracechurch Street.

The door to the house opened as the carriage came to a stop before it. Mr. and Mrs. Gardiner appeared on the step, awaiting the appearance of their niece. Mr. Darcy stepped down and assisted Elizabeth. She rushed up the stairs to greet her aunt and uncle, as Darcy and the others followed. Elizabeth finished hugging her relations and turned to make the introductions. Before she could say anything, Mrs. Gardiner said, "Please do come in." She and her husband led the way, and the others followed them into the house. Servants were waiting to take their outerwear, and then the guests followed their hosts into the parlor. Upon entering, Darcy and Elizabeth both noted the others in the room. Elizabeth ran to hug her sister and Darcy greeted Bingley with a firm handshake and a clap on the back.

Before anyone took their seats, Elizabeth made the introductions. "Aunt, Uncle, Jane, Mr. Bingley, allow me to introduce Miss Anne de Bourgh of Rosings Park, Kent; Colonel Andrew Fitzwilliam, second son of the Earl of Matlock; and Mr. Fitzwilliam Darcy of Pemberley, Derbyshire. Miss de Bourgh, Colonel Fitzwilliam, Mr. Darcy, my aunt and uncle, Mr. and Mrs. Edward Gardiner, my elder sister Miss Jane Bennet, and Mr. Charles Bingley, whom I believe some of you already know."

Everyone exchanged greetings along with bows and curtsies. Once finished, Mrs. Gardiner offered seats to the newcomers. Darcy looked at his hosts and said, "It is a pleasure to meet you both. Miss Elizabeth speaks of you with great fondness."

"It is a pleasure to meet you as well. Lizzy's letters have been full of the kindness of her new friends," said Mrs. Gardiner.

"Thank you, Mr. Darcy, for sending word of your late arrival. My wife would have worried terribly had we not known you would be late. I hope whatever caused your delay in arriving was nothing serious," said Mr. Gardiner.

Darcy and Andrew exchanged a glance, but neither spoke immediately.

Lizzy spoke in response to her uncle's question. "It was quite an adventure, Uncle, but I shall leave the telling of it to Mr. Darcy or the colonel.

Andrew looked at Darcy with raised brows. Seeing his cousin's expression, he relayed the details of their adventure, including the events at Rosings that led up to the preparations for their trip. Gasps escaped both Jane and Mrs. Gardiner at several points during the recounting.

"I am very grateful to both you gentlemen, for your care of my niece," commented Mr. Gardiner. "I am glad to say we have never experienced such a thing during any of our travels. I can only assume it was made worse by knowing it was someone of your acquaintance wishing to cause you harm."

"Lamentably, Wickham has caused trouble for my cousin for most of his life," Andrew said.

"It is hard to imagine such a pleasant young man could be so deceitful and wicked," added Jane. "He certainly presented himself differently when we made his acquaintance in Meryton."

"I, for one, am glad he cannot cause further harm to anyone," said Elizabeth decisively. "Both Lydia and Kitty were quite enamored of the officers, and Mr. Wickham in particular. Perhaps if I wrote to Papa of the events, he would caution my sisters to be less accepting of the militia officers."

Changing the subject, Mrs. Gardiner spoke. "As you were not able to join us for tea, would you and your family consider staying to supper, Mr. Darcy? Mr. Bingley is staying, and your presence will help round out the numbers."

Looking at his cousins for their opinion, Darcy turned back to his hostess, saying, "We are pleased to accept your invitation."

A clattering on the stairs caused everyone to look toward the door to the parlor. A small blur with dark chestnut curls very like Elizabeth's flew into the room and into the arms of her cousin, with cries of "Lithy, Lithy, I am tho glad you are here!"

The youngest Gardiner child did not notice the others in the room as she raced to greet her favorite cousin. However, the older children followed, pausing in the doorway, eyes wide, as they noted several strangers in the parlor with their parents and cousins, and, of course, Mr. Bingley, who visited almost daily.

Lizzy hugged the child to her, whispering in her ear, "What have your mother and governess taught you about rushing into a room?" Pushing the child back a little, she turned her to see their visitors.

"Come here, children," Elizabeth called, extending her hand toward the two in the doorway. When they moved to stand beside their younger sibling, Elizabeth said, "Margaret,

Michael, Amelia, please meet my friends Miss Anne de Bourgh, Colonel Andrew Fitzwilliam, and Mr. Fitzwilliam Darcy. Miss de Bourgh, Colonel, Mr. Darcy, may I introduce to you my young cousins, Miss Margaret Gardiner, Master Michael Gardiner, and Miss Amelia Gardiner." Margaret and Michael gave a credible curtsey and bow, while Amelia's curtsey was a tad wobbly.

"It is a pleasure to meet you, Miss Gardiner, Master Michael, and Miss Amelia." It was Darcy who spoke first. Looking at Miss Amelia, he remarked, "You are very fond of your cousin, Miss Elizabeth, I take it."

"Oh, yeth," cried Amelia. "Lithy is the betht cousin. Thhe plays gameth with uth and readth thories, and takes uth to the park. I love it when thhe cometh to vithit!"

"I would have to agree. Your cousin is wonderful company." Elizabeth blushed when Darcy looked at her as he said these words.

Amelia looked from Mr. Darcy to Elizabeth, confusion on her face. "Lithy, why ith your face red? What kind of gameth do you play with Mr. Darcy?"

Amelia's words only made Elizabeth's blush deepen, but caused several of those present to chuckle. "Mr. Darcy and I are friends, Amelia. We sometimes play cards together, but most often, we discuss books we have read."

"Children," said Mrs. Gardiner, "it is time to return to the nursery. Please say good night to everyone." The children bowed and curtsied to the guests, then moved to hug Elizabeth, Jane, and their parents.

As they followed their nurse from the room, Amelia stopped in the doorway and said, "Lithy, will you come and read uth a thory?"

"I shall be up as soon as we finish supper," Elizabeth promised.

"Thinthe you like thorieth, you can come too, Mithter Darthy."

"I would be honored to join you, Miss Amelia."

The child smiled broadly and rushed to catch up with her siblings.

"Your children are charming, Mrs. Gardiner," said Anne.

"Thank you."

At that point, the housekeeper appeared in the doorway and announced dinner. Mr. Gardiner offered his arm to his wife and led the way to the dining room. The others paired off and followed.

As the meal progressed, the conversation flowed. The group discussed plays presently running and special exhibits that were available. The gentlemen talked about the war with France, while the ladies spoke of the best dressmakers. "Though my modiste is not well-known in the ton, she is indeed one of the best in town, and my husband gives her the first pick of fabrics when he receives a new shipment. I always treat the girls to a new gown when they visit, so I planned to visit her on Monday, as Lizzy just arrived. You would be welcome to accompany us, Miss de Bourgh."

"If my cousin, Miss Darcy, is not otherwise engaged, might she join us, as well?"

"That is an excellent idea, Anne," said Darcy. "I have long wished she could make Miss Elizabeth's acquaintance."

"I should love to meet her." Elizabeth's face glowed with pleasure that the protective Mr. Darcy wanted her to meet his precious sister. When the ladies separated from the gentlemen, they set a time for their shopping trip. The gentlemen did not sit long over their port, as Darcy and Elizabeth had a date with the children.

When he appeared in the parlor doorway, Darcy said, "I believe we are required in the nursery, Miss Elizabeth." She stood and joined him, then led the way to the children's rooms. Darcy took the largest chair in the nursery, moving it close to the sofa on which Elizabeth sat surrounded by the children. Seeing her thus caused Darcy's heart to beat faster. He could not help but picture her surrounded by their children one day, and a beaming smile spread over his face.

Elizabeth took the book Amelia handed her and began to read. It charmed Darcy to hear her change voices for the characters, and the children's enraptured faces delighted him. Elizabeth would make a wonderful mother.

When the story ended, the children hugged Elizabeth again and moved to their beds. Amelia was the last to say goodnight. She turned from Elizabeth, hesitating, then turned to Mr. Darcy and hugged his legs. She let go with a giggle and jumped into her bed. The look of pleased surprise on his face caused Elizabeth's heart to beat a little faster as she wondered what type of father he would be.

Shortly after Darcy and Elizabeth returned downstairs, the guests departed. Both families planned to enjoy a quiet Sunday before they began their busy schedule of shopping and events.

8. Unpleasant Encounters

Promptly at the appointed time on the designated morning, the Darcy carriage arrived in front of the Gardiner residence. Darcy stepped out first and handed down Anne and Georgiana. They mounted the steps to the house and followed the butler into the parlor, where the other ladies were waiting to welcome them. Darcy introduced Georgiana to Jane Bennet and Mrs. Gardiner before Anne engaged them both in conversation.

Turning to Elizabeth, he said, "Miss Elizabeth, allow me to introduce my sister, Miss Georgiana Darcy. Georgiana, this is Miss Elizabeth Bennet."

The ladies both made their curtsies, but Elizabeth spoke first. "It is a pleasure to meet you, Miss Darcy. Your brother and cousins speak quite highly of you."

"Thank you," said Georgiana shyly. "Darcy, Andrew, and Anne told me many wonderful things about you, as well. My brother wrote of you during his stay at Netherfield, and Anne and Andrew spoke of their enjoyment in making your acquaintance while at Rosings."

Elizabeth led the young lady to a nearby settee and took a seat to one side of Georgiana. Darcy sat on Elizabeth's other side, where he beheld both of his ladies. They chatted for a short time about music before Mrs. Gardiner reminded them of the time. With an impertinently raised brow, Elizabeth asked, "Do you plan to accompany us to the dressmaker today, Mr. Darcy? I am sure you would find shopping even more tedious than I do." She laughed.

"Though I doubt I would consider any time spent in your company tedious, Miss Elizabeth, I shall leave you ladies to your shopping. I wished to personally make the introduction of Georgiana to you and your family."

"I am sure my aunt and sister would agree that we are delighted with our new acquaintance. We anticipate spending the day in Miss Darcy's company so that we might become better acquainted. Do you need us to drop you somewhere on our way to the dressmaker?"

"Thank you, but no. I tied my horse to the back of the carriage. I thought you might enjoy using the larger vehicle today. It will bring the ladies home after you complete your outings."

"How thoughtful of you, Mr. Darcy," said Mrs. Gardiner. "Mr. Gardiner returned his carriage for our use today, but I daresay, yours shall be more comfortable for five ladies and their packages at the end of a busy day of shopping." Everyone laughed at Mrs. Gardiner's quip.

Darcy waited as the ladies gathered their outerwear and prepared to depart. Offering his arm to Elizabeth and Georgiana, he led the ladies from the house. Darcy stopped at the carriage door for the footman to open it. He handed in Georgiana and Elizabeth before turning to assist the remainder of the ladies into the vehicle. Darcy then untied his horse from the back and stood waving to the occupants as the carriage moved away from the Gardiners's home. When it turned the corner, he mounted his horse and headed for his club, where he would meet Bingley and Andrew to plan some outings for the ladies.

As the carriage moved through the streets of London, the ladies discussed how many and which types of dresses they would need. "I already ordered one for you, Lizzy, that only needs a fitting," said Mrs. Gardiner. "However, your uncle and I discussed the matter last evening and we would like to purchase an additional half dozen gowns for each of you. I believe we should get one ball gown, two evening gowns, and three walking or afternoon dresses. Then, whatever events the gentleman plan, you will have the appropriate attire."

"Aunt, you need not go to such expense," said Elizabeth. "I am sure Mr. Darcy will not mind what I wear. He knows Father does not possess the funds for such extravagance."

"I quite agree. Mr. Darcy shall not mind what you wear, for he clearly finds you lovely no matter the circumstances. However, Lizzy, and you as well, Jane, this is London society into which you will be mixing. The ladies of the ton can be quite harsh on newcomers, especially when they appear in public with one of the city's most eligible bachelors."

"Your aunt is quite right, Lizzy," said Anne. "William has been the most sought-after bachelor of the ton since he first appeared at eight and ten. Things became worse when he went from being the heir of Pemberley to its master. Your aunt wishes to protect you from the vitriol of the many young ladies who unsuccessfully tried to capture

William's attention over the years. In fact, it would be my honor if you would allow me to purchase a dress or two for you as well. You are the first friend permitted me in a very long time. You made the time at Rosings much more enjoyable. Now you are sharing your family with me, and your aunt is kindly introducing me to her dressmaker. I wish to repay the kindness that all of you are extending to me. You know what my life with Mother is like. Can you deny me this simple pleasure?"

Elizabeth felt guilty when she remembered how tightly controlled Anne's life was. How could she deny either of these wonderful women something that would give them pleasure?

Before she could respond, Georgiana added her opinions. "For the happiness you bring William, I would offer to do the same as Anne, but I do not wish to make you any more uncomfortable than you seem. However, like my cousin, my life has not abounded with friendship and good company. At school, I learned most of the girls I thought were my friends only pretended to be so to meet my brother. When he showed no interest in them, they no longer wished to associate with me." Thinking of how Miss Bingley spoke of Georgiana, Elizabeth understood her feelings and experienced sadness for the wonderful young lady seated across from her. "Because William introduced you, I need not worry about that where you are concerned. I do hope we can be friends."

Elizabeth had to strain to understand Georgiana's softly spoken words. "I would like that very much. And I do understand your meaning. I had the--ah--pleasure of making the acquaintance of Miss Bingley while her brother resided at Netherfield." At Elizabeth's words, Georgiana and Anne both rolled their eyes. Upon seeing their action, Elizabeth contained her mirth as long as possible. However, soon Elizabeth, Anne, and Georgiana were laughing so hard, tears streamed down their cheeks. Mrs. Gardiner, who had twice briefly encountered Miss Bingley, tried to contain her laughter as she recognized the uncertainty in Jane's eyes.

When Elizabeth noted her sister's expression, she took a deep breath to calm her amusement. "I am sorry to speak so bluntly, Jane, but you learned of her perfidy in separating you from her brother and her bad manners when you called and when she returned your call. You cannot still believe Miss Bingley is your friend?"

"I am aware of her true nature, Elizabeth, but she will be my sister someday. It does not seem appropriate to make fun of her in this way." Jane's cheeks were scarlet in her embarrassment.

"Oh, please forgive us, Miss Bennet," said Georgiana contritely. "I could not help myself. My brother is not aware I learned of this incident, but I learned Clarke ejected Miss Bingley from Brother's room during her last stay at Pemberley." Elizabeth's eyes widened at the younger girl's words. "His valet caught her in my brother's bed, waiting for him. She intended to compromise him and force him into a marriage. Miss Bingley gives no thought to what anyone else wants or feels. Her actions are always selfish. I would urge you to be cautious in all your interaction. I believe she is at her most conniving when she is *helpful*. I realize how fond Mr. Bingley is of you, and I would not wish either of you hurt because of her actions or wishes."

Anne looked at Georgiana in wonderment. It was unlike her shy cousin to share such information or to speak so forcefully. "William would be shocked if he knew you were aware of that, Georgiana. He told me of the events during his visit this Easter. William is extremely fond of Mr. Bingley but would like to avoid his sisters altogether. He endures them only for his friend's sake. However, were she ever to cause trouble for someone Darcy loves, he would take whatever steps necessary to exclude her from his life. Fortunately, Mr. Bingley is also aware of his sister's manipulations. If she pushes him too far, she shall find herself living in the north with a maiden aunt, from what William tells me."

"It is hard to conceive of a woman acting in such a fashion. I thank you, ladies, for your words of caution. I shall do my best to be kind, but keep Miss Bingley at arm's distance."

"I think your decision is a wise one, Jane," said Aunt Gardiner. "Well, ladies, shall we turn our thoughts to a more enjoyable subject? We are here. Let us not keep Mrs. Hartfield waiting. There are measurements to be taken, fabrics, trims, and patterns to be selected, and good company to enjoy." Mrs. Gardiner hesitated for a moment, then added, "Jane, Elizabeth, please describe to the modiste the ideas you would wish for your wedding dress design. I realize they are not needed right away, but she can work up sketches for your approval, thus making the gowns easier to have ready in a timely fashion when required."

For the next three hours, the ladies were busy ordering the new clothes they would need.

Elizabeth, who tended to not be overly fond of shopping, found she enjoyed the experience much more than usual. Each of the ladies offered suggestions and compliments to the others as they made their selections. Jane ordered a ball gown of sky blue, a walking dress in a similar shade, and one in light blue trimmed with sapphire ribbons. Her evening dresses were pale pink and deep blue. Elizabeth chose a ball gown of lavender trimmed with silver lace. Her evening gowns were deep rose and aqua, while her walking dresses were pale yellow and mint green. She agreed to allow Anne to purchase two day dresses for her--one white with pale green and blue stripes and the other white with a pattern of clusters of lavender and yellow flowers and green vines. Anne ordered the same number of gowns as Elizabeth. Georgiana did not need anything new but was thrilled to be asked her opinion on the styles and colors that the other ladies chose.

When they finished at the dressmakers, the ladies, in high spirits, journeyed to a teashop two streets over. They found a table near the window and seated themselves. Once they ordered their tea and treats, they discussed other shops they should visit to find the items they needed to accompany their new gowns. So engrossed were they in their conversation, they did not notice the woman who stopped at the window upon recognizing Miss Darcy with two elegant companions. The woman turned to her companion, but whatever she said received a negative reply. Tossing her head and raising her nose higher into the air, the woman turned and left her companion on the sidewalk. Entering the shop, she scurried to Georgiana's table and interrupted the conversation taking place.

"My dear, Miss Darcy. How lovely to run into you today. Do tell me you are well." Everyone turned to stare at the newcomer, at which time Caroline Bingley noted the others at the table with Miss Darcy. Before Georgiana could reply, however, Miss Bingley continued. "How did you come to be in company with such people? I am sure your brother would not approve. You must allow Louisa and me to accompany you home now. You would not wish your reputation to be sullied by consorting with those so far below you in consequence."

In a tone reminiscent of her mother, Anne looked at her young cousin and asked, "Is this interloper known to you, Georgiana?"

The younger lady recognized the hint of wicked amusement lurking in her cousin's eyes but kept her tone composed. "Yes, cousin, this is Miss Caroline Bingley. Miss Bingley, this is my cousin, Miss Anne de Bourgh."

"It is a pleasure to meet you, Miss de Bourgh." Caroline's tone did not convey pleasure as she sized up the woman before her. She understood Miss de Bourgh to be sickly, but the lovely young lady sitting before her seemed to glow with good health. Caroline wondered why the woman was in town. She understood Darcy's intended never left her estate.

Still sounding like Lady Catherine, Anne continued, "I wish I could say the same, but I have heard much about you. I should like to understand why you are insulting Georgiana's and my friends."

"I claim a prior acquaintance with the Misses Bennet," said Miss Bingley with a sneer. "And their aunt is married to a tradesman. I am sure Mr. Darcy would not approve." Caroline sniffed as she finished speaking.

"I will be sure to inform William of your opinions when we return to Darcy House later today." Caroline's eyes widened at the fact that Miss de Bourgh resided with the Darcys. "After all, he escorted us to the Gardiners's home and made the introductions. Miss Elizabeth became a dear friend of mine while she and William were both in Kent over Easter."

Miss Bingley narrowed her eyes and glared at Elizabeth. "Was Mr. Darcy's hasty departure from Netherfield not enough to indicate his lack of interest, Miss Eliza? Why did you find it necessary to follow him to Kent? I suggest you leave the poor man alone. Mr. Darcy could never be interested in someone so far beneath him. And you, Miss Bennet, should keep your distance as well. You are aware of where my brother's interests lie."

The ladies all gasped, but Anne had had enough of the pretentious upstart. "When I encounter Darcy, I will be sure to inform him of your insults to the lady he is courting. I doubt he will be pleased to learn of your actions."

Caroline's eyes widened in disbelief. "He would never stoop to such behavior. How dare you suggest such a thing?"

"It is you who dares too much. Good day, Miss Bingley. I hope we shall not meet again."

The ladies all turned away from Miss Bingley and returned to their conversation. Caroline's fury nearly overwhelmed her and, by a happy chance, robbed her of speech as well.

Several of the other patrons in the shop had witnessed her receiving the direct cut from the ladies at the window table and began whispering amongst themselves. Hearing the murmur of conversation and seeing the many who stared at her, Caroline started, particularly as she recognized one or two of the faces. Drawing back her shoulders, she turned on her heel and, head held high, marched from the shop. When she exited, Louisa hurried to her side and spoke in an urgent undertone. "I told you, you should not interrupt. When will you learn, Caroline? You will not gain acceptance in the first circles if you continue as you are. Charles will be most displeased, and I dread to think what Mr. Darcy might do when he learns of this."

Realizing her sister might be correct, Caroline said, "My head aches dreadfully and I wish to return home immediately. You continue your shopping, and I will take a hackney."

"Nonsense, my errands can wait. Allow me to take you home."

"Louisa, I just wish for quiet time alone to recover. I shall be well as soon as I am lying down."

Mrs. Hurst looked at her sister for several moments before acquiescing. She did not know if she believed Caroline, but perhaps it was time to let her sister learn from her own mistakes. Being a married woman protected Louisa from Caroline's missteps, but only if she did not support her sister in her actions. Nodding, she said, "I hope you feel better. I shall see you at dinner this evening." Louisa had the footman accompanying them hail a cab for her sister. The footman did as requested and handed Miss Bingley into the vehicle before giving the coachman the address to the Hurst townhouse. Louisa watched for only a moment before turning to continue her errands. She rushed past the teashop window, looking the other way so the ladies at the front table would not recognize her.

When the hackney left Bond Street, Caroline said, "Driver, I must make one additional stop before returning home. Please take me to number Eighty-four Park Lane." After giving the driver the address, Caroline, her back rigid for fear of the dirty squabs, began to plan what she would say to convince Darcy to marry her and not Elizabeth Bennet or his cousin. If need be, she would throw herself into his arms and kiss him before his staff. However, that may not garner her the desired effect, as his staff had the reputation of being notoriously close-lipped and loyal.

When the carriage stopped in front of Darcy House, Caroline paid the driver and stepped down from the vehicle. Looking about, she straightened her gown and smoothed the wrinkles from her skirt before mounting the stairs. She knocked on the door and slipped inside before acknowledging the butler. "I must see Mr. Darcy on an urgent manner concerning Miss Darcy. She is in great danger."

The butler's eyes grew round as he listened, but before the opportunity to acknowledge her request arose, Mr. Darcy stepped from the small parlor off the front hall. He and Bingley had just returned from lunch at the club. Outside of Caroline's view, he gestured for his friend to remain hidden while they discovered what Miss Bingley wanted.

"Miss Bingley, what is this about my sister?" asked Darcy sharply.

Looking relieved at being received so quickly, she stepped toward the gentleman, but he took a step backward to keep the distance between them. She did not speak directly but glanced at the butler and footmen nearby. Noting at whom she looked, Darcy gave a quick hand signal to the butler, and the servants disappeared from view. Darcy knew they would still be within hearing, as he had given orders to his servants to never leave him alone with Miss Bingley. As Darcy's staff thoroughly disliked her, they would never allow her to entrap him into marriage.

"Oh, Mr. Darcy, while shopping with Louisa, we happened across Miss Darcy. I went to pay my addresses to her only to be rebuffed in the rudest of manners. I then noticed her companions included the eldest Misses Bennet from Hertfordshire and their lowly aunt, who lives in Cheapside. You must come with me to remove her from such company. Her response to my pleasant greeting can only be the result of her being with such unsophisticated women. If she is allowed to remain under their influence for any length of time, word will get out and her reputation will be ruined in society."

Darcy did not for a minute believe her but wondered why she did not mention Anne. "Was my cousin, Miss de Bourgh, not also present?"

Thinking quickly, she said, "Another lady was with them, but she did not match the description I have always heard associated with your cousin."

"And did this other lady express any concerns at my sister's company?"

"Well, no." Caroline knew she must tread carefully. She had to be honest but still press home her point. "However, the other women's behavior was even more unseemly than Miss Darcy's."

Darcy crossed his arms over his chest. "I doubt there is cause for concern, Miss Bingley. I escorted my sister and cousin to the Gardiners's this morning, as the ladies planned to shop together today."

"Oh, Mr. Darcy, you so obviously need the help of a wife," said Caroline with a sharp, shrill laugh. "Countrified ladies such as the Misses Bennet have no idea how to dress to fit in with your sister's social circle. She will be humiliated if seen in something Miss Eliza Bennet would consider appropriate."

"Please desist in your nonsense, Miss Bingley. It is unseemly of you to call here unchaperoned. Please do not return. I shall inform my staff that you are not welcome unless you are in your brother's company."

Caroline's look changed to one of cunning. "Now, we both know you do not wish Charles to always be underfoot. I know you have feelings for me, Mr. Darcy. Your little infatuation with Miss Eliza will pass, and you know you need someone more appropriate as your wife." Caroline started forward again, but Darcy knew her tricks. He knew what she intended. She started forward, planning to throw herself at him, but at the last moment, Darcy sidestepped and Caroline landed face-first on the tile floor. She looked at him, startled he would do such a thing. Then Caroline heard a snicker coming from the room Darcy had exited. Looking up, she saw her brother standing in the doorway, leaning against the frame. "Charles, what are you doing here? I thought you had an appointment at your club. Otherwise, I would not have accepted Mr. Darcy's invitation to meet him here."

"Nice try, Caroline, but I met with Darcy. We just returned a short time before you arrived. As he told me of his courtship over luncheon, I doubt he invited you to meet him." Caroline's face flushed. "I also know you kept the knowledge of Jane Bennet's presence in town from me. Not only that, you also sent her a letter upon your departure from Netherfield, telling her I did not plan to return and indicating I would soon be marrying Georgiana Darcy." Caroline's face went from red to white and her eyes widened in surprise. "Despite your best efforts, Jane and I are together again, and she has accepted my proposal of marriage. I have already received her father's blessing. We were only awaiting the arrival of Miss Elizabeth and Darcy to discuss the dates."

"Now, Charles, how could you believe she cares for you? How many times must Louisa and I tell you, she is only after your money?"

"You are not looking out for me when you say such things, Caroline. You are only concerned with getting your way. However, I will not allow you to influence me ever again."

"I am your sister. Of course I am concerned for your best interest."

"So, in your opinion, marrying the woman I love is not in my best interest?"

"Just because you love her does not mean she loves you. I overheard her mother crowing about the match the night of the Netherfield ball. If Miss Bennet is chasing you, it is at her mother's direction."

"I happen to know she was heartbroken at my departure."

"How could you know such a thing?"

"Because Darcy told me so."

"Mr. Darcy agreed with Louisa and me that she only wanted your money."

"I did not say that, Miss Bingley," said Darcy, his tone frosty. "I only observed that Miss Bennet did not outwardly appear to have any particular interest in your brother. However, after seeing them together last evening, I would have realized my mistake, had another not already brought it to my attention."

"So now we are to believe the word of an even greater social climber. Miss Eliza set her sights on you, Mr. Darcy. Of course, she would want her sister to catch your friend." Caroline's voice dripped with derision.

"That is enough, Miss Bingley. It is time for you to depart and remember what I said. You are not welcome here without your brother. Do not think to get around this by asking to visit Georgiana or if accompanied by Mrs. Hurst alone. I know my sister is not comfortable with your insincere fawning and flattery. She will be relieved to not have to entertain you."

"I know you do not mean that!" exclaimed Caroline in desperation.

"Indeed, I do. Now you can leave under your own power, or my footmen will toss you from the house. The choice is yours."

Throughout the conversation, Caroline had remained on the floor where she had landed. She sat waiting for one of the gentlemen to assist her to her feet, but she finally had to admit no help would be forthcoming. When she saw the footmen move in her direction, their usually impassive faces showing slight smiles, Caroline scrambled from the floor with as much dignity as she could muster and rushed to exit the house.

Bingley's voice called to her as she stood in the open doorway. "I believe you should begin packing when you arrive home, sister. You will be going to stay with Aunt Bingley for an extended visit."

His sister's face took on an expression of panic and her eyebrows rose nearly to her hairline. She rushed out, closing the door behind her as if chased by the hounds of hell.

It was fortunate for Miss Bingley that her brother would be sending her away. By tomorrow afternoon, the cut she received from a table of ladies, including Miss Darcy and Miss de Bourgh, would be making its way through the drawing rooms of London.

9. An Engagement

When Anne and Georgiana arrived at Darcy House, William waited for them. "I understand you encountered Miss Bingley during your outing. Are you both well?"

"How could you possibly know that!" cried Georgiana in surprise. Anne merely rolled her eyes.

"I will explain later, but please tell me what took place."

Anne noted Darcy's worried expression, but could not resist saying, "May we at least be permitted to remove our wraps and take a seat before doing so?" Her brow arched in a manner reminiscent of Elizabeth, distracting Darcy for a moment.

"Of course, you can. Please forgive my lapse in manners, but my concern is for the wellbeing of those in your party."

"You need not be concerned, William," said Anne. "Between us, we were more than a match for that upstart." Darcy visibly relaxed.

Offering an arm to each lady, he led them to the drawing room, where Andrew and Bingley waited. Once everyone had taken a seat, Georgiana began the tale, with Anne contributing when she felt that Georgiana had glossed over something worthy of the gentlemen's interest.

"And knowing Caroline, her voice was anything but quiet," muttered Bingley. "How will Jane or Mrs. Gardiner ever forgive me for my sister's unpardonable words?"

"You need not fear, Mr. Bingley," said Anne. I believe the ladies, even your sweet Miss Bennet, are fully aware of what your sister is capable. They will not hold her behavior against you."

"Now, William," said Georgiana, "you must tell us how you knew we had met Miss Bingley during our outing."

"She presented herself at Darcy House, claiming to be worried over your presence in such unsuitable company."

"Alone?" asked Georgiana, her concern unmistakable.

"Yes, Georgie, but you need not worry. Bingley and the servants were all close at hand and heard everything she said."

"What did you do?" asked a wide-eyed Georgiana.

Darcy recounted the events and his warning to the young lady to never darken his door again.

"The woman must be delusional," said Anne after Darcy finished his explanation.

"I am beginning to believe that myself," said Mr. Bingley. "If a stay with my Aunt Bingley cannot correct my sister's behavior, then nothing will. Perhaps I should ask her to watch for signs of instability. My aunt is a dear, sweet woman, but she does not tolerate nonsense or haughty airs easily. Surprisingly, Caroline is slightly afraid of her. Perhaps because my aunt has never allowed

Caroline to have her way, especially at the expense of others."

"What will you do if Miss Bingley does not improve her ways?" Anne asked.

"After what Caroline did to separate me from Miss Bennet, I will not allow her into my home again unless she sees the error of her ways. Perhaps it will be necessary to purchase a home for her somewhere and allow her to manage her future."

As agreed during their shopping expedition, the Bennet sisters and Mrs. Gardiner arrived for tea at Darcy House the next morning. Darcy and Bingley were waiting to greet their ladies and Mrs. Gardiner. As they mounted the stairs, Darcy leaned close and spoke to Elizabeth. "I hope your encounter with Miss Bingley left you unscathed, Miss Elizabeth."

"You need not worry, Mr. Darcy. I am well. I learned long ago to ignore Miss Bingley's behavior. While she prides herself on the education she received at the exclusive finishing school she attended, her actions are more like those of a low-born fishwife. For all my mother's faults, she would never speak so unkindly to another, other than me." She spoke the last words under her breath, not meaning for William to overhear, though he did. Glancing behind them, Elizabeth suspected a similar conversation was taking place between Jane and Mr. Bingley.

When they arrived at the sitting room door, both Anne and Georgiana rose to greet the ladies with welcoming hugs. Fiona, too, rushed to sit at Elizabeth's feet. Her tail wagged rapidly with her excitement at the presence of her new friend. While Mrs. Gardiner and Jane spoke of their delight at the well-behaved animal, Elizabeth stooped down and rubbed the dog's ears. After receiving the attention she desired, Fiona sniffed the other women before returning to her basket by the fire. The tea arrived as everyone settled themselves.

The two couples sat on loveseats facing each other across a low table. At one end, Anne and Andrew sat in a pair of matching chairs. Opposite them, Mrs. Gardiner sat beside Miss Darcy. Georgiana served everyone and they settled in to make plans for the upcoming weeks.

"What entertainments are available during our remaining time in London?" asked Elizabeth.

Darcy listed the most notable happenings as the ladies listened. "Do you have any preferences?" He laughed when the ladies all began speaking at once.

"I wish to attend the opera," said Anne. "I have always wished to do so, but Mother calls it nothing but 'caterwauling.'"

"I should love to view Mr. Turner's exhibit," said Elizabeth. "Though I am not an art expert, there is something about the light in his pictures, which is both moving and fascinating."

"May we please go to the concert?" begged Georgiana.

Ever the peacemaker, Jane said, "Everything sounds delightful. I care not what we do with such pleasant company around me." She spoke to the group, but her eyes were on Mr. Bingley.

Mrs. Gardiner smiled benevolently as she studied her favorite nieces with their friends. Contentment filled her to realize others appreciated both Jane and Elizabeth for the delightful young women they were--without regard for their lack of fortune.

"There is also a ball to be given by the Millbrookes. Bingley, Andrew, and I received invitations. We hope you ladies will accompany us."

"Mr. Gardiner and I are also invited to the ball. Lord Millbrooke and Edward met at school. He invested with my husband several years ago. The return on investment was excellent, and through him, my husband was able to grow his business. Lord Millbrooke's success brought several other members of the peerage to Gardiner Imports as investors."

"I believe one of those is my father," added the colonel. "He mentioned having a meeting with Mr. Gardiner in the near future."

"Yes, Lord Matlock also invests with my husband. After finding unique, high-quality gifts for his wife for three years in a row, he decided to learn more about the business. Impressed with what he found, he invested with us as well. In fact, Lady Matlock and I serve on the same board of a charity for young ladies here in town."

"What charity is that, Aunt Gardiner?" wondered Elizabeth.

"We assist abused young ladies who are left in difficult circumstances. It is called A New Hope."

"Perhaps you would permit me to help the next time I come to visit. I could teach the young women to read or sing," offered Elizabeth.

Knowing young maidens should not be aware of the seedier side of life, Mrs. Gardiner said only, "We will consider the matter on your next visit."

"Well," said Darcy, bringing the conversation back to the discussion of their plans, "there is no reason why we cannot do all of those things and more. With the beautiful spring weather, we should visit several of the gardens in the afternoons, perhaps even enjoying a picnic one day. There is also a production of Shakespeare's 'The Tempest' if anyone would care to attend."

"Oh, I would enjoy that," said Elizabeth. "I never tire of seeing Shakespeare's plays brought to life. I relish seeing how the actors' interpretation of the characters differs from what I imagine."

As they continued drinking their tea, Georgiana moved to the writing desk near the window. She pulled out a sheet of paper and listed the events they wished to attend. As Darcy had a box at both the theater and opera house, they could attend whichever night they chose. They agreed their first official outing would be next Monday--allowing time for the ladies' gowns to be ready--to visit the exhibit by J. M. W. Turner. However, there would be a dinner at Darcy House on the Friday before, just three days from now. Those invited would include the Darcy House residents, Lord and Lady Matlock and family, the Bennet sisters, Mr. and Mrs. Gardiner, and Mr. Bingley.

With the majority of the plans set, the conversations devolved into the pairings around the table. Mrs. Gardiner shared with Georgiana some memories from her youth of meeting Mr. Darcy and Lady Anne Darcy.

Jane and Bingley quietly spoke about their desires for their wedding. Looking across at the couple on the other love seat, Bingley chuckled.

"What do you find so amusing, Charles?"

"I cannot recall ever seeing Darcy so besotted. In the past, he would often tease me about-." Bingley broke off abruptly, realizing Jane would not wish to hear about times he fancied himself in love with another young lady. "It will be fun to be able to tease him for a change." Jane could not understand what brought the blush to his cheeks, so she did not comment. Shifting her focus to Elizabeth and Mr. Darcy, she whispered, "I wonder how soon they will become betrothed?"

"From something Darcy said, I believe he is ready now. I guess the decision depends on Miss Elizabeth."

"Perhaps I will speak to Lizzy. We always spoke of standing up for each other when we married. It would be better still if we could share our wedding ceremony, if you would not mind, Charles."

"What a wonderful idea! You talk to your sister, and I will drop a hint with Darcy."

With pleased smiles, they continued discussing the future, including the possibility of seeking a home farther to the north.

Darcy again required reassurance from Elizabeth that she had experienced no injury from Miss Bingley's actions of the previous day. "I was quite put out with her reprehensible comments about Jane and me, but we had a staunch defender in Anne. It was almost like listening to Lady Catherine when she spoke." The two chuckled before Darcy told her of Miss Bingley's visit to Darcy House. "Anne questioned whether Miss

Bingley might not be quite right in the head," said Darcy with a smile.

"I have often wondered the same thing myself. Miss Bingley possesses all the traits she denigrates in others, yet she cannot see them in herself. It reminds me of the verses in the bible found in Matthew."

3 And why beholdest thou the mote that is in thy brother's eye, but considerest not the beam that is in thine own eye?

4 Or how wilt thou say to thy brother, Let me pull out the mote out of thine eye; and, behold, a beam is in thine own eye?

5 Thou hypocrite, first cast out the beam out of thine own eye; and then shalt thou see clearly to cast out the mote out of thy brother's eye.(2)

Darcy could not help but laugh at Elizabeth's reference. "I could not agree more. It is unusual to hear you quoting scripture, though it would not surprise me to hear Miss Mary make such a reference. I know you attend church regularly, but what importance do you place on faithfully living the church's teachings?"

"It is vital to me, though, unlike Mary, I do not make my faithfulness quite so obvious. We are required to forgive others their offenses against us. Laughing at absurd behavior helps me to keep from judging others or becoming offended by their sometimes less-than-kind pronouncements."

"I wonder why that did not work for you upon meeting me?" He raised his brow as he watched her face.

"Most likely due to an unacknowledged attraction to you from the start. My anger served as a shield against further hurt." Elizabeth could not meet his eyes as she answered his question.

Darcy crooked his finger and placed it under Elizabeth's chin, forcing her face up so that he could see her eyes. "I hope you no longer suffer from that hurt and pray I have left you in no doubt of my feelings."

"I do not, and you have, Mr. Darcy." She finally lifted her eyes to his. He could see the joy and love shining from them.

The light in her eyes made him wonder if, perhaps, it might again be time to offer her his hand. Not wishing to waste a moment, he said, "Mrs. Gardiner, would you permit me to show Miss Elizabeth a painting of Pemberley that I keep in my study?"

She had been watching the couple as they sat together, talking in low tones. If her suspicions were correct, there would be another engagement in the family very soon. "I believe that would be acceptable, but please do not be gone too long." She directed a look at Darcy that could not be mistaken: He should behave like a gentleman.

Darcy stood and offered his hand to Elizabeth. When she regained her feet, he wrapped her hand around his arm and led her from the room. They descended the stairs and turned to the right. Pausing at the first door, Darcy opened it and held out his arm for her to precede him inside. He left the door open as propriety required but positioned them beyond the view of anyone passing.

Dropping to one knee, Darcy held both her hands in his. "I know we have not been courting long, but my heart is yours and has been since early in our acquaintance. I love you and wish nothing more than to spend the rest of my days in your joyous company. Will you make me the happiest of men, Elizabeth, and accept my hand in marriage?"

With a brilliant smile and tears glittering in her eyes, she smiled down at the humble man before her. Her opinion of him had changed dramatically in the last few weeks. Knowing she had felt an attraction to him from the beginning left only one possible reply. "Of course, William. Nothing would make me happier than to share my life with you. You are the best man I know, and I love you, too."

William rose from his knees, though he kept possession of her hands. "May we seal our engagement with a kiss?" His eyes appeared to darken and glisten with a light she did not quite understand. Overwhelmed with emotion, she nodded her agreement. He dropped her hands and put one arm around her waist, pulling her closer. He lifted his other hand to caress her face before cupping her cheek and leaning in to capture her lips. The kiss began gently with the merest brush of his lips against hers once, twice, thrice, but when her hands moved to rest on his chest, he deepened the kiss. As if by instinct, her hands moved further to wrap around his neck and she buried her fingers in his hair. Elizabeth moved her lips in a mirror action of his.

Soon, new emotions flooding through her left her legs feeling like jelly. She had to grip his shoulders to stay upright.

Then and only then did Darcy break the kiss. They stared at one another, their breath coming in ragged gasps.

Then, as she always did when feeling overwhelmed, Elizabeth teased: "That was nothing like the kiss I received from John Lucas when I was nine. I must say it was far more impressive and much more fun!"

They both laughed breathlessly as they recovered. "I believe we should return to the drawing room before Mrs. Gardiner comes looking for us. But first, let me show you the picture in case she asks about your impression of Pemberley." He led her to stand before an enormous watercolor on the wall across from his desk.

"This is your home?" asked Elizabeth in awe. Darcy nodded. "I cannot imagine such a beautiful place, and I look forward to seeing it someday."

He offered her his arm and they mounted the stairs to return to the group. "May we announce our engagement to the others, though we still need your father's permission?"

"I would be surprised if they cannot tell from our appearance what occurred, so yes, you may announce our betrothal. However, the subject should not leave the group until you have spoken to my father."

"I did hint to him that I must speak with him when I return you to Hertfordshire, so he may not be too surprised. Thank you, my love. I will be sure they understand the need for discretion." He gifted her a brilliant smile as he spoke, and Elizabeth's heart rate doubled. Upon reaching the top of the stairs, he stopped her. When he did not see anyone else, he reached into his jacket pocket and pulled out a small velvet bag. "Would you please accept this as a sign and token of our engagement?" Darcy dumped the contents of the bag into his palm and held the ring out to her.

Elizabeth looked in awe at the large double brilliant cut diamond in a gold setting surrounded by perfectly matched white pearls that were surrounded yet again by a ring of smaller diamonds. "William, it is stunning!" I will happily wear it while in London, but I will not permit my mother to see if before we receive my father's permission."

As they continued walking, Darcy asked, "Should I make a quick trip to Longbourn for permission?"

"I believe it would be best for us to go together, for the last my father knew, I did not possess any fondness for you. I will write to him of my changed feelings and what led to them, but I am sure he will wish to speak to me before giving his final permission."

By this time, they had reached the drawing room. Everyone turned to look at the couple when they entered. Colonel Fitzwilliam spoke first. "Congratulations, Darcy. I see you gathered your courage and proposed, and as I can distinctly see the ring worn by the last four mistresses of Pemberley on Miss Elizabeth's hand, I assume she accepted your offer!"

Everyone jumped up and rushed to offer their congratulations to the newly engaged couple, who beamed in delight. Shortly after this, the visitors rose to depart. They exchanged farewells, and Darcy and Bingley escorted the ladies to the door. Darcy handed Mrs. Gardiner into the carriage first and then stepped back to allow Bingley to assist Miss Bennet. While they waited, Darcy took Elizabeth's hand and raised it to his lips. "You have made me the happiest and most fortunate of men, Elizabeth. I cannot wait to announce our engagement to the world. However, waiting until we will no longer need to part at the end of the day will be an even greater challenge. I hope you do not wish for a long engagement."

"I have never cared much about the wedding, only the man who stands beside me. I could not have found a better man if I searched the world over. I, too, look forward to the time we no longer must separate at the end of the day. Will you call on me tomorrow? We have a dress fitting in the morning, but should be at home all afternoon."

"I shall be sure to call. I do not know how I will survive should I not see you every day."

Elizabeth blushed at his words. When he handed her into the carriage, she smiled at him and said, "I understand you completely, and I will eagerly await your arrival."

Darcy watched until the carriage was out of sight. When he returned to the house, he excused himself, stating that he needed to write a letter to be sent express.

"Is anything the matter, William?" asked Anne.

"No, I just thought of a gift I would like to get for Elizabeth. I wish to have it sent here as soon as possible." They all knew Darcy to be very generous with his loved ones, but the smile on his face left them wondering what this particular gift might be.

10. Sealing Her Fate

Despite having seen Elizabeth every day since their arrival in town, Darcy anxiously paced the entrance hall, awaiting her appearance. He almost beat Travers, the Darcy House butler, to the door when the first guests knocked. However, he recalled himself in time and stepped back, allowing Travers to open the door. His face fell at the sight of his Fitzwilliam relations.

The earl and countess exchanged a look before the earl's hearty laugh broke forth. "You need not invite us to dine, nephew, if you do not wish to see us."

Darcy looked confused until Andrew added, "Your crestfallen appearance will not make your other guests feel any more welcome than we do." Darcy's face flushed as he realized what his relations meant, which only caused Andrew to bark in laughter.

"Please forgive me, Aunt, Uncle. I was just hoping for another guest's early arrival. I hope you know you are always welcome at Darcy House."

"Of course we know that, William. Is the arrival of Miss Bennet what you anticipate so eagerly?" asked the countess. "From what Andrew told us, I look forward to making her acquaintance. Just tell us where we are gathering this evening, and we will take ourselves off to greet our nieces while you await your other guests." Darcy gave his aunt the information. She stopped and smiled at him as she patted his face before mounting the stairs to the green drawing room.

The next to arrive was Bingley. Again, Darcy's face showed his disappointment, but his friend understood as he waited in the hall with Darcy to greet his betrothed.

"Did you receive a reply from your aunt yet?" Darcy asked.

"Not yet, but I imagine my letter has already reached her. I hope to receive her reply by Tuesday. I stopped by the Hursts before coming here to finalize the arrangements for Caroline's travel. Everything is in place for her dawn departure on Wednesday. I included in my letter all of Caroline's recent behavior--from separating Jane and me to the attempted compromise. My sister will be kept from all company until Aunt Bingley sees substantial improvement in Caroline's behavior."

"Are there any changes in her since my pronouncements during her last visit here?"

"No, she is still not taking responsibility for her actions. Instead, she blames the influence of Miss Elizabeth for everything wrong in her life since our stay in Hertfordshire." Darcy rolled his eyes and encouraged his friend to continue. "Miss Elizabeth corrupted Miss Darcy and Miss de Bourgh, causing their rudeness. She also stole all of Caroline's dreams by turning your attention away from my sister. Of course, Miss Elizabeth is responsible for Caroline's name being bandied about the drawing rooms of London. She is a laughing-stock, and that too is Miss Elizabeth's fault."

"I am glad you are sending her away, for I am beginning to agree with Anne that Caroline is perhaps not in her right mind. She cannot accept it when she hears the truth."

"I will send an additional letter to my aunt with information on all further happenings before her departure. I will ask one of Hurst's footmen to deliver it, as two of them will accompany the carriage north."

"I shall be greatly relieved when she is gone. I dread to think what might happen should we encounter her as we escort the ladies about town."

"She keeps close to home these days. Louisa brought back the gossip she learned on Tuesday about Caroline's set down by a table of ladies at a tea shop. I must agree, Darcy, I will be relieved when Caroline is no longer a part of my day-to-day life."

At that moment, the doorbell rang. Darcy and Bingley held their breath as Travers opened the door. Upon seeing who stood on the threshold, Travers did not open the door wide enough for the visitor to recognize his master's presence. The gentlemen's mouths dropped open in astonishment at the voice. Moving to peek through the crack in the door, they saw an overdressed Caroline Bingley dripping in jewels and standing on the steps of Darcy House. They stepped back quickly before she became aware of their presence in the hall.

"I am here with my brother for dinner," stated Caroline.

Travers blocked the door as he looked at the young woman. "I do not believe you received an invitation for this evening, Miss Bingley."

"How dare you refuse me entrance! I have met the demands of Mr. Darcy to only come in my brother's presence. I was not quite ready when he departed, but I am here now."

"I am sorry, miss, for you were not on the guest list provided to me for the evening."

"Do you actually mean to deny me entrance?" challenged Caroline.

"I am merely following my master's orders."

"I demand you take me to Mr. Darcy this instant!"

"There is no need for me to disturb my master while he attends to his guests. I received a list of the invitees for tonight, and your name is not on it. Now, will you go under your own power, or shall I call the footmen to assist you from the steps?"

"You will be sorry for this when I am mistress of this house. I guarantee I will make you pay for your insolence." Caroline glared at the butler for a few moments before turning on her heel to depart. Behind the open door, Darcy and Bingley stared at each other, astounded at the brash behavior of the uninvited guest. Caroline had provided the answer to Darcy's earlier question.

Unfortunately, what no one perceived during the interchange was the arrival of the Gardiner party and several other bystanders who stopped to witness the scene on the steps of Darcy House. When Caroline saw Elizabeth Bennet standing at the bottom of the steps, her vision turned red. Before anyone could realize her purpose, Caroline smacked Elizabeth's face with all her might, causing Elizabeth to stagger from the impact. "This is all your fault. You caused me to lose all my dreams for the future. You should watch out, for one day, I will pay you back for this," shouted Caroline in a voice of menace. Caroline marched away with a last glare at Elizabeth and a derisive sniff at the rest of the group. She was not aware of the others who had observed her actions until the murmur of voices reached her ears. Having snuck out of the Hursts's home and taken a hackney to Darcy House, Caroline departed with what dignity she possessed. *How do I find myself in this position again so soon?* Repeating her actions from the tea shop, Caroline Bingley marched down the sidewalk and around the corner, out of sight.

Travers alerted Darcy to the arrival of his final guests, but not quickly enough to protect Elizabeth from Miss Bingley's attack. He rushed out the door and to her side. Elizabeth held one hand to her cheek as she stared after the departing Miss Bingley. Once she disappeared from view, everyone seemed to react at once. Before Charles could reach her, Jane sagged against her aunt at the violence she had witnessed. Bingley wrapped an arm around Jane's waist before assisting her inside. Mr. and Mrs. Gardiner and Mr. Darcy all spoke at once, asking, "Elizabeth, are you well?" Darcy removed her hand from her cheek and saw a bright red handprint on her face. Not wishing to add to Darcy's guilt, Elizabeth nodded. Darcy offered his arm and helped her into the house, with Mr. and Mrs. Gardiner following.

"Travers, please arrange for some ice for Miss Elizabeth's face, to be brought to the drawing room right away."

"Of course, sir."

He whispered the instructions to a nearby footman and then led the latest arrivals up the stairs. Pausing at the door to announce the guests, Travers stepped aside to allow them entry.

Anne and Georgiana, instantly noting the mark on Elizabeth's cheek, rushed forward.

"Elizabeth, what happened?" exclaimed Georgiana.

"Who did this, Elizabeth?" pressed Anne.

Lord and Lady Matlock looked on in surprise as Darcy led an injured young lady into the room, while Bingley appeared to support the young woman beside him. He sat Jane in a chair and rushed to retrieve a small glass of wine to steady her nerves.

Appalled at so many witnesses to her embarrassment, Elizabeth blushed brightly from her décolletage to her hairline, causing the handprint to appear even redder. "I had the misfortune to encounter Miss Bingley upon our arrival. The butler would not admit her, and when she saw me at the bottom of the stairs, she could not control her anger."

"What did that harridan do now?" demanded Lady Matlock. Andrew stepped to his mother and whispered to her about the recent events. "Well, I hope you will ban her completely after this display, William."

"I shall, Aunt. I shall also give her the cut direct, should I encounter her in public." He turned to his friend. "I am sorry the situation has come to this, Bingley, but I shall make it understood that she is the only member of your family to lose my goodwill. Perhaps you should restrict her to the house until she departs for Scarborough."

"After her display tonight, I certainly shall." Few in the room had ever seen Bingley this angry.

Fortunately, at that moment, the footman arrived with ice for Elizabeth. Everyone took a seat, and Darcy made the introductions. "Aunt, Uncle, Nicholas, and Andrew, allow me to present to you, Mr. and Mrs. Edward Gardiner, Miss Bennet, and Miss Elizabeth Bennet. Mr. and Mrs. Gardiner, Miss Bennet, Miss Elizabeth, these are my relations, Duncan Fitzwilliam, the Earl of Matlock, Ellen Fitzwilliam, the Countess of Matlock, Nicholas Fitzwilliam, Viscount Gilchrist, and you know Colonel Andrew Fitzwilliam." They exchanged proper greetings before settling in to converse.

Allowing Elizabeth some time to recover, Lady Matlock spoke with her nieces to learn more about their confrontation with Miss Bingley. Lord Matlock struck up a conversation with Mr. Gardiner, while Mrs. Gardiner drew near to Jane to ensure she was recovering from the shock she had received, thus giving Darcy a chance for a private conversation with Elizabeth.

Darcy leaned close to Elizabeth and said, "I am so sorry for what occurred. I cannot believe Miss Bingley would go so against the rules of propriety. She desperately wishes to be a member of the first circles, but her recent public behavior ensures that London society will never accept her.

"I did not expect such a surprising start to the evening. I am embarrassed to be making your aunt and uncle's acquaintance looking as I do."

"Do not be embarrassed, Miss Elizabeth, for you did nothing wrong," said Lady Matlock. "Though my husband and I consider ourselves quite liberal when it comes to mixing with people in trade, Miss Bingley's actions will, without question, set back the acceptance of those who must earn their living by the majority of the upper classes."

"Perhaps it would be best if my family and I left, Mr. Darcy," Elizabeth said. "I am sorry to bring such an incident to your front door, which will cause your name to be bandied about in society. How can you ever forgive me?"

"Elizabeth, no!" cried Darcy in anguished tones.

"Now, none of that, Miss Elizabeth. Miss Bingley's actions will reflect poorly only on herself and her family if they do not distance themselves from her. I can assure you that no harm will come to either your name or those of my niece and nephew."

"How can you possibly do such a thing?"

"I am certain I shall receive many callers tomorrow as word spreads of what occurred on the steps of Darcy House. I will be sure the correct information circulates, and the displeasure of the ton will be on the one deserving of it."

"My thanks, Aunt, for your assistance."

"I am happy to help, William. Now, please tell me a little about yourself, Miss Elizabeth. Darcy informed us of your courtship. Though from the ring on your finger, it appears to now be a betrothal." A wide smile accompanied the lady's words.

Across town, a shocked Hurst and Louisa watched as Caroline, dressed for an evening out, stepped into the drawing room.

"I hate that conniving witch. I will make her pay if it is the last thing I do," muttered Caroline.

"What did you say, Caroline?" asked her sister in concern.

Mr. Hurst almost bellowed, "Where did you go? You did not receive any invitations for tonight."

"Of course I did. Charles was to dine with Mr. Darcy, and as I am allowed at Darcy House only in Charles's company, I went as well."

"Oh, Caroline! Tell me you did not do such a thing," said a beleaguered Louisa.

"Tell me, did you receive an invitation to such an event, or were you gauche enough to arrive uninvited?" asked Mr. Hurst.

"Why should I not be invited? Charles is there, and we are very close to the Darcys."

"Louisa, I believe we need to call the doctor to evaluate your sister. I believe she is delusional and must be put away for her good and the protection of others."

"How dare you speak to me in such a fashion? What are you but a drunken lout?"

"I am drunk only when I have to put up with your ridiculousness," Hurst jeered in return.

"Tell me what happened, Caroline," inquired her sister, her tone weary.

Caroline related the experience, blaming the butler, and, of course, Elizabeth Bennet.

"So, let me understand you," said Hurst. "You were thrown from the steps of Darcy House, in front of a crowd, and you were not at fault? I am convinced, Louisa, that your sister is not of her right mind."

"That is not helping, Oliver," said Mrs. Hurst with a reproving look. "Caroline. Miss Elizabeth did not force you to show up to a dinner to which you were not invited. Nor did she prevent you from entering the house. Nor is the butler responsible. You invited yourself to a dinner at someone else's home. Are you trying to tell me you learned such behavior in school? You must learn to accept responsibility for your actions, Caroline. Charles repeatedly tells you that Mr. Darcy is not interested in you, yet you continue to believe otherwise. You drown the man in flattery and attention, to which he barely responds. You cling to him like a leech, and he is constantly removing you from his arm or standing in such a way so as to make it almost impossible for you to attach yourself to him. Are you really so blind that you cannot recognize his feelings for you?"

"But why should he not desire me? I am beautiful. I attended the right school. I know how to manage a home and plan social events. Why does he not realize when the perfect woman is before him?"

Hurst could not prevent a loud guffaw from escaping him. "The man detests society, and you love the social whirl. Why would he wish to marry the type of woman he has avoided for over five years? He realizes your only interest in him is his money, his name, and the prominence that comes from being Mrs. Darcy. You care nothing for the man."

Stomping her foot, she wailed, "But such is the way of our society. Why must he be different?"

"Do you never listen to what the man says? He frequently speaks of desiring a relationship like the one his parents had. They married for love, and Mr. Darcy desires the same. As Oliver said, Mr. Darcy is aware you do not love him, only what he can do for you."

Caroline looked at her sister and brother-in-law as though they spoke Greek. She could not understand a word they said.

"You cannot be serious. Mr. Darcy never shows emotion. He is a refined gentleman, and love is a ridiculous, messy affair." For the first time, her tone showed uncertainty.

"Caroline," said Louisa in a kind but firm tone, "you must accept the fact that Mr. Darcy will never marry you. If you hope to have a home of your own, you must direct your focus elsewhere. You must also lower your expectations. No one in the first circles is going to offer for the daughter of a tradesman. If you continue to behave as you have in the past, you will find yourself alone as you grow old. Also, if you continue as you are, Charles will never allow you back into his life. Is that what you want?"

"Nor will you be allowed to live with us," said Hurst. "You cause too much drama and stress."

"Louisa would never permit you to throw me out!" declared Caroline in shocked tones. She expected her sister to support her statement without hesitation. When no words came, she looked at Louisa, who sat sharing a smile with her husband.

"Am I truly so awful?"

"At times, yes. You can be pleasant when the mood strikes you, but because such behavior is infrequent, most recognize it is false," said Hurst. "Would you wish to be friends with someone like you? Someone who is polite to your face and mean and unkind behind your back?"

"I can tell you from experience, such actions are very wearing on a person and are quite tiresome," Louisa said. "I believe you should take the days between now and your journey northward to consider this conversation. You should also realize your behavior tonight will probably cause Mr. Darcy to refuse you admittance to Darcy House permanently. We will all be lucky if he does not cut you in public after causing a scene at his door and striking Miss Elizabeth."

Caroline blanched at the thought of Darcy taking such an action. "But why did Mr. Darcy never make his intentions clear? Why would he lead me on in such a way?"

"Are you not listening? Short of coming out and telling you he would not marry you if you were the last woman on earth, which is something he has said to Charles and me," said Hurst, causing Caroline to shrink at his words, "Darcy shows his lack of interest in every way he could within the bounds of gentlemanly behavior, but you refuse to see it, or to believe us when we tell you of his disinterest."

"He really dislikes me so much?"

"Yes," responded Hurst in his usual blunt manner. Caroline stared blankly, thinking about what her brother by marriage had said.

As she turned to depart, Louisa softly added, "I am sorry to tell you this, but Charles mentioned that the Matlocks would be dining with

Darcy this evening to meet Miss Elizabeth. Lady Matlock never held any fondness for you. She will ensure word of the scene you created tonight reaches the ton. I suggest you remain at home until your departure. If you do nothing else to cause tongues to wag, perhaps you will be able to return to town in several months or a year."

Caroline looked horrified that such a thing might happen to her. Was her family correct in what they said? Was she failing to act responsibly? Had she caused the downfall of her dreams? She did not know what to believe. Without speaking further, she turned and trudged from the room.

When her footsteps faded away, the couple remaining behind shared a look.

"Do you think we finally got through to her?" asked Mr. Hurst.

"For her sake, I hope so," said his wife.

11. Unwanted Attention

Visits between the group of young people took place nearly every day, either at the Gardiner residence, at Darcy House, or in one of the local parks. They visited the Turner exhibition the previous day and enjoyed their outing to the park on this beautiful spring morning.

Though wrapped up in their private concerns, Darcy and Elizabeth both noted what appeared to be a growing closeness between Anne and Andrew.

"I wonder if they are aware they are falling in love?" asked Elizabeth as the group walked in Hyde Park one afternoon shortly after the dinner at Darcy House.

Darcy was wool-gathering as they walked, recalling his aunt and uncle's expressions of pleasure at making Elizabeth's acquaintance.

'I believe you made a wise choice, William," said Aunt Ellen. *"Your personalities complement each other perfectly.'*

'Yes," added his uncle, *"I believe your parents would both be pleased with your choice. Though Miss Elizabeth is more outgoing than my dear sister was, she possesses the same kindness and caring heart. I believe she will be an outstanding mistress of Pemberley.'*

'Thank you, both. I am pleased you agree with my choice, though I must tell you, the lack thereof would not have changed my course if you disagreed.' The older couple smiled at his determination.

Patting his arm, Elizabeth returned his attention to the present. "You were very far away, Mr. Darcy. What were you thinking about?"

"I pondered the dinner at my home and the words of my family after your party departed."

"Is there cause for worry?" Darcy noted the evenness of her tone, but her eyes contained a hint of concern.

"Not at all. The Fitzwilliams all expressed their delight with my choice and offered us their full support in introducing you into society." Elizabeth smiled and Darcy could feel the tension leave her at his words. "Now, what shall we discuss?"

"You obviously did not hear my question."

"What question was that?"

"Do you realize the relationship between Anne and Andrew is changing?" Darcy's confused gaze rested on Elizabeth's face, so she continued. "They are often thrown together when accompanying us. To me, they appear to be falling in love. I wondered if you had recognized it, too."

Darcy stared at her in surprise. "Surely not! They have known each other forever, but I have never remarked any signs of intimacy."

"Perhaps they could not be open with their feelings around your aunt, or maybe the emotion is something new due to the increase of time they spend in each other's company. I suppose I could be wrong, but I suggest you become more observant of them. If Anne and Colonel

Fitzwilliam were to fall in love, it would be a blessing for both. Anne would have someone who cared for her without the smothering ways of her mother. The colonel would be able to resign from the army and become the master of Rosings. With his years in the army, he is undoubtedly capable of keeping Lady Catherine in her place. Keeping him safe from the risk of death in service to king and country is an added benefit."

"I cannot say if you are right about their feelings for one another. I always found it necessary to avoid Anne during my visits to Rosings to prevent Aunt Catherine from believing she would get her way on the matter of our marriage. Andrew did always spend more time with Anne during our visits, so perhaps there is something in what you say."

"What would her mother do if Anne should choose to marry someone other than you?"

"Aunt Catherine would likely cause a big fuss and try to prevent Anne from finding her happiness."

"In that case, they will need our support to ensure they are allowed to find happiness should they see that in each other."

"I find your concern for Anne delightful. You know you will likely receive a large share of my aunt's displeasure for stealing me away from my cousin." They both laughed at Darcy's words. Darcy drew Elizabeth closer to his side, pressing her arm between his body and the one she held before placing his other hand over hers. They continued to meander through the park, following the other couples, all of whom walked at intervals that allowed them to enjoy private conversation while keeping them close enough to chaperone one another. Georgiana was with her music master during the outing but would join them for tea upon their return to Darcy House.

Though Darcy kept his focus primarily upon Elizabeth, he did sneak a few glances at Andrew and Anne. Andrew appeared much as he always did, but for an odd bit of seriousness in his focused gaze. As for Anne, she seemed to blossom brightly under Andrew's attention. *I shall have to speak to Andrew about this when a moment presents itself. Though I do not wish to marry her, I would not wish Anne to be hurt if Andrew's intentions are not serious.*

They parted company reluctantly as they would be apart for most of the next day. The ladies had an appointment for fittings with Mrs. Hartfield while Darcy and Bingley met with their solicitors. They would meet for tea on Thursday at the Gardiners's. Then they would attend the theater together, dining at Matlock House afterward on Friday evening.

Friday evening arrived and the Gardiner carriage made the trip from Cheapside to Darcy House. They would be meeting the gentlemen there and then making their way to the Royal Theater Covent Garden to see the production of Shakespeare's *The Tempest*. Getting such a large group to the theater required two carriages. Mr. and Mrs. Gardiner and Jane rode with Bingley in his carriage. The Darcy coach carried Mr. and Miss Darcy, Miss Elizabeth, Anne, Andrew, and Mrs. Annesley, Georgiana's companion. They would be meeting the Matlocks at the theater, and the party could spread out between the two adjacent boxes.

Upon arriving at the theater, Andrew and Darcy stepped out first. Andrew assisted Anne and

Mrs. Annesley from the carriage while Darcy handed down Georgiana and Elizabeth. He offered an arm to each of his favorite ladies, and they mounted the steps to enter the building. The ladies stepped to the side to hand off their wraps and Darcy caught his breath when Elizabeth rejoined him. He had always enjoyed the flecks of green in Elizabeth's eyes, but tonight they vividly reflected the beautiful aqua color of her evening gown. Tonight the specks stood out like the first sign of spring flowers after the winter's long sleep. "You look stunning tonight, Miss Elizabeth. That color is exceptionally becoming on you."

Elizabeth blushed and smiled shyly at his enthusiastic compliment. "I told you the color would be beautiful on you, Lizzy," said Georgiana.

The Bingley party and the Matlocks soon joined them. Lady Matlock also voiced her agreement on the appearance of Elizabeth, Anne, Georgiana, and Jane, though Lizzy wondered why her voice seemed a bit loud when doing so.

"Thank you, Lady Ellen. It is a pleasure to see you again," said Elizabeth.

The lady took Elizabeth's hands and kissed her cheek in welcome before doing the same with all the other ladies except Georgiana's companion. As the group moved to mount the stairs, a tall, angular matron pushed her way through the crowd, dragging a pale young woman behind her. Practically forcing Elizabeth out of the way to stand in front of Darcy, the woman blocked his ability to ascend the stairs.

"Ah, Mr. Darcy, how fortunate we are to run into you this evening. You remember my daughter, The Honourable Phoebe Plowman."

Darcy ignored the woman until he determined Elizabeth's well-being and pulled her closer to his side. "Good evening, Lady Plowman, Miss Plowman. We cannot stay to chat, as the rest of our party is already on their way to my box. Please excuse us."

He maneuvered around the two women and mounted the stairs. The daughter looked relieved at not being required to speak to the intimidating man. Lady Plowman, however, was extremely frustrated. She had seen Darcy earlier at the Turner exhibition, and once in Hyde Park. He was always in company with a large group and too far away for her to speak to him. The elation induced by his presence at the theater filled the woman with hope. Dorothy Plowman could not fathom the man's rudeness. It also distressed her to recognize the young woman on his arm—the same one who had been with Darcy the previous times she encountered him. *Could this mean he is off the market? Since I have not seen a notice in the papers, he is still fair game. I must find a wealthy husband for Phoebe before my wretch of a husband loses her dowry at the gaming table. Perhaps we should call on Darcy House tomorrow, as we did not get to speak tonight.* Her mind made up, Lady Plowman dragged her daughter toward their box, all the while admonishing her of the need to impress Mr. Darcy.

As they climbed the stairs, Darcy apologized to Elizabeth for the lady's behavior and for failing to introduce her. "Please do not believe I am embarrassed by our betrothal. Nothing would make me happier than to shout it to the world. However, the woman's inability to take the hint of my disinterest sometimes requires that I be abrupt with her. She is a particularly determined matchmaking mama. I understand her husband experienced some heavy gambling losses. She is looking for someone wealthy to take her daughter and save her from the poorhouse."

"I am not offended, Mr. Darcy. I am sorry you must endure such behavior. I understand from Anne and Georgiana that this has been normal since you first appeared in society. I also understand it grew worse after you became the master of your estate. I find it easier to understand your behavior in Meryton after having seen how so many treat you when in public," Elizabeth added with a laugh.

Darcy blushed at her remark before giving her a sheepish smile. His expression made Elizabeth laugh again, but she gave his arm an understanding, compassionate squeeze.

"There you are, William," said Lady Matlock as he entered his box. "I was beginning to wonder what happened to you."

"Lady Plowman nearly knocked down Elizabeth in her attempt to speak with me."

"That woman is the most determined, scheming female I've ever encountered. You did not give her any attention, I hope, as it will only convince her of her eventual success."

"Indeed not," said Elizabeth with a smile. "Mr. Darcy greeted her politely and excused us to catch up with the rest of you. I think at least three others called out his name, but he did not acknowledge them."

"William does hate receiving so much attention," said his aunt.

With a rakish glance at Elizabeth, Darcy said, "I do not hate attention when it comes from a certain source, but I do detest all the unwanted attention I receive simply because I am Fitzwilliam Darcy of Pemberley." Everyone in the group laughed heartily at Darcy's words.

The Gardiners, along with Georgiana and her companion, sat in the box with Lord and Lady Matlock. The other couples sat in the Darcy box, with the ladies in the front row and each gentleman behind his particular lady. To see the stage, Elizabeth's face was situated in profile to Darcy. Enraptured by the enjoyment on Elizabeth's face as she took in the performance, he could do naught but stare. Her eyes sparkled with delight, and the smile never left her visage. They remained in their box during the first intermission, discussing the performance with their companions. Two couples dropped into the Darcy box, both accompanied by an eligible daughter, but when their polite overtures met with monosyllables, they did not remain long. However, all of them overtly studied the young woman whose hand Darcy held tight to his arm.

During the second intermission, the Darcy party and all those with them exited the boxes in search of refreshments. Due to the size of Darcy's party, no one attempted to approach the group, though both Darcy and Elizabeth could feel the eyes upon them. Feeling confident in her new gown, Elizabeth easily handled the almost continuous scrutiny. However, when she noticed the tenseness in the arm she held, she looked up to find the same haughty, closed expression on her companion as he had worn at the Meryton assembly. Though he had explained his feelings and apologized for his behavior, Elizabeth's compassion grew for the discomfort this shy gentleman experienced.

Squeezing his arm to garner his attention, Elizabeth smiled up at the man who held her heart. "Fear not, Mr. Darcy, I promise to use my wit to keep at bay all those who cause you distress." She gifted him a broad smile, her brow arched in a challenge.

Darcy could not help the smile that overspread his face. He looked down at her, love shining from his eyes. At Darcy's smile, several gasps sounded from those nearby, but the couple was oblivious as they stared into each other's eyes. Darcy lifted the hand that held his arm and raised it to his lips, kissing the back tenderly. Lord and Lady Matlock followed the interchange between the two, also sharing a look and a smile. They spoke to several friends who asked about Darcy and the young lady. Lord and Lady Matlock spoke of the couple as courting and how happy they were with Darcy's choice. Before long, the ton would be buzzing with the news of Darcy's courtship. When the play ended, the group returned to Matlock House for a late dinner.

Despite the brevity of Mr. Darcy's greeting the previous evening, the very next afternoon, Darcy sat with his sister and cousin, awaiting the arrival of Elizabeth and Jane, when Travers came to notify them of the visitors. "Can the woman not take a hint?" grumbled Darcy.

"Do you wish to depart while Georgiana and I receive the ladies? You can sneak down to your study after they are here with us. I will discourage her for you," offered Anne.

"Good luck with that. Lady Plowman seems determined to find someone to keep her and her daughter before her husband loses all they possess."

Darcy exited the room and hid in the music room across the hall. He heard Travers announce their visitors and waited until he heard the click of the door firmly closing after they entered. Upon hearing the rumble of voices through the door, Darcy quietly moved to the stairs, descending to the safety of his study.

While Darcy avoided the unwelcome guests, Anne and Georgiana greeted the ladies. "Good afternoon, may we help you?"

"We requested to see Mr. Darcy," said Lady Plowman, disappointment evident in her tone.

"My cousin does not receive ladies alone, especially now that he is involved in a courtship," replied Anne

"I have seen no such announcement in the papers."

"My brother is a private man," Georgiana said. "He does not like to have his name in the paper."

"Continuing to call will do you no good, Lady Plowman, as Mr. Darcy is aware of your situation. He knows you search only for someone to care for you and your daughter because of your husband's gambling losses. Now, we must ask you to depart, as we are expecting other visitors." Anne and Georgiana rose, waiting for their guests to do the same. "As we are not acquainted, and Miss

Darcy is not out, I do not expect you will call again. Have a pleasant afternoon, ladies."

Lady Plowman's face showed her outrage, but Miss Plowman, who found Mr. Darcy to be quite intimidating, spoke, despite knowing she would have to endure her mother's wrath later. "Please give Mr. Darcy my best wishes for his future happiness. We shall not bother him again." Lady Plowman grabbed her daughter's hand and dragged her from the room.

Later the same afternoon, the Darcys, Anne, Elizabeth and Jane Bennet, Andrew Fitzwilliam, and Charles Bingley shared tea and pleasant conversation in the blue drawing room at Darcy House. The walls of the room were pale blue with white woodwork. The room contained varying shades of blue striped settees and dark blue chairs. The rug had a dark blue border, with a center pattern in varying shades of blue. Artwork with water views adorned the walls.

The two weeks Anne resided at Darcy House were some of the happiest she could remember. Therefore, with trepidation, she watched as Travers crossed the room with a letter on a tray, which he held out to her.

"This just arrived express, miss." Thanking the butler, she took the letter. Her face fell as she recognized her mother's writing.

At her expression, Georgiana asked, "Is anything wrong, Anne?"

"Not really, though I have dreaded this day."

"What do you mean?" asked Elizabeth of her dear friend.

"It is a letter from Mother. I knew she would write as soon as she was able, but I dread reading her words."

12. Because of Lady Catherine's Letter

Elizabeth rose to give her friend a moment of privacy. Jane and Bingley followed her to the far end of the room.

While her cousins looked on, Anne opened the letter and began to read.

Rosings Park
Kent
3 May 1811

Dear Anne,

> *How dare you leave me in my hour of need? Have I not always tended to you when you were ill? Have I not always provided you with loving care? How could you abandon me?*
>
> *Not only did you leave me on my own, but you traveled without my permission and left Mrs. Jenkinson behind. Are you sure your health was up to a trip? Who will care for you if you become ill, and neither Mrs. Jenkinson nor myself are present? I shall worry about you until you return, which I think you should do without delay. I need you to attend to me.*

Your Mother

P.S. I insist Darcy return, too, so we can begin the wedding plans.

It surprised Anne to read that her mother thought of the care she gave her daughter during periods of illness as loving and tender. Lady Catherine never set foot in any sickroom. Mrs. Jenkinson acted as the go-between when Anne's health was not its best. Anne considered her companion a dear friend whose affection for Anne was much more motherly than that of the woman who gave her life. This recollection brought other thoughts to mind.

As far back as Anne could remember, Lady Catherine had never shown tenderness to her only child. Anne's father, Sir Lewis, adored his daughter. Shortly before his death, Anne questioned him about her mother's lack of love and care. Though not a pretty tale, her father explained his history with her mother. After having spent five seasons on the marriage mart, Lady Catherine had received no offers of marriage. She was striking rather than beautiful, though what deterred most men was her less-than-feminine behavior and superior attitude. Being the eldest, Lady Catherine strove to meet and exceed her parents' expectations, assuming her parents would recognize, despite her sex, her ability to succeed her father upon his death. Catherine Fitzwilliam was starting her sixth season when Sir Lewis de Bourgh, a childless widower, reentered the marriage mart after his year of mourning his wife and dearest friend. The older gentleman worked hard to build a friendship with his betrothed, but the resentful woman rebuffed most of his efforts.

However, Lady Catherine possessed an impressive dowry, and Sir Lewis needed an heir, so he persevered. Fearing this would be his eldest daughter's only offer, her father, the earl, approved the marriage. Though never an obliging companion, the new bride did her duty and became with child early in their marriage. She lost the first child but promptly became pregnant again. Anne was a healthy, happy child at birth and the apple of her father's eye. At age eight, Anne contracted scarlet fever. The case appeared mild, but a couple of weeks after her recovery, she began to experience a stutter in her heart rate. In the following year, Anne experienced frequent periods of trouble with her heart and often took ill. Appalled by the lack of tenderness his daughter received from her mother, even when very sick, Sir Lewis hired Mrs. Jenkinson to serve as his daughter's governess, and then companion.

Before he passed away, Sir Lewis took the woman aside and said, "No matter what, I want you to promise me you will care for my daughter and protect her from her mother. Tell Lady Catherine what she needs to hear, but always do what is best for Anne. I will speak to the doctor and the apothecary as well. I recognize how demanding my wife can be, and I do not wish Anne to suffer from her mother's lack of care when I am gone."

To Anne's misfortune, her father soon passed away. Lady Catherine believed now was her opportunity to prove to the men in her family she was not only their equal at estate management but also their superior. She became more demanding of all those around her and dictated to everyone what they should and should not do. So began the grand conspiracy. Anne, her companion, the doctor, and apothecary had successfully maintained the façade for over ten years. Anne's health improved over the years, but because of her mother's demanding attitude, Anne still *took ill* on occasion to gain a respite from the overbearing woman. Most of the tinctures the apothecary prescribed were nothing but colored sugar water.

Anne was tired of living a pretend life--not only pretending ill health to escape her mother but also pretending to enjoy her limited world. How she wished for a life of her own, one that her mother did not dominate.

Watching Anne's expression as she read, Darcy realized it was more important than ever for him to speak to Andrew and find out about his feelings and plans in regards to Anne.

"What does she say?" wondered Georgiana with trepidation. Anne read the brief message to her cousins.

Andrew could not help the loud bark of laughter that escaped him. "Is Aunt Catherine delusional? She never tended you, and I doubt she has any concept of what love is. Our aunt avoids the sick room for fear of catching even the mildest of illnesses."

Though too polite to say such, Darcy could not help but wonder the same thing. Instead, he offered something more useful. "Perhaps if you write back informing her that you are staying here and obtaining a new wardrobe for the many outings we are taking, she will not mind and will allow you to stay."

"If I do so, you will want to speak with someone at the newspaper about not accepting any announcements of your wedding that you have not personally delivered. With a reply like you suggest, Mother would not hesitate to send a notice of our engagement to the papers." The cousins all laughed at Anne's words.

Hearing the laughter, the others rejoined the group. "I hope your humor means all is well, Anne?" said Elizabeth.

"Mother wishes my immediate return, to provide her with the same tender care she affords me when I am ill." Andrew snickered again. Elizabeth raised a questioning brow to the colonel, who explained his aunt's all-consuming fear of being near anyone ill. Knowing Lady Catherine, this caused Elizabeth to emit a giggle as well. Bingley and Jane simply observed the merriment of the others.

"What will you do? Must you return right away, or may we still enjoy our planned outings?"

"Darcy offered an excellent suggestion." Anne related his idea and her comment.

"I believe Anne is correct, sir. I should hate for your aunt to steal you away from me." The look Lizzy bestowed on Darcy left him in no doubt that she would be heartbroken should their relationship end.

"You all discuss some additional outings we can add to our scheduled events to further delay Anne's return. Aunt Catherine will not be able to travel for at least another six weeks to two months. I imagine your friend, the doctor, will keep her down longer were you to ask. Aunt Catherine can send letters, but she cannot force you to return. If you will excuse us, I must speak to Andrew for a moment. We shall join you again momentarily."

Andrew looked at his cousin in confusion but followed him from the room. *What did Darcy want with him?*

The two gentlemen stepped down the hall to the study. "What is the matter, Darcy?"

"Nothing, as far as I know. Is there anything you need to tell me?"

Andrew stared at the man who knew him better than any other, trying to determine what Darcy wished to discuss. After a moment or two, his face turned red. Was it possible someone else had noticed his changing affections for Anne?

Knowing that going on the offensive often confuses your opponent," Andrew said, "I cannot think of anything I need to share with you."

Darcy chuckled. "You are not as subtle as you think, cousin. Elizabeth pointed out to me the way you and Anne look at one another."

"Anne looks at me in a particular way?" Andrew's voice held a touch of wistfulness.

"I believe she is as besotted as you are."

"I am not besotted. A colonel in his majesty's army would never behave in such a manner."

Again, Darcy chuckled. "What I want to know is what you are going to do to protect Anne from her mother. Or will you allow her to return to Rosings when Lady Catherine regains her health?"

"What can I do? I would like to marry her, but Lady Catherine would never allow it."

"Lady Catherine can do nothing for another month or more. I am sure arranging a magnificent wedding on short notice is within your mother's ability."

"Yes, but Lady Catherine would just annul the marriage as long as you remain unmarried. Have you and Miss Elizabeth set a date? Perhaps having a double ceremony would be best."

"I would not object to your suggestion, but I am sure Elizabeth would like to marry with her sister and best friend, Miss Bennet."

"Do you think we can pull off a triple ceremony?" Andrew asked with a chuckle. "It would spare you the trouble of returning to Hertfordshire and dealing with Mrs. Bennet."

"You need to focus on you and Anne and thwarting Aunt Catherine. Have you and Anne discussed your feelings for each other?"

"No, I assumed she would not wish to settle for a lowly second son who must remain in the army to support himself and a wife."

"Did you forget Anne is an heiress who will one day inherit an estate of her own? You would no longer need to remain in the army. You could become a gentleman farmer, like myself. When we rejoin the others, why not ask our cousin to take a stroll in the conservatory? Once you and Anne settle what is between you, we can make plans to stop Aunt Catherine's manipulations."

"I will take your advice, Darcy."

The two men returned to the drawing room. Andrew chose a seat beside Anne while Darcy moved to sit between Elizabeth and Georgiana. With the majority of the group deep in a discussion of upcoming offerings, Andrew whispered to Anne, and the two disappeared from the room. When they reached the conservatory, the colonel led his cousin to a secluded bench in the back corner.

Andrew cleared his throat as he thought about how he should proceed. When nothing came to mind, he did it a second time and, then, a third.

"Is everything well, Andrew? You are not to be sent back to the front, are you?"

The fear in Anne's voice settled his nerves. "Would it disturb you if I were?"

"Of course it would! I worry tremendously when you are abroad."

"Anne, the time we have shared since your mother's injury has been some of the most enjoyable of my life. Watching you bloom as you took charge of Rosings, and even more so since our arrival in London, has been remarkable. Why do you allow your mother to treat you so, since you are of age?"

"I must appear to fall in with mother's plans until Darcy marries. Only after he takes a wife will I be free to live my life as I please."

"You are of age. Did you ever think of marrying someone of your choosing?"

"There is someone I always admired, but I am unsure if he thinks well of me."

"Is this someone from Kent?" Disappointment and concern were easily discernable in his voice.

"No, the only young men I meet at Rosings Park are the fortune-hunters who need a large infusion of cash or who are seeking an estate because they do not possess one of their own."

"Are you like Darcy? Do you suspect everyone who meets you is only after your dowry?"

"No, but probably only because I spend little time in town and have not had to suffer the attention for as long as Darcy." Anne's flash of humor caused a chuckle to escape from Andrew.

"I want you to know I greatly enjoy the time we spent together lately. I always knew you had intelligence and humor, but you have grown in surprising ways since your mother's accident."

Blushing brightly at Andrew's words, Anne managed only a whispered, "Thank you."

"Are you looking forward to finding a mate from among the ton during your visit to town?"

"No. Much like our cousin, I enjoy the cultural aspects London offers, but I would find it exhausting and tedious to go out night after night and deal with the falseness of the ton." Taking a deep breath, Anne dared to add, "I do not think I will need to examine the ton to find someone who interests me." She held Andrew's eyes for as long as possible, but as a blush spread over her cheeks, she broke the connection.

Andrew grasped both of her hands in his. "Anne, I have always been fond of you, and we often spent time together at Rosings while Darcy took care of the estate business. However, observing you in London has been a revelation. You are poised, charming, and witty. Perhaps your mother's treatment of you did serve a purpose, as you can handle the Miss Bingleys of the ton with ease. However, the thing that surprised me the most is the change in my feelings. They are no longer cousinly but something much, much more. I love you, Anne, and I am asking you to marry me."

"Oh, Andrew. Yes, of course, I will marry you. You always held my heart. Darcy and I are too much alike to ever make a good match. He needs his Elizabeth, just like I need you! You have always brought joy to my life. You tease me and make me laugh, no matter how difficult Mother makes things for me. Do you think your parents will support us in this?"

"I am sure they will. Mother and Father always knew no arrangement existed between you and Darcy. My parents will be relieved I can resign my commission, but I would retain my rank rather than cause you to think I am marrying you for your money."

"Do not be ridiculous, Andrew. I do not want a husband who will always be gone or who risks his life because his pride insists that he support me."

"How I will support you is of great concern. How will we live until you inherit the estate from your mother?"

"Mother is not aware I discovered this, but I found Father's will one day--the one she keeps hidden from the family. The document states I am my father's sole heir upon my twenty-fifth birthday. By the time we return to Rosings, married or not, the estate will be mine."

"Do you think your mother will just hand over the property to you?"

"Probably not, but with a strong, commanding husband by my side, and the support of the family, coupled with getting our hands on the will before my mother recovers, she will have no choice."

"I believe we should talk to my parents as soon as possible. Then, I can ride to Rosings tomorrow to recover the will. Do you remember where she keeps it?"

"Yes."

"We could go to your father's solicitor, which would be faster."

"Perhaps, but as I have not received notification of my inheritance, I would imagine that either Mother has the only copy or she paid the solicitor to hide the matter from me. Why would he cooperate with us?"

"I believe the influence of the house of Matlock can be of assistance in gaining his cooperation."

"I hope things go well and we can arrange a marriage without Mother's interruption or attendance. Andrew, when did you realize your feelings changed from cousinly to deep love?"

"You must thank Darcy for making me speak. I feared you would not consider a second son who is unable to support you in the manner you deserve. Elizabeth asked if he noticed our changed behavior. After you read your mother's letter aloud, he encouraged me to speak my mind. You do not have to return to Rosings alone unless it is your desire."

"Do you think Aunt Ellen would welcome my presence at dinner this evening?"

"You know you are always welcome."

"Shall we rejoin the others and share the good news?"

When the couple returned to the drawing room, Darcy and Elizabeth instantly noted their bright smiles. They looked at each other before turning back to the couple, a question in Darcy's eye and Elizabeth's brow raised.

"Ladies and gentlemen, I am thrilled to announce that my dear Anne just accepted my offer of marriage." The other couples and Miss Darcy rushed to congratulate Andrew and Anne.

"This is so exciting," said Georgiana, "another wedding!"

"Do you plan to marry soon so your mother cannot interfere?" This question came from Elizabeth.

"Yes, that is our plan," said Anne. "I hope, Elizabeth, you can remain in town until the wedding. You are the first friend ever allowed me. I would be pleased if you would stand up with me at my wedding."

"I will do my best to convince my father to permit me to do so. However, his last letter spoke of his desire for the return of intelligent conversation to his home," said Elizabeth with a laugh.

"Why do we not send for my aunt and uncle to join us now so that we can begin preparations?" suggested Darcy

While Andrew sent a footman with a note requesting his parents' immediate presence at Darcy House, Georgiana ordered fresh tea and more refreshments.

"Perhaps Jane and I should depart, as this is a family matter."

"But you are almost family. Both of you should remain," said Miss de Bourgh.

"I appreciate your thoughtfulness, Anne, but there will be some family matters you must discuss regarding your mother. I wish to allow you the privacy to do so. However, I will look forward to hearing about any plans you made on the morrow."

13. Wedding Plans

From the time the letter left Darcy House to the time Lord and Lady Matlock arrived, not fifteen minutes passed. Jane and Elizabeth were still waiting for Darcy's carriage to return them to the Gardiners's residence.

"Is everything well?" inquired a breathless Lady Matlock upon rushing into the room. She looked around, but everyone appeared to be well.

"Actually, Mother, Father," Andrew said, "I asked Anne to marry me, and she accepted." His parents' eyes widened, but smiles appeared on their faces. Observing the expressions with which their younger son and their niece regarded each other, they were quite pleased.

"Congratulations!" exclaimed Lord Matlock with a hearty pat on his son's back and a kiss to his niece's cheek.

"I wish you both every happiness," said Lady Matlock, pulling them into a group hug. "When do you plan to wed?"

"We would like to marry quickly, but there is another issue we must address first."

"What is that?" asked his Lordship.

"Aunt Catherine always claimed that Sir Lewis made her his sole heir. According to Anne, who came across her father's will one day while in the study, she is to inherit everything upon her five and twentieth birthday in a couple of weeks. However, she also said she has not heard from the solicitor to notify her of her inheritance. How can we verify what is in the will? If I go to Rosings to look for the will, it might alert Aunt Catherine to our plans. I would not doubt she would make the trip to London despite the doctor's orders."

"I will send a letter to Lewis's solicitor requesting a meeting first thing Monday morning. I will get the necessary information, do not worry." The earl spoke in a firm tone, one with the merest hint of menace. "In the meantime, you should plan the wedding so you can be ready to marry quickly. Anne is of age to marry, no matter the conditions of the will. We shall find a way to make this work."

"Thank you, Aunt, Uncle. I have long had feelings for Andrew and am delighted he returns them. With William marrying, I think this is my chance to seize my happiness, as well. After Darcy marries--particularly if against Mother's wishes--she would most likely barter me to the wealthiest peer she could find. She will insist I marry her choice to ensure that my standing exceeds that of Elizabeth. Since Papa's death, there has been little love in my life. Marrying for love will ensure those painful days remain in the past."

Andrew stepped closer to his betrothed and wrapped an arm around her waist, pulling her closer. Recognizing his love for Anne left him feeling guilty he had not done more for his cousin since her father's passing. He often spent time with Anne when visiting Rosings, but usually to prevent Darcy from needing to do so, which would lead Aunt Catherine to believe her wishes for a union would come true. "I am sorry, Anne. In trying to protect Darcy from your mother's machinations, we all failed to give you the love you needed."

"That is not true, Andrew. You are always kind to me, as is William, when Mother is not around to interfere. Your mother and Georgiana are both faithful correspondents. My mother would not have allowed more."

Changing the subject to something more uplifting, Lady Matlock questioned, "When and where would you like to marry?"

"Mother is demanding my immediate return, so we must do so before she is well enough to travel here and retrieve me." Anne relayed Darcy's suggestion and the precaution he took by making an appointment to visit the newspaper office in the morning.

"Yes, but if she did not see the announcement appear soon after, would she not try to find out why? We must prepare for all contingencies," said the earl.

"Why do I feel like we are planning a battle strategy instead of a wedding?" chuckled Andrew.

"Well, then, let us begin planning. Do you wish for a large wedding or something smaller and more intimate?" asked Lady Matlock.

"I would prefer something more intimate, but perhaps larger is better, so there are too many witnesses for Mother to bribe when she attempts to annul the marriage."

"What a brilliant idea, Anne, dear," said Lady Matlock. "However, I believe we can accomplish the same thing with a small, select group of attendees. Your mother manages to ruffle the feathers of most with whom she comes into contact. Many of our friends would enjoy seeing her put in her place."

"I wish William and Elizabeth would marry at the same time, so their relationship is also protected from mother's machinations."

As Elizabeth and Jane were still in the room, Jane asked, "Do you really believe your mother would attempt to cause trouble for Lizzy and Mr. Darcy even after the wedding?"

"I do," said Anne, "and I wish to prevent her from ruining my cousin's and your sister's happiness."

"I think you should consider this, Lizzy." Jane's earnest expression and tone gave Elizabeth pause.

"But Jane, William must still ask Father for permission for our marriage. People will get the wrong impression if we rush into marriage. You know how gossip flies around Meryton. I do not wish to have our names bandied about because of unpleasant speculation and gossip."

"I am sure we can find a way around that, Miss Elizabeth. Andrew and I share a godfather. The Bishop of Derby went to school with both our fathers. I am sure he would be delighted to perform the ceremony, and we can say the date selected was what worked for him."

Elizabeth looked from Darcy to her sister. "That is not my only concern, Jane. We always spoke of standing up for each other when we married."

"We can still do so. Besides, Lizzy, you do not wish for the grand ceremony Mama will demand for a man of Mr. Darcy's consequence. I doubt Mr. Darcy would wish such either." Elizabeth saw the slightly panicked look on

Darcy's face at the thought. "You do not possess the patience to deal with all her nervous flutterings during the planning. Do you wish for Mama to oversee your trousseau or determine the style of your wedding dress? She would dress you in an excessive amount of lace." Jane recognized her sister's hesitation as she pointed out what Elizabeth would be required to endure from their mother. "We can still stand up for each other, just not in a double wedding."

Elizabeth turned to Anne. "I thought you wished me to stand up with you?"

"I would be just as delighted to marry beside you. Perhaps Jane would stand as a witness for both of us, or if she is not comfortable doing so, I will ask Georgiana to stand up with me. Please consider the matter, Elizabeth."

Looking at the faces around her, Elizabeth felt herself weakening. "That still does not solve the problem of needing Father's permission."

"I would be happy to write your father and invite him to town, or perhaps your Uncle Gardiner would do so?" offered Darcy. "Then your father could stay to give you away. If you wish the rest of your family to be in attendance, we can send for them the day before the wedding," offered Darcy. At this, Elizabeth's eyes widened in horror at the thought of her mother and younger sisters meeting Lord and Lady Matlock.

With the pleading looks on both Anne's and William's faces, as well as Jane's reminder of what her mother would demand of her, Elizabeth made her decision. "I will agree on the condition that my father agrees to the plans. I would suggest we request that Uncle write that letter."

"Do you know if your aunt and uncle have plans for the evening? Perhaps you should remain, and we might continue discussing the matter while getting input from your aunt and uncle upon their arrival," suggested Lady Matlock.

"Very well," said Elizabeth, "but I should send the message to my aunt now."

"You write the note and I will arrange for its delivery," said Mr. Darcy. "Since the carriage is ready, why not let the driver deliver your letter and bring back your aunt as well as proper attire for dinner? Then she will be able to be more involved in the planning. Your uncle can come at his convenience after sending the express to your father."

Elizabeth smiled at her betrothed. "Well, I must get busy, as I now must write two letters. Perhaps I should also write a third to Father to be included in Uncle's letter, explaining the change in my feelings."

"By all means, do so if you think it would help," encouraged Mr. Darcy. "I am happy to write one as well, which can include my feelings for you and an outline of your settlement."

Lady Matlock smiled at the group. "It seems we all have much to do. Andrew, I would suggest *you* write requesting an appointment for you and Darcy at Doctors' Commons for Monday to apply for special licenses. Husband, perhaps you should write to the bishop, explaining the plans and settling a date with him. If all goes well, the wedding can be in less than two weeks. I also suggest that while Mrs. Gardiner and I handle the wedding plans and details, all of you must be seen in public as often as possible. If you are always in a large group while in public, the gossips will find it difficult to determine who is interested in whom. You can use the time to become better acquainted with your new relations. I will ask Nicholas to join you and walk with Georgiana. Another member of the group will add to the confusion for the gossips. Mrs. Annesley will, of course, still accompany the group to provide proper chaperonage."

While a footman gathered writing supplies for all those in need, Darcy arranged several others to prepare to deliver the messages. In all, there were five to deliver. The four messengers delivering within the city were to await replies. Once everything was in order, Darcy set about writing his letter to Mr. Bennet, including in it a surprise for Elizabeth.

Less than an hour and a half later, Mrs. Gardiner arrived. She joined Lady Matlock, Elizabeth, and Anne to assist in the planning. Mr. Gardiner came about half-past six and learned the reason for the many hurried plans. He offered hearty congratulations to both couples. Just as his wife had done earlier, he expressed his agreement with the couples' decisions. By the time the group sat down to supper, they had received replies to Lord Matlock and Andrew's letters agreeing to appointments Monday morning at ten o'clock. Darcy and Andrew would need to depart at half-past eight to visit the newspaper office before heading to Doctors' Commons.

Much laughter was heard and many toasts were made over the evening meal. The group discussed and discarded many events before agreeing on what to do. Lady Matlock was insistent they hold a wedding ball for the two couples the evening of the wedding. She was also emphatic about providing trousseaus for her niece and soon-to-be niece.

"Lady Ellen, it does not seem appropriate for you to purchase my trousseau," argued Elizabeth.

"Would you deny me the pleasure of having young ladies to dress, Elizabeth, dear? I have no daughters of my own, so dressing my nieces is the closest I shall come. You are entering a new level of society and will need to look the part. I will not allow anyone to think poorly of you or William for his choice. Besides, saving your father from this expense will allow him to allocate more for Miss Bennet, who, like you, will need much more, as her marriage will raise her in society, as well. I sent a letter to Madame Delacour earlier, along with all the other letters. I am sure she will agree to see us Monday at ten o'clock in the morning."

To prevent Elizabeth from arguing further, Mrs. Gardiner spoke. "You are incredibly generous, Lady Matlock, but you must allow my husband and me to participate, as well. I took all the girls to my modiste when they arrived in town. She is currently making about a dozen dresses each for Elizabeth and Jane. Anne also ordered several gowns from her."

"Who is your modiste, Mrs. Gardiner?"

"Her name is Mrs. Hartfield, and her shop is in Cheapside. Our husbands were friends. When her husband passed away, she had to support herself and two small children. Edward helped her locate the shop and gives her the first pick of the fabrics he imports. The excellent assortment of fabrics made her shop grow in popularity. In exchange, she gives me an excellent discount on the gowns she makes for me."

"Did she make the gowns you wore to the theater?" asked Lady Matlock. Elizabeth and Anne answered in the affirmative. "Well then, she is of great skill indeed, and with two brides, we shall be able to split the work between the two modistes."

Once the group planned to meet at Matlock House after church on Sunday to continue with the wedding plans, the visitors departed. Everyone would need a good night's rest for the busy week ahead.

14. So Many Engagements, So Little Time

Monday morning began early for the members of the Darcy, Matlock, and Gardiner homes. Everyone had many tasks to finish in a short period. Darcy and Fitzwilliam went first to the newspaper office, where Darcy made it clear that any announcement of his betrothal or marriage not signed by him should be verified before being printed. He warned that legal action would follow if this request went ignored. From there, they visited Doctors' Commons to apply for the special licenses they needed. After completing those errands, Darcy suggested they write to the family solicitor and arrange a meeting to begin working on the marriage settlements for their brides. Darcy suggested that Bingley join them for this so he would have a better understanding of what to include when he prepared Jane's settlement.

Lord Matlock brought his family solicitor along to meet the one for the de Bourgh estate, to ensure he learned all he needed to know and how to best proceed with the information learned.

For the ladies, the morning dragged on until almost time for tea. They visited with Madame Delacour and selected patterns and fabrics for morning, afternoon, and evening gowns. Elizabeth and Anne also ordered undergarments and nightwear, including something special for their wedding night, and outerwear they would require. During their previous planning, the women had decided Mrs. Hartfield would design their wedding gowns and several ballgowns for each lady. They had an appointment with her the following morning. After leaving Madame Delacour's shop, they visited the cordwainer for shoes and boots. They would need to return for dancing slippers after selecting the fabric for their ballgowns. Then they went to the milliner for hats to match the new gowns and outerwear. Their final stop for the day was at a shop catering to the accessories women needed to complete any ensemble. They selected ribbons, fans, gloves, and a few other necessities. As they returned to Darcy House, Lady Matlock made note of some particular items she thought Darcy and Andrew might enjoy purchasing for their new wives.

The ladies arrived at Darcy House in time for tea, and Elizabeth thought it not a moment too soon. They had ordered more clothing today then she had owned throughout her life, and the process exhausted her. The gentlemen, except for Mr. Gardiner, were there ahead of them. Mr. Gardiner had sent a note saying Mr. Bennet would arrive the next afternoon.

As they entered the drawing room where the men waited, they heard the sound of angry voices. "How could a mother treat her child in such a fashion?" demanded Andrew.

"Aunt is more selfish than even Caroline Bingley, which is hard to fathom." This time the voice belonged to Darcy. Elizabeth hurried to discover what had caused his anger. Anne was close behind her.

Darcy looked up at the sounds of someone coming to join them. He and Andrew rushed to greet their ladies. Elizabeth studied his eyes as she asked what had upset him.

"We were discussing Uncle's findings. I am sure you will be equally disgusted when you learn what he discovered." Elizabeth held her tongue as he led her to a settee and took the seat beside her. Moments after the ladies had settled themselves in the room, Mrs. Hadley, the housekeeper, entered with the tea service. She was followed by two maids carrying trays laden with fruit, sandwiches, biscuits, and the like.

Georgiana poured tea for everyone as the others fixed small plates of refreshments for themselves. Silence reigned for a brief while as everyone ate enough to sate their hunger. Lady Matlock finally broke the silence. "What did you learn from the solicitor, Duncan?"

Andrew and Darcy scowled as the topic of their earlier discussion resumed. Lady Matlock, Anne, and Elizabeth noted the gentlemen's expression and expected the news was not good. "The will is as Anne said," began Lord Matlock. "However, the reason Anne received no notification of her inheritance is despicable. Catherine told the solicitor Anne was too weak, in both body and mind, to take control of her inheritance." All the women gasped at such a blatant falsehood.

"How could Mother do this to me?" Anne's voice trembled as tears welled up in her eyes and spilled onto her cheeks. Andrew immediately clasped her hand in his and whispered soothing words.

"I asked the same thing," said her uncle. "I demanded to know what proof he had of her assertion. Based on his answer, Anne, I would suggest you find a new solicitor when you gain your inheritance."

"What did he answer, Uncle?"

"He said that, as your mother, Lady Catherine would know you best, so why should he bother to verify her words."

"I can see what you mean. Can the man be trusted to look out for my best interests when he did not attend to my father's final wishes? I trust you and Andrew can help me find a competent solicitor?"

"Of course we will," Andrew avowed.

"You shall receive all the help you need, Anne, as you take up your inheritance," her uncle assured her.

"How did you fare at the newspaper office, William?"

Elizabeth looked at him as she waited for an answer. "I believe we need have no concerns about them. The threat of a lawsuit was enough for them to give me their promise."

Andrew laughed, adding, "The head of the announcements section went quite pale at Darcy's threat. It made me wonder if he may not have done so in the past and remembered the problems which arose."

"Were you able to procure the special licenses we will need to marry?" asked Anne.

"The clerk promised they would be ready by Friday," replied Andrew.

"Now, we only need to receive a reply from the bishop to set the date. The express should reach him by tomorrow morning, which means we should receive a reply in three days. If he leaves at the same time as his letter, we can marry by Monday at the latest."

"What can we do if he is not available to marry us?" wondered Elizabeth. "Particularly as that was the reason provided for not allowing my mother to participate in the preparations. I dread hearing her complaints about being excluded from the planning, as she has dreamed of nothing so much as marrying off her daughters since Jane turned five and ten."

"We shall lay the blame on my sister-in-law and point out the advantages," said Lady Matlock. "You will be married by special license, along with the son of an earl, and in the presence of many peers. Surely, your mother will accept such a situation."

Elizabeth looked doubtful, as there was little she did which pleased Mrs. Bennet, but Jane spoke reassuringly. "Think of the bragging Mother will be able to do when she tells everyone about the special license and peerage present. She may be briefly disappointed, but you shall not be present to hear it."

Lady Matlock changed the subject. Looking at the two couples, she said, "Would you like to have the ceremony in our ballroom, or do you prefer to have it at St. George's? I am sure Mr. Edgecombe would allow the bishop to conduct the service in his stead."

"I would prefer to marry in a church," said Elizabeth quietly, "but other than my aunt and uncle's parish near Cheapside, I have no affiliation with any London church."

"A special license makes a home parish unnecessary, as there is no need to post the banns," the countess reminded her.

"Would holding the ceremony in a church make things more difficult for my mother?" asked Anne.

"With the bishop performing the service, I doubt there will be any trouble in any case," said Lord Matlock, "but you may marry at St. George's if you wish, as both Darcy's family and mine attend the parish."

Anne looked at Elizabeth and thought for a moment. "I believe I, too, would prefer to marry in the church."

"Then as soon as we hear from the bishop, Darcy and Fitzwilliam will visit with Mr. Edgecombe to finalize the date."

Elizabeth looked at her aunt. "Do you think Mrs. Hartfield can finish two wedding gowns in such a short period?"

"You and Jane spoke to her about this upon our first visit. Perhaps Miss Darcy would help Anne sketch her design in advance to save Mrs. Hartfield some time."

"I would love to help," cried Georgiana.

"Mrs. Gardiner, please inform Mrs. Hartfield I will pay for any additional seamstresses she needs to complete the projects," said Darcy.

When everyone finished their tea, Georgiana gathered her sketchpad and pencils to sketch the wedding gown of Anne's dreams. After an hour, when Anne had approved the final sketch, they began to discuss colors for their attendants and flowers.

   With the arrival of the fashionable hour in Hyde Park, the couples left the house to stroll. They spoke as much as possible, though they tried to follow Lady Matlock's suggestion and changed partners regularly. Friends and acquaintances frequently hailed the gentlemen, but introductions were rarely requested, nor were they offered. The unknown ladies drew considerable interest and attention as they accompanied two of the most eligible bachelors in London--Fitzwilliam Darcy and Viscount Gilchrist, heir to the Earl of Matlock. After their walk, they returned to Darcy House for farewells before Mrs. Gardiner and the Bennet sisters returned home.

15. Gaining Mr. Bennet's Permission

For Elizabeth, the next day proceeded much like the previous one, with more shopping to do. Mrs. Hartfield, delighted with the sketch for Anne's gown, helped the young ladies select the best fabrics for their dresses. Elizabeth chose pale yellow silk and Anne a blush pink silk. As a tribute to her future home, Elizabeth selected Derbyshire lace to trim the gown. Both gowns were simple yet elegant and utterly lacking in furbelows. Elizabeth doubted very much that Lady Catherine—or her own mother, for that matter—would approve of either gown.

The men spent the morning with their solicitors. Upon their return to Darcy House, another group outing took place. It took two carriages to transport the group to the shopping district. Here, they visited a shop filled with items for ladies. The gentlemen had both received a list from Lady Matlock of things their wives would soon need. Though they made no purchases at the time, Darcy and Andrew could determine which items Elizabeth and Anne preferred. They returned to Darcy House in time to change for dinner. Mr. Gardiner would stop by his home to retrieve Elizabeth's father.

Surprise filled Mr. Bennet when he arrived at an empty house to be greeted by only servants. Having received an express requesting his attendance, he expected to find things in an uproar of some sort. Mrs. Blake, the Gardiners's housekeeper, took care to provide him with refreshments, and Mr. Bennet lost himself in a book from Mr. Gardiner's study, happy for the peace and quiet.

Elizabeth changed rapidly and returned to the drawing room to await her father's arrival. When Darcy arrived in the room, he found her staring out the window. Moving to stand behind her, he asked, "Are you worried about your father's reaction?"

"Only a little, but I think we should talk to him together. Though I sent the letter about my changed feelings for you, I expect he will wish to discuss the matter in person before granting his approval. There is also the matter of explaining the need for the quick wedding. Father can be contrary, sometimes for the sheer enjoyment of watching others' discomfort. I would like to spare you some of the teasing you might experience."

Using the hand away from the door, Darcy reached down and took her hand, entwining his fingers in hers. "I am not afraid of anything your father might say, Elizabeth. You are more than worth any teasing he might inflict. I would endure that and so much more for the privilege of marrying you." The intense look accompanying his words brought a blush to Elizabeth's cheeks. Darcy offered her an arm and led her to the settee. They sat, their heads close in a whispered conversation, so lost in each other that Mr. Bennet's voice took them by surprise.

"Is Mr. Darcy's company why no family members greeted me upon my arrival at the Gardiners's home?" Mr. Bennet's face showed no expression except for an eyebrow quirked in wonder.

The two startled apart, a blush spreading over each face. The couple jumped up, and Elizabeth rushed to hug her father.

"Welcome, Papa. I am happy you arrived safely." Mr. Bennet's intense scrutiny of his daughter did nothing to ease the blush on her face.

Darcy stepped forward and bowed in greeting. "Welcome to Darcy House, Mr. Bennet. It is a pleasure to see you again."

"Good evening, Mr. Darcy. My astonishment knew no bounds when Gardiner informed me we would be dining at your home this evening."

"I am grateful you could join us on such short notice." Darcy glanced fleetingly at Elizabeth, a question in his eye. Finding what he was looking for, he turned back to Mr. Bennet. "I understand from Miss Elizabeth that she got her love of reading from you, sir. Would you allow me to show you my library? I believe you will find it interesting."

Mr. Bennet's eyes widened at the offer and he agreed with alacrity. Darcy offered his arm to Elizabeth and led Mr. Bennet from the room. As they moved down the hallway, they passed Andrew. He nodded at Darcy and continued on his way, without stopping for an introduction. Darcy dropped Elizabeth's arm and threw open both doors, stepping aside to allow Mr. Bennet to enter first. He reclaimed Elizabeth's arm and they followed the older gentleman into the room.

Elizabeth's father stepped to the center of the room and stood looking about him in awe.

"Never before have I seen such an extensive personal library, Mr. Darcy. How do you find time for your responsibilities with so much temptation before you?"

"It can be a challenge, but it is also a great joy to have so many options at my fingertips."

"I do not believe I would get any work done. I am often distracted by my smaller selection."

"Before you get lost in my collection, sir, might Miss Elizabeth and I request a few moments of your time?" Mr. Bennet looked at the two and believed he knew the subject, though he would not allow things to be too easy for the gentleman.

"Is that not usually a discussion between just the petitioner and the father? Why do you wish to include my daughter?"

"It is my wish, Papa, for us to speak to you jointly. There is a great deal to discuss, and some important decisions must be made rather expeditiously."

"Are you here because this marriage must take place, Elizabeth?" charged her father.

"Papa, how dare you ask me such a thing?"

"It is not a lack of trust in you, but I know much about the reputation of men of the ton."

Darcy's lips thinned and Elizabeth could see him clench his teeth, but he said not a word.

Clasping her hand over his, where it rested on her other hand, she spoke more sharply than intended. "Papa, you could not be more mistaken. Mr. Darcy is the best man I know and a perfect gentleman." Again, Mr. Bennet regarded his daughter with a quizzical expression.

"Shall we sit?" asked Mr. Darcy, gesturing toward the furniture before the fireplace. Darcy led Elizabeth to the settee and settled himself beside her. Mr. Bennet took the chair across from them, resting his elbows on the arms and steepling his fingers in a thoughtful pose. Darcy cleared his throat and began to speak. "Mr. Bennet, I recognize my behavior and actions during my time in Hertfordshire did not give you and your neighbors a good opinion of me, for which I am sorry. However, that is when I fell in love with your daughter. As you are aware, Miss Elizabeth and I met again during her stay in Kent. Conversation helped us overcome our differences and discover how many common interests we share. Our personalities complement one another perfectly, and we would like your permission and blessing on our marriage."

Mr. Bennet studied the pair before him. He knew Elizabeth had possessed an extreme dislike of the gentleman the previous fall. Was this new feeling a result of Mr. Darcy's rescue of her rather than love? Her father knew he had to ask. "Elizabeth, are you sure what you are feeling is affection for Mr. Darcy and not gratitude that he saved you from Mr. Collins?"

"I am sure, Papa. I had already accepted a courtship from Mr. Darcy at the time of Mr. Collins's poor behavior."

Mr. Bennet's eyebrows rose further up his forehead. "You proceeded from dislike to courtship to betrothal in less than a month?"

"No, Papa. Once Mr. Darcy and I discussed our misunderstandings, I acknowledged to myself that my injured pride caused my supposed dislike. The more time we spent together, the quicker we realized our many common interests. It did not take me long to realize that Mr. Darcy is the best man I know. He is exactly the man who in disposition and talents most suits me." Elizabeth looked at him when she finished speaking. Darcy's delighted smile showed his dimples, and she could not help smiling in return.

The look they exchanged, more than any words spoken, convinced Mr. Bennet this marriage was indeed what his daughter desired. Clearly, she would be happy and loved throughout her life.

"I give you my consent and my blessing on your marriage," he said.

"Thank you, sir, but there is one more thing we must discuss."

"What might that be?"

"Miss Elizabeth told me Mr. Collins made mention of a supposed engagement to my cousin, Miss de Bourgh." Mr. Bennet nodded. "The engagement is solely my aunt's desire. Neither Anne nor I ever wished to marry each other. Anne and another cousin, Colonel Andrew Fitzwilliam, discovered their affection for each other. Anne declared her affection for Andrew was longstanding, but could not express it due to her mother's desires. When I made my interest in Elizabeth known, Anne felt free to be more open with her feelings. The problem arises because my aunt would protest this if she knew of Andrew and Anne's desires. As a result, they wish to marry before she recovers, to avoid her interference."

"I can understand why they might wish to do so, but how does that affect your wedding to Elizabeth?"

This time, Elizabeth answered. "Anne requested we marry in a joint ceremony. She does not wish to allow her mother the opportunity to make trouble for Mr. Darcy and me. Mr. Darcy's aunt, Lady Matlock, is arranging things so that there are no grounds for Lady Catherine to demand the annulment of either marriage. I accepted the offer based on your approval."

"When were you planning to marry?"

"We can review the preliminary settlement today if you wish. Our special license should be ready in a few days, and we hope to marry by the end of next week at the latest."

"My, that is quick. Did you consider your mother's reaction?" asked Mr. Bennet.

Elizabeth's concern for the subject showed on her face, so Darcy answered while she arranged her thoughts. "Miss Bennet encouraged Elizabeth to consent. She also suggested that being married by special license with the son of an earl, before several other members of the peerage, might satisfy Mrs. Bennet's need for--" Darcy paused to find the appropriate word, "excitement. We are hoping to be married by my godfather, the Bishop of Derby. We can say the date selected best fit his schedule."

Elizabeth added, "We will come home to allow Mama to throw a party, which should satisfy her." She glanced at William, pleading in her look.

"Of course we will," added Mr. Darcy. Elizabeth smiled in gratitude, as she knew Darcy would be very uncomfortable being the center of attention at such a gathering. She reached over and squeezed the hand resting beside her on the settee, something that did not go unnoticed by her father.

"Would you be willing to stay until the wedding, Papa, to give me away?" Elizabeth's hopeful expression met with disappointment.

"Do you wish for your mother and younger sisters to attend the wedding?"

Elizabeth hesitated, considering how best to answer her father's question.

Before she could speak, he said, "I understand your hesitance. I never expected one of my daughters would marry so well. If I had, I might have restrained your mother and younger sisters to make them acceptable to higher society. I think I must decline and stay at home with them, but I am sure your uncle would happily accept your offer."

It pained Darcy to behold Elizabeth's unhappiness. However, he much appreciated the fact that Mr. Bennet recognized his wife and younger daughters' behavior would not be acceptable to high society and would cause problems for Elizabeth. "Perhaps, Mr. Bennet, you might return the day before the wedding and stay for only a day or two. Then Miss Bennet would be able to return home with you. I would be happy for you to stay and enjoy my library for those couple of days." Darcy could see him wavering. "In fact, you may borrow some books to read before you return, if you would care to do so."

"I believe that would be an acceptable compromise. Though no father truly wishes to give his daughter away to another man, having the opportunity to do so is a great honor."

"Thank you, Papa. It will make the wedding perfect with you and Jane here."

"I will return to Longbourn tomorrow, so be sure to send me a letter confirming when I must return."

"Of course, sir. If I may, there is one more thing we need to discuss, Mr. Bennet."

The confused expression on his daughter's face raised Mr. Bennet's interest.

"Miss Elizabeth mentioned that Miss Lydia wrote of an invitation to Brighton with the colonel of the militia and his wife. I must tell you something about which I should have warned the citizens of Meryton while staying in the area." Darcy took a deep breath and continued. "I am aware Mr. Wickham told a tale, to Miss Elizabeth and several of your neighbors, of my denying him a living."

"True, but I do not put much store in gossip."

"I am relieved to hear it, sir, but I feel it necessary to relate to you my history with Mr. Wickham for the safety of your family."

"The safety of my family?" the elder gentleman repeated, looking surprised.

Darcy proceeded to tell Mr. Bennet of his history with Wickham. He did not mention Georgiana's attempted elopement, but he did speak of the other young women of all classes whom Wickham had sweet-talked and then abandoned after having taken his pleasure with them.

Looking quite shaken, Mr. Bennet said, "I appreciate your honesty, sir. I believe you helped me decide Lydia is far too young to travel with only the colonel's young wife as a chaperone. I will not get a moment's peace when Lydia learns my decision, but I believe it will save my family from ruin. The current gossip indicated Mr. Wickham vanished without a trace."

The couple shared a look, not wishing to say more about the man at present. "Even should the story be true, I am sure he is not the only blackguard wearing a militia uniform. Now, dinner will be ready soon. Would you care to come and meet the rest of my family?"

They returned to the drawing room, where everyone awaited them. Anne and Andrew wore expectant expressions. Darcy gave them a broad smile and both relaxed. Hadley appeared in the room to announce dinner before Darcy completed the introductions. Not standing on formality, Darcy sat at the head of the table with Elizabeth to his right and Mr. Bennet on his left. The earl sat beside Elizabeth, and Lady Matlock sat beside Mr. Bennet. The Gardiners were next. Mr. Gardiner's acquaintance with the earl and his brother-in-law's idiosyncrasies allowed him to keep the conversation flowing appropriately. While they sat over dinner, Mr. Bennet discovered Lady Matlock's intent to purchase Elizabeth's trousseau.

"It is not necessary, my lady. I am capable of meeting my daughter's requirements."

"I am sure you are, Mr. Bennet, but William is like a son to me, and it would give me great pleasure to do this for Elizabeth. As another of your daughters will soon require a trousseau to purchase, my gift will allow you more for Miss Bennet's needs."

Bennet realized he could not afford everything Elizabeth would need, so arguing would be churlish. "You are exceedingly kind, Lady Matlock. I must admit I am surprised at Elizabeth's easy acceptance." Elizabeth glared at her father and Mr. Gardiner kicked him in the ankle.

"Elizabeth is the daughter of a gentleman, the same as my nephew," said the earl.

"More importantly, she is intelligent, witty, and beautiful. She is just what William needs, and I expect her to make a splash in the ton upon her presentation," added the countess.

Humbled at the words of Elizabeth's future family, Mr. Bennet determined to improve not only himself but the rest of the family, so they would never be an embarrassment to his eldest daughters.

16. Intruders

"Where is my daughter? Why did she not return as commanded?" bellowed Lady Catherine.

Her lady's maid shifted from foot to foot, clasping and unclasping her fingers as she responded, "I am afraid Miss de Bourgh is still in London, my lady."

"How long since you mailed my letter?" The lady's imperious tone did nothing to soothe the maid's unease.

"You sent the letter ten days ago. Do you not remember? Miss Anne replied that her busy schedule of events with the Darcys prevented her from returning at this time."

"Of course, I remember," snapped the ill-tempered patient. "Then why have I not seen an announcement of their engagement in the paper? Are you sure we have received the London papers each day?"

"Yes, your ladyship."

"Send for Mr. Collins, then. I demand to see him this instant."

Eyes wide, the servant gulped. "I cannot, your ladyship. You know the doctor does not wish you to receive visitors as of yet."

"Then send for the doctor post-haste."

"Yes, your ladyship." The maid scurried from the room. Upon reaching the hallway, she leaned against the wall and took a deep breath before rushing below stairs to find someone to carry out Lady Catherine's request.

Dr. Walker took his time in arriving at Rosings. It had been about six weeks since the accident, and he did not think he would be able to keep visitors away from Lady Catherine for much longer. He hoped Miss de Bourgh would marry very soon so she would be beyond her mother's reach.

At the knock, Lady Catherine's maid crossed the room and opened the bedchamber door to admit the doctor.

"It took you long enough," complained Lady Catherine.

"I am sorry, an emergency with another patient prevented me from arriving sooner. There was no indication of a problem, so what is the trouble, Lady Catherine?"

"I wish you to lift the ban on visitors. I am lonely and would like my parson to visit. Let him make himself useful by reading to me."

"Should he not be attending to parish duties? I would be happy to stop by the parsonage and ask Mrs. Collins to come read to you if you would like."

"Perhaps some other time, but for now, I wish Mr. Collins to attend me."

"The gentleman is overwrought by your illness. I do not think it is wise for him to be around you, as he may cause you to become agitated as well. Should you move about too much, it will only delay your recovery."

"Then I shall order him to be still, but I must discover the parish's needs so I might offer whatever assistance is required."

The doctor knew she wished for the latest gossip so that she might force others to her will. He attempted to repress a smile as he replied, "You are unable to assist anyone at this time."

"I know my physical limitations," barked the lady, "but it is still within my power to offer assistance through my steward or Mr. Collins. I demand you allow him to visit me."

"Very well, Lady Catherine, but you must wait until tomorrow before seeing him. It is late in the day, and I do not wish his visit to distress you before you retire. Sleep is the best thing to ensure you recover to your fullest."

"Very well." The pout on the older woman's face almost made Dr. Walker laugh. Turning away to hide the smile that her expression conjured, he picked up his bag to depart. Turning back, he said, "I shall visit you on Monday next week as usual. Please remember to remain still so you will recover without causing permanent damage to the joint."

"Yes, yes," said the lady as she shooed him out the door.

As Dr. Walker stepped up into his carriage to return home, he murmured, "I pray you accomplish your goal soon, Miss Anne. There is nothing else I can do to assist you."

The next day, a footman from Rosings appeared at the parsonage door with the message that Lady Catherine wished Mr. Collins to attend her without delay. As it happened, Mr. Collins was out on parish business, and Mrs. Collins was visiting several of the sick and elderly parishioners. As a consequence, not until late afternoon did the parson return to his home and receive Lady Catherine's message. Without stopping to freshen his attire, he rushed to Rosings. When Jackson tried to turn him away, Mr. Collins pushed his hand against the door to keep it from closing, crying, "Lady Catherine demanded my presence."

Jackson looked skeptical and reluctantly opened the door wider. Mr. Collins rushed past the butler and directly up the stairs to Lady Catherine's chamber. He knocked on the door and tapped his foot as he waited for it to open. When the maid admitted him, the parson practically raced across the room and bowed abjectly to his patroness.

"Why did you keep me waiting so long, Mr. Collins? I sent for you early this morning."

"Your pardon, Lady Catherine, I was out attending to duties and only just arrived home. I did not even stop to change, as I have been so anxious to verify for myself your well-being. Do you need my comfort and succor? How can I help you?"

"What transpired since I became ill? Do you know when Anne went to town and in whose company she traveled?"

"I tried to counsel Miss de Bourgh about the newcomer in her company, but she would not heed my words."

"Why would my daughter need your advice? Her cousins were here to assist her in any way she needed."

"That was the problem. She did not realize she was taking a snake to her bosom by inviting Miss Bennet to stay here with her. When I tried to tell her Miss Elizabeth was attempting to steal Mr. Darcy from her, she said there was no engagement between her and her cousin. She expressed pleasure that Mr. Darcy had found someone to love." Mr. Collins hoped Lady Catherine would not wonder why Cousin Elizabeth had to leave his home, but the hope was short-lived.

"Why would Miss Bennet need to stay at Rosings when in the area to visit her friend and stay with you?"

His face a mottled red, his voice hard, the parson replied, "The vixen manipulated Mr. Darcy into believing I harmed her and that she was not safe in my home."

"Why did you not just send her away if the wretch caused trouble?"

"I tried, but Mr. Darcy intervened and said Miss de Bourgh would welcome her at Rosings until her scheduled departure."

A suspicion growing in her mind, Lady Catherine pressed, "With whom did my daughter travel to London?"

"Miss de Bourgh departed in Mr. Darcy's carriage." The woman smiled at his words, then began to wonder at his hesitation to continue.

"Who else departed with her and Darcy?" Lady Catherine's tone informed the man he could not fail to answer.

"The two you mentioned traveled with the colonel and my cousin."

"This is all your fault," howled Lady Catherine. "You brought a jezebel into our sphere and my home."

"I had no way of knowing she would behave in such a manner."

"If you had the sense God gave a pig, you would know a woman who turned down a worthy proposal to a parson was a troublemaker. Now you shall make things right. I demand you go to London. You will take a letter I give you to the newspaper, announcing Darcy and Anne's engagement, and you will ensure she returns to me immediately. You must leave in the morning. I will expect you and Anne to be back the day after tomorrow. You should insist Darcy return as well. Then you can read the banns beginning on Sunday. They will wed in three weeks."

"But--but--Lady Catherine, how shall I make her come home? She ignored my advice before. What will make her listen now?"

"You will tell her that if she does not return, I will disinherit her."

Mr. Collins looked appalled at the words of his patroness. "You would do such a thing to your daughter?"

"If Anne refuses to return, then you are to go to the office of my solicitor and deliver to him a letter that I will also prepare."

"Y-y-y-yes, your ladyship. I will do as you say." The parson again bowed almost to the ground and backed toward the door. When he bumped into the wall, he nearly pitched forward on his face. Struggling to regain his balance, he wobbled through the door that the maid held open.

While Lady Catherine met with the physician, Elizabeth arrived at Darcy House. She received a cryptic message from William, requesting her presence briefly. As Georgiana and Mrs. Annesley were in residence, Mrs. Gardiner allowed her to go with only a maid to accompany her.

Upon her admittance to Darcy's study, the door of which stayed open for propriety's sake, Darcy led her to the chairs before the fire. Once seated, he said, "Elizabeth, close your eyes."

"What are you up to, William?"

"Just close your eyes." Elizabeth did as requested and felt him set something on her lap. "All right, you can open them."

On her lap sat a basket containing a black Scottish terrier puppy with a bright red bow around his neck.

"Oh, William, she is beautiful!" said Elizabeth as she placed a kiss on the dog's head and began to scratch the puppy's ears.

"She is a he. You seemed to enjoy Fiona so much, I thought you might like one of your own. This little fellow came from the same litter as Anne's puppy. Since the females are a bit smaller, I chose her for Anne, but I thought you might like this sturdy fellow to accompany you on your rambles at Pemberley."

"We were never allowed to have a pet at Longbourn. I love him. What is his name?"

"You get to decide."

Elizabeth thought for a moment as she absently petted the dog. Then she lifted his head to study his face while scratching his chin. "I believe I will call him Angus."

"You chose a name that pays honor to his heritage. It suits him admirably," agreed Darcy. I shall keep him here at Darcy House until after the wedding, but he can travel with us to Rosings if you wish."

Elizabeth picked up the puppy and cuddled him to her as she buried her face in his fur. After a few more minutes with the animal, Elizabeth returned Angus to his basket. He licked her hand as she gave him a last pat and said goodbye. Standing, Elizabeth moved closer to Darcy. She reached out and placed her hands on his chest.

"Thank you for my gift, William." She stood on tiptoe to place a kiss on his cheek. He promptly wrapped his arms around her, pulling her even closer, before bending to capture her lips with his. The kiss began gently, but their passions soon built into a raging fire. Darcy regained his senses when his hands began to slide down her side to cup her rounded *derriere*. He took a step back, his breathing labored. Looking disappointed, Elizabeth struggled to get her breathing under control as well.

"You are irresistible, my dearest, loveliest Elizabeth. I nearly let my feelings run away with me. In two short days, I will be able to show you the depth of my love."

"I cannot wait to be your wife, William." Darcy offered his arm to Elizabeth and led her to her carriage. He helped her in and then kissed her hand before letting it go. He closed the door and watched the carriage until it disappeared from view.

Rushing into the house, he called, "Andrew, Georgiana, we cannot be late for our appointment." Then Darcy disappeared into his study. He returned, holding the lead attached to Angus as Georgiana descended the stairs. Andrew soon followed, holding the lead attached to Fiona.

Leaving the house through the mews, they quickly entered the carriage and were on the way to their destination. After an hour of working with the dogs, Darcy and Andrew were happy with the animals' success and the surprise they had for their ladies.

On the night before the wedding, the Bennets, the Gardiners, the Darcys, Charles Bingley, and the Bishop of Derby gathered at Matlock House for a celebratory dinner. The next day, the ladies would take up residence in their new homes. Two days after the wedding, the Fitzwilliam family, including its latest member, would return to Rosings to deal with Lady Catherine. Elizabeth expressed the desire to be of assistance to her friend and new cousin. Darcy, fearing the harsh words his aunt would hurl at Elizabeth, tried to convince her that the others would deal with Lady Catherine and that Elizabeth's presence might only provoke the older woman, making the situation worse. Knowing she could be helpful without Lady Catherine's knowledge of her being there, she insisted they go. Elizabeth hoped to foster a relationship between Charlotte and Anne, thinking they would enjoy each other's company and probably become good friends.

The earl and Andrew would deal with the legalities. Elizabeth would oversee the servants as they prepared the dower house for its new tenant, and the countess would help Anne with staffing and redecorating.

The group had an early dinner and said their goodnights sooner than the lovers wished. For ease in preparing everyone for the upcoming nuptials, Georgiana, Elizabeth, and Jane would spend the night at Matlock House with Anne. Andrew and Nicholas would move to Darcy House for the night.

While Mrs. Gardiner and Lady Matlock spoke to Elizabeth, Jane, and Anne, respectively, about what to expect on their wedding nights, the gentlemen retired to Darcy House for a game or two of billiards. As Andrew was also to marry in the morning, they did not overindulge in liquor--a trick he would have attempted to play on his staid cousin had circumstances been different. However, the lack of imbibing did not mean the two soon-to-be-grooms enjoyed a peaceful evening. They received a monumental amount of teasing about giving up their freedom. However, Darcy reminded Bingley that, with his wedding fast approaching, he should expect payback.

After two games, Darcy wished to retire. He stopped by the library to check on Mr. Bennet and his godfather, the bishop, before making his way to his chamber. Once ready to retire, Darcy dismissed Clarke and sat beside the fire, a brandy in his hand.

Darcy could not believe that all of his dreams would come true in less than twelve hours. A restless excitement filled him, so he stood and moved to the door leading to the mistress's chamber. Opening the door, Darcy looked about. When first shown her new room, Elizabeth had found it pleasant and said she did not see the need to make changes, as everything appeared to be in good condition. However, Darcy wanted only the best for his beautiful Elizabeth, so he decided to make some changes to refresh the room as a surprise. The delicate furniture in the room-- cherry wood, finished in a rich, deep shade fashioned in the graceful Queen Anne style--would appeal to Elizabeth. Knowing the colors she favored, Darcy had the walls done in pale yellow silk. Filling the picture frame trim on the walls around the room was a fabric with a white trellis pattern on a pale blue background. Climbing the trellis were small clusters of yellow and deep blue flowers. The same material covered the settee before the fireplace, flanked by a pair of light blue and white striped chairs. A writing desk sat near one window and a deep yellow brocaded chaise lounge near the other. The bedding matched the settee, and dark yellow velvet drapes hung at the windows. Imagining her look of pleasure, Darcy closed the door and retired to bed, dreaming of his dearest, loveliest Elizabeth.

Half an hour before sunrise, one of Lady Catherine's carriages arrived at the parsonage. Mr. Collins stumbled from the house, a small travel bag in hand. As he reached the door, the footman handed him two letters addressed in Lady Catherine's firm, angular script. He tucked them into his coat pocket before stepping into the carriage. Collins fell onto the bench as the driver slapped the reins and the horses sprang forward. He dreaded the trip and wondered what the consequences would be should he fail. However, the man experienced a sense of satisfaction that he would be delivering the letter announcing Mr. Darcy and Miss de Bourgh's engagement; the parson looked forward to causing pain and embarrassment to his wretched cousin.

Having a four-hour journey ahead of him, Mr. Collins settled into the corner of the carriage and was soon snoring louder than the rattle of the vehicle. At the half-way point, the carriage stopped to change horses, and the gentleman took the opportunity to break his fast before continuing his journey.

17. Interrupted Weddings

The day of the wedding dawned bright and beautiful. In late May, spring flowers bloomed everywhere one looked. The azure sky, dotted with puffy white clouds, lifted the brides' spirits, as they would not be required to battle a spring shower, which would have dirtied their gowns and shoes.

Elizabeth experienced mixed feelings. She felt peaceful at the knowledge that she would soon marry the only man she could ever love. There was also a sense of excitement at beginning this new phase of life and seeing her new home, as well as helping her friend find a life of freedom, love, and joy. When making the journey to Hunsford, Elizabeth could not imagine things would end in this way. Interrupting Elizabeth's thoughts was the arrival of Jane and Aunt Gardiner, accompanied by the maid to help her prepare for the day.

In her room, Anne was also experiencing mixed emotions. She could not believe she would marry the man of her choice--one for whom she had long-held affection. However, until the ceremony ended, Anne would not be able to relax. Only after the 'I do's' would she be free of her mother's tyranny.

A knock at the door pulled Anne from her thoughts with the arrival of Aunt Matlock and

Georgiana, along with Anne's maid. Georgiana felt torn about whom to attend. She did not wish for Anne to be alone but she also desired to see her new sister. As a result, she spent much of her time darting between the two rooms, showering the brides with compliments.

The Darcy carriage pulled up before the columned front of St. George's. The four men exited the carriage, mounted the steps, and entered to find Mr. Edgecombe. They walked into an anteroom, where they would wait for the service to start. Darcy sat looking out the window at the back of the church and watched the traffic on the streets below. Andrew, however, paced the small room like a caged animal. Like Anne, he would not be able to relax until they were husband and wife and beyond the reach of Lady Catherine.

"Andrew, would you please stop pacing? Watching you is making me sick to my stomach," said Nicholas. "Everything will be fine. Aunt Catherine is not suddenly going to appear."

"From your lips to God's ear, my brother." Andrew's fervent desire was evident in his reply.

Charles opened the door and peeked into the sanctuary, where he saw people beginning to fill the rows. As he listened, the organist began playing prelude music. Bingley closed the door and looked at his companions. "The guests are arriving. It should not be long now."

Nicholas crossed the room to a tray where sat a decanter and glasses. He poured a finger's worth of brandy into each and raised his glass. "To the grooms. May your lives be filled with joy and the comfort of your beautiful wives."

Just as the last glass returned to the tray, the door opened and Mr. Edgecombe announced it was time for the gentlemen to take their places. Darcy stepped out first, followed by Bingley, Andrew, and Nicholas. The bishop smiled down at his godsons before they all turned to face the rear of the church to watch the brides approach.

Andrew's eyes widened as Anne walked down the aisle. She glowed, her bonnet and gown of blossom brightening her complexion as she progressed on the arm of her uncle, Lord Matlock. In her hand, Anne carried a bouquet of pink and white roses.

Darcy glanced momentarily at his cousin, but then his eyes looked behind her, searching for Elizabeth. When she appeared, Darcy forgot to breathe. Elizabeth, in a gown of primrose, walked beside her father. Instead of a bonnet, Elizabeth wore white rosebuds, primrose, and evening primrose in her hair and carried a matching bouquet.

Following the brides, the two terriers walked side-by-side down the aisle. Each wore a ribbon to match its bride and sat at the feet of their respective grooms. The congregation, shocked into silence at the scene, soon buzzed with conversation when someone noted the gold bands tied to the dogs' ribbons. The realization that the dogs carried the rings caused a few chuckles.

Georgiana and Jane followed the dogs. Both wore cream-colored gowns trimmed in ribbons to match their respective bride. When they took their positions at the altar, the service began.

The ceremony proceeded much as every other wedding was performed. When the bishop asked for any objections, both couples held their breath until the celebrant continued speaking. However, just as the bishop was about to pronounce the two couples husband and wife, a voice asserted, "Stop! This marriage cannot take place."

As the carriage transitioned from the dirt roads of the countryside to the cobbled streets of London, Mr. Collins awoke. He stretched and yawned as he rubbed his hands over his face. He watched the passing scenery until the carriage stopped before a tall, narrow building. The sign above the door read "The Times Newspaper." Mr. Collins climbed out of the vehicle and paused, pulling the two letters from his pocket. Selecting the one he wanted, he put the other back inside his coat. Approaching a desk just inside the door, he asked for the editor.

"Do you have an appointment?"

"No, but I am here to deliver an important marriage announcement from Lady Catherine de Bourgh."

"The editor does not see anyone without an appointment."

"B-b-b-but I have been sent by one of the most important peers in the kingdom," shrieked the affronted parson.

The man at the counter laughed. "The wife of a baronet is hardly an important peer."

"She is also the daughter of the late Earl of Matlock!" exclaimed Mr. Collins. "A more perspicacious and benevolent lady you will never meet. How can you call her unimportant?" The man's indignation grew by leaps and bounds at the insults to his patroness. "I demand to see the person in charge of betrothal and wedding announcements."

"You can sit there while I send someone to find out if he will receive you."

Mr. Collins took the seat indicated, wearing his indignation like a cloak. After fifteen minutes, a gentleman stood before him. "I understand you wish to run a betrothal announcement?"

Mr. Collins stood and held out Lady Catherine's letter. The man opened the missive and perused it. Remembering his conversation with Mr. Darcy, he now understood why the gentleman had made such threats. "I will be sure the message about Mr. Darcy runs this afternoon." He did not consider his statement a lie, as the announcement about the double wedding was set to appear in that afternoon's edition of the paper.

Satisfied he had accomplished his task, Mr. Collins turned and stormed from the office. Stepping into the coach, he told the coachman to take him to Mr. Darcy's home. Upon reaching the magnificent house, he climbed the stairs and knocked at the door.

Opening the door, Hadley stared at the squat, ugly parson before him. "Away with you. We do not allow peddlers at the front door."

"I am not a peddler!" Indignation caused Mr. Collins to quaver. "I am here to see Miss de Bourgh. I come with an important message from her mother."

"Miss de Bourgh is not at home this morning."

"Where is she?" demanded the parson.

Hadley turned to look at the longcase clock in the entry hall. It was now a quarter past ten. Knowing the man would be unable to stop the wedding at this point, he said, "I can tell you she should be arriving at Matlock House shortly for the wedding breakfast."

"Wedding breakfast!" shouted the parson in dismay. "In whose honor is this event?"

"There are four guests of honor, Colonel Fitzwilliam, Miss de Bourgh, Mr. Darcy, and Miss Bennet."

Mr. Collins's face went white at the butler's words. Without taking his leave of the butler, he ran down the stairs, calling out to the coachman to take him to the Earl of Matlock's family church. Mr. Collins jumped from the carriage, almost falling on his face in his hurry. He ran up the stairs of St. George's church as fast as he could. His breathing labored, Mr. Collins pushed himself to go faster. The parson flung open the door and, without giving any thought to what he should do, opened the door to the nave and rushed in, calling for the wedding to stop.

Everyone in the church turned at the voice, and Mr. Collins hesitated to see so many eyes cast in his direction, many of them with angry looks. He hurried up the aisle, crying, "This wedding cannot take place. Mr. Darcy is already promised to Miss de Bourgh. It was the dearest wish of both of their mothers."

He paused to catch his breath, and his eyes fixed on the minister. It was then that he realized the man wore the robes of a bishop. Mr. Collins also noticed the bishop's expression was one of extreme displeasure.

However, the first person to speak was Darcy. "Begone, Mr. Collins. No one invited you or desired your presence."

"I am here at the direction of Lady Catherine, tasked with returning her daughter to her without delay."

Then came the voice of the earl. "You do not have the authority to remove my niece from here, sir. I suggest you depart as my nephew advised."

Mr. Collins tried a different tack. "Your lordship, I fear you do not know what kind of woman it is who entrapped your nephew into a marriage."

"How dare you speak of my daughter in such a way?" Mr. Bennet's voice joined the discussion. "In fact, you possess no authority over any of the people involved in this ceremony. Unless you wish certain unpleasant facts to reach the bishop's ears, you should depart."

Mr. Collins glared at his cousin until a deep, commanding voice addressed him. "I know not who you are, but you are too late to object. You will take a seat and I will listen to what you have to say after finishing the service."

Then, ignoring the interruption, the bishop continued. "As I was saying, *Forasmuch as Andrew and Anne and Fitzwilliam and Elizabeth have consented together in holy Wedlock, and have witnessed the same before God and this company, and thereto have given and pledged their troth either to the other, and have declared the same by giving and receiving of a Ring and by joining of hands; I pronounce that they be Man and Wife together, In the Name of the Father and of the Son, and of the Holy Ghost. Amen."* (4)

The group at the altar followed the bishop to the office, where the gentlemen had waited earlier. After they all signed the register, the bishop looked at the two couples. "Do you wish for me to deal with him alone or do you want to stay?"

The men looked at their wives and then at each other. With nods all around, Darcy said, "We will stay, but, Jane, Bingley, perhaps you would be so kind as to invite my uncle and Mr. Bennet to join us."

The bishop nodded. "I am glad you explained all that led to this point. I believe I know exactly how to handle Mr. Collins. I also think it would not hurt if the new master and mistress of Rosings should decide to address him as well."

Everyone took a seat. The bishop sat behind Mr. Edgecombe's desk as the rector left with Jane and Mr. Bingley to retrieve the other parties. The bishop directed both the earl and Mr. Bennet to seats, leaving Mr. Collins standing before the desk.

"You are the parson at Hunsford, a living in the gift of the estate of Rosings, correct?"

"Yes, your eminence. I am the fortunate--"

The bishop cut him off. "And have you conducted any wedding services since your ordination?"

"I have, and I look forward to reading the banns for Miss--"

Again, the bishop interrupted the verbose Mr. Collins. "And is there, or is there not, a specific point in the service where objections are sought?"

"There is, bishop, but under the circumstances--"

"If no one speaks at the permitted time, are any other interruptions allowed?"

"No, but it was necessary--"

"If you did not arrive in time to object when it is permitted, you cannot object later. As a clergyman, you should know this."

"I do, sir, but I had to object, as Mr. Darcy is already betrothed to Miss de Bourgh. An unworthy woman such as my cousin does not deserve to marry into such a prestigious family as that of my patroness."

"Miss Bennet did not become a de Bourgh. She became a Darcy. Mr. Darcy and his uncle explained to me Lady Catherine's desire for this wedding, but that is all it is. There are no marriage articles signed nor any documentation of any kind to require Mr. Darcy to offer for Miss de Bourgh. Also, as a third party with no real connection to those being married, you do not have any right to object. Everyone involved is of age or has parental permission. There are also marriage articles for both of the ladies signed by the appropriate persons."

"Such is not possible," cried Mr. Collins, "Lady Catherine would never sign any papers for her daughter to marry unless it was to Mr. Darcy. As her recent injury prohibits her from traveling, I know she signed no such papers."

"My wife did not need her mother's permission to marry. She is of age and had my father sign as her witness," Andrew said.

"Then, I hope you can support her on your army salary, sir, for I have a letter here from Lady Catherine vowing to disinherit her daughter if she does not return home with me tomorrow."

"My sister does not have the power to do such a thing, though she believes she fooled us all."

Mr. Collins looked at the earl in confusion, but it was Andrew who spoke. "My aunt tried to hide her husband's will from us to retain charge of Rosings Park illegally. However, my wife recently discovered she is the rightful mistress of Rosings Park, something confirmed by the de Bourgh family solicitor. Per the will, Anne inherited it from her father effective today, her five and twentieth birthday. Should you wish to keep your position, I believe you should decide where your loyalty lies."

Mr. Collins's mouth fell open and his eyes nearly bulged from his head. Colonel Fitzwilliam's implacable stare made the parson speechless for perhaps the first time in his life, so he merely bowed.

The bishop decided to bring this discussion to a close. "Now, you are aware of the truth of this matter, and I expect your concerns are no more." Mr. Collins glared at his cousin but held his tongue. "Good. Now there are other matters which we must discuss. It recently came to my attention that you laid hands upon a woman in anger. For a man of the cloth, such behavior is utterly unacceptable. I do not expect to ever learn about such a thing happening again. Should you so forget yourself in the future, you shall face judgment from the church and possibly lose your position." Mr. Collins's face paled and beads of sweat formed on his brow. He pulled his handkerchief from his pocket and wiped it across his forehead.

"Yes, your eminence."

"The church will be keeping an eye on you. I hope you begin to put your attention where it rightly belongs--on your parishioners, not on Lady Catherine's wishes."

"Yes, bishop."

"Now, Mr. Collins, I suggest you return to Hunsford and attend to your duties." The parson looked particularly uncomfortable and tugged at his collar. "Do you have something pertinent to say, sir?"

"I, uh, I, uh, that is to say, when I first arrived in the city, I stopped at the office of the Times and delivered an announcement of Mr. Darcy's betrothal to Miss de Bourgh."

The others eyed one another as they struggled to refrain from laughing. "And what were you told would be the result of this announcement you delivered?" challenged Darcy, his tone harsh.

"The man said the announcement about Mr. Darcy would appear in this evening's edition of the paper," muttered Mr. Collins. Now all but Mr. Edgecombe and Mr. Bennet burst into laughter. Mr. Collins looked at them as if they had lost their senses. "I do not know what you find funny," accused the parson. "The announcement's publication will cause great embarrassment for my patro--for Lady Catherine."

"It is not the letter you delivered that the paper will publish," laughed Anne. "Knowing my mother as I do, I thought my reply about spending time with Darcy might push her to such an announcement."

"Consequently," maintained Darcy, "I spoke to the editor and the person in charge of the announcements section. I threatened both with legal action should they publish any announcement that I did not sign and deliver. The announcement to be published this evening is the announcement of our two weddings. Everything we have done is to prevent Lady Catherine from attempting to annul the marriages. As she is losing her position as mistress of Rosings Park and will have a much smaller income at her allowance, I do not think she will be in a position to cause any further trouble."

"True," said the earl, "very soon I will be joining my son and new daughter in breaking the news of her new circumstances to my sister. I would advise you to follow the bishop's advice and return unannounced to Hunsford. It will only go badly for you if you make Lady Catherine aware of what is coming. She will take out her anger and disappointment on the person who brings her the news."

"I believe you should depart now, Mr. Collins. The rest of us have a wedding breakfast to attend. And remember what I said. We will be watching you." Andrew's tone was hard, his stare unwavering.

Mr. Collins bowed low, saying, "Yes, sir. I shall do as you suggest. It will be my great pleasure . . ." The man continued to drone on. Ignoring him, the others exited the room and walked to the carriages waiting to take them to Matlock House for the wedding breakfast. When the parson finally finished his lugubrious speech and straightened up, he discovered he was alone in the room except for Mr. Edgecombe.

Realizing Lady Catherine did not expect his return until the next day, he decided to stay the night in London. However, being miserly, he did not wish to pay for a room. Looking at Mr.

Edgecombe, he asked, "Might I impose upon your hospitality for the night?"

After hearing the previous discussion, the gentleman wished he could deny the request, but Christian charity forced him to answer in the affirmative.

18. Confronting Lady Catherine

The wedding breakfast delighted all in attendance, except perhaps for the eager grooms, who desired nothing more than to be alone with their beautiful new wives.

Anne and Elizabeth met several of the patronesses of Almacks as well as two dukes, three marquesses, and several other prominent members of society and parliament. Both ladies received the promise of a voucher to Almacks during the next season. Finally, the breakfast came to an end. Elizabeth said farewell to her father and Jane. Jane and Bingley planned to marry in late June. Darcy and Elizabeth would return to London when Anne and Andrew no longer needed their assistance at Rosings. They would wait for the completion of Elizabeth's trousseau. Elizabeth also wanted to purchase gifts for her mother and sisters. Then they would travel to Meryton to stay with Mr. Bingley at Netherfield until the wedding.

Both couples would spend the next two nights at Darcy House. Georgiana would remain with the Fitzwilliams. On the third day, they would depart for Rosings. Georgiana and Mrs. Annesley would stay at Darcy House while the others traveled to Kent.

The servants at Darcy House did not line up to greet their new mistress. Darcy requested they wait to do so until the couple returned from assisting Anne. Other than the wedding ball scheduled for that night, the Darcys would spend the next two days alone in the master suite on the second floor. The Fitzwilliams would have a suite on the third floor on the opposite side of the house. Their personal servants would be the only ones to attend them, and Mrs. Reynolds and cook would ensure all meals were simple and could easily be delivered to the newlyweds' suites.

After experiencing the joys of the marriage bed for a good portion of the afternoon, the couples, of necessity, had to rejoin the world to attend the wedding ball. The gentleman bemoaned the situation but, with the promise they would not remain too late, finally agreed to bestir themselves. The newlyweds arrived ahead of the other guests to participate in the receiving line.

Light streamed from the windows of Matlock House, brightening the street when the Darcy carriage pulled up in front. When they entered the house, Lord and Lady Matlock were momentarily speechless at the beauty of the brides. Elizabeth wore a gown of emerald green, and the Darcy emeralds adorned her neck, along with a matching bracelet and earbobs. Her maid had piled her hair atop her head in a mass of curls. In the candlelight, pins to match the jewels sparkled in her dark hair. Anne's azure gown brought out the color of her eyes. Her light brown hair, braided with matching ribbons, wound around her head, with soft curls framing her face and dancing along her neck. A smaller set of the

Fitzwilliam diamonds graced her neck, ears, and wrist.

"Anne, Elizabeth, you are both breathtaking!" said Lady Matlock. "I daresay you shall outshine everyone tonight! Darcy, Andrew, how appropriate and thoughtful of you to coordinate with your wives." Darcy wore a gold brocade vest shot with emerald green threads. His cravat bore an emerald stickpin. Andrew's waistcoat was silver-gray embroidered with azure in a simple geometric pattern around the edges. His cravat boasted a diamond stickpin.

"I must agree with my wife," said Lord Matlock, "you are stunning, ladies. There shall be many jealous eyes of both sexes turned upon you all tonight."

The viscount, also in attendance, bowed over the hands of his female cousins. My parents are correct. You, ladies, look magnificent. I hope to someday be as fortunate as my brother and cousin in finding such an exceptional woman to be my wife."

The earl's words proved correct as the newlywed couples greeted their guests. However, most of the displeasure was reserved for Elizabeth, who was astonished by the number of ladies, and their mothers, with disappointed hopes. However, as the evening wore on, these women realized their dreams had been in vain, for everyone could see William and Elizabeth made a love match. While many ladies were jealous of Elizabeth's good fortune, many men wondered how an untitled, lowly second son had managed to capture the heart of one of the most elusive and wealthiest heiresses in the kingdom. Many an impoverished peer would welcome her dowry, but the rumors of the long-standing engagement between Darcy and Miss de Bourgh had kept them at bay--that coupled with the fact that she rarely visited town. As promised, the newlyweds remained long enough for all those in attendance to meet them and see the loving relationships between the two couples. It was not long before they found themselves back in their suites at Darcy House. They did not step from their chambers until the morning they departed for Rosings Park.

When the Fitzwilliam carriage pulled up before Darcy House at ten o'clock in the morning on the third day after the wedding, the Darcy vehicle stood ready at the curb. The viscount descended from his parents' carriage and mounted the steps. When he knocked at the door, it opened and the newlywed couples appeared ready to depart. Both brides fairly glowed, and the smug smiles on the men's faces indicated everyone was supremely happy. The viscount returned to his family carriage, and the two couples mounted the steps to Darcy's. When the footman closed the door and climbed on the back, the two vehicles took off, headed southwest to Kent.

Halfway to their destination, the carriage stopped to change horses and for the passengers to eat. They would need to be fresh and at full strength for the battle to come. They resumed their journey and arrived at Rosings Park at three in the afternoon. Darcy's carriage stopped at the parsonage. Anne and Andrew joined the others in the Matlock carriage while Elizabeth sought out Charlotte. After greeting her friend and explaining the situation, she recruited her help in preparing the dower house. Charlotte agreed and joined Elizabeth in the carriage. They continued to

Rosings, where Darcy met with the housekeeper and requested three maids and two footmen to join his wife in preparing the dower house for its new occupant. Though surprised at her orders, Mrs. Creeley did not hesitate to comply. As they waited for the servants, Elizabeth told Charlotte of her husband's appearance at the wedding and the bishop's words regarding his conduct. Mrs. Collins shook her head at learning of her husband's misstep.

She knew Lady Catherine had charged him with an errand, which took him from home for two days. However, since returning, he could not be induced to speak about his time away. Upon learning what had transpired, Charlotte blushed, saying, "I am sorry, Eliza, for his disruption of such a special event. I will apologize to Mr. Darcy and Mr. and Mrs. Fitzwilliam as well."

"No one holds you responsible, Charlotte, but you may need to remind him of his proper place going forward. I would hate to see you lose your situation because of your husband's ridiculous belief in his patroness."

When the servants joined them, the ladies headed to the dower house in the Darcy carriage. While Elizabeth and Charlotte oversaw the work at Lady Catherine's new home, Anne faced her mother. Though Andrew argued, Anne insisted on meeting her mother alone. He agreed only if the others could remain in the hallway to listen.

Taking a deep breath, Anne opened the door and entered. "Hello, Mother. How is your recovery progressing?"

"Far too slowly, particularly as you left me with no one to keep me company."

"That is not true, Mother, I left Mrs. Jenkinson here to assist you. She always takes wonderful care of me, so I know what comfort she can be."

"I desired more than a servant for my comfort. I am Lady Catherine de Bourgh, and only the very best should attend me--not one lone servant."

"I am sure others, besides my companion, assisted in your care. I am sorry you are displeased, but it is much like the care you gave me. You never attended me when I took ill. You feared the sick room and never visited. I lived under your thumb all of my life. Now I intend to take my rightful place as mistress of my estate. I am aware of the contents of Father's will. I am also aware you told the attorney I was too weak of both mind and body to assume my inheritance." Anger tinged Anne's voice. Her tone implacable, she resumed speaking, "Servants are currently cleaning the dower house to receive you. As soon as Dr. Walker says it is safe to move you, you will take up residence in your new home. Your income will be one thousand pounds per year, as per the terms of Father's will. You will pay all of your expenses--including any servants' wages--from the stipulated amount."

"How dare you speak to me like that? I am your mother, and I demand your respect."

"Respect is earned, Mother, not demanded. You controlled every aspect of my life and attempted to control my future. I realize you hoped to keep my inheritance by forcing me to marry Darcy, but your plans were for naught."

"You know nothing about running an estate. You will fail and be bankrupt in no time.

You would do better to allow me to remain as mistress of Rosings Park."

"I will not fail, and I will not face this alone. I will have a husband at my side, a man I love and respect. We will work together, and Rosings will thrive under our management."

"If you married Darcy, there is no reason I should not continue to run the estate."

"I did not marry Darcy. I married Andrew. He is no longer in the army. With the assistance of his family and Darcy and his wife, we will succeed in our endeavor. Rosings will become an even greater estate under our care. Now I shall leave you to rest. A great many things require my attention, and I have guests to whom I must attend."

Anne turned to walk away as a stream of curses and criticism followed her. When she reached the door, Andrew stepped into the opening, rage suffusing his face. Fiona was at his side and began barking at the woman. "Enough!" His bellow quieted both the woman and the dog. "Lady Catherine, how dare you speak to your daughter, my wife, in such a way? You are a heartless, selfish virago. If you wish to continue living at the dower house, you will never again speak in such a way to Anne or anyone else. According to the will, Anne is not obligated to allow you to live on the estate grounds. As you have alienated everyone else in the family, you will not find a home with any of them. Also, the townhouse is part of the estate, and you will not be permitted to reside there either. Now, unless you wish to find yourself alone and friendless--perhaps having to work for a living--I suggest you think before you speak in the future." Turning his back on the woman, Andrew offered his arm to Anne. They left the room, closing the door soundly behind them.

Anne leaned against the hallway wall, exhaling forcefully. "Are you well, my love?" asked her worried husband.

"I am fine, Andrew. I dreaded the first encounter, but now that it is behind me and I survived while holding my own, I know I can face anything she may try."

"You did a masterful job, Anne," complimented Lord Matlock. His wife nodded in agreement. "You handled things like a mature adult, not the petulant child my sister showed."

"I recommend you put yourself in your mother's place and try to determine what complaints she will make," said Darcy. "If you can resolve those issues before they arise, you will pull the rug from under her feet, so to speak."

"An excellent suggestion, nephew," agreed the countess. "For instance, Anne, do you like the furniture in the mistress's chambers? If not, you may wish to send it to the dower house. Lady Catherine cannot complain about being uncomfortable if familiar things are around her."

"I see what you are saying. There are several unattractive pieces here that Mother adores. Allowing her to keep them will solve one of my problems with the house."

Anne and Lady Matlock began a tour of the house, noting pieces Anne did not wish to retain. The gentlemen retired to the study to meet with the steward. Darcy had recently reviewed the books, so looking them over did not take long. They discussed what had to be accomplished between now and the harvest. Andrew learned about collecting the rents, the status of the repairs begun on the tenant homes during their April visit, and what went into planning for the following year.

Anne and Lady Matlock employed an army of footmen to move furniture from several rooms of the house. They took the items to the waiting wagons. The carts, in turn, delivered them to the dower house with a letter to Elizabeth from Anne as to their placement.

The family, without Lady Catherine, reassembled for supper, where everyone reported on the progress of their activities. Anne received several angry notes from her mother, making demand after demand.

Andrew took the last one and marched up to his aunt's room. "You can desist in these ridiculous games, Aunt. We intend to ignore your demands. The longer you continue your abominable behavior, the greater the chance you will need to find your own home--one you can afford on your much smaller income. I will not repeat this, Aunt, if you cannot treat your daughter with the respect she deserves, you will find yourself out on your ear."

Lady Catherine glared at Andrew, but the implacable expression on his face eventually convinced her he was in earnest.

When the family retired that evening, Darcy took Elizabeth to the suite he always used while residing at Rosings Park. Upon locking the door behind them, he said, "You haunted my dreams every night during your stay at Hunsford. I tired of Aunt Catherine's ridiculous demands to marry Anne and dreamed of loving the woman of my choice here, in her home."

"As you made all my dreams come true when we married, I am happy to fulfill one of your dreams, my sweet William."

After a week at Rosings, everything was well in hand. Andrew understood the basics of estate management. Lady Matlock and Anne had removed many of the gaudy and uncomfortable furniture pieces to the dower house or the attic. The largest drawing room, formal dining room, and music room were receiving a fresh coat of paint. Lady Matlock would send fabric samples from London for Anne's review.

On the day of her removal from the Rosings Park manor house, Dr. Walker sedated Lady Catherine. The maids washed, cleaned, and dressed her, while her furniture made the trip to her new room at the dower house. Then they loaded her into the well-padded bed of a wagon and conveyed Lady Catherine to her new location. She awoke in her usual bed, but the room did not appear familiar. Standing about her bed, she saw her brother, nephew, and daughter.

"What is going on here? Where am I?"

"You are in your room, Mother."

Lady Catherine glanced about the space. "The furniture is mine, but I do not recognize this room. The colors are hideous."

"Well, if your income allows, you may change them, but this is your room in the dower house. I have filled the dower house with many of the pieces from Rosings you so loved. I always found them unattractive or uncomfortable. You should feel quite at home here."

"Rosings Park is my home. I demand you return me to my room."

"That will not happen, Aunt Catherine. I advise you to take my words to heart. It is only by Anne's grace that you receive the dower house as a home. If you bother us at the manor or appear without an invitation, you shall lose the privilege of living at the estate altogether. You sought to control Anne and denied her many of the basic comforts of life. Your only control now is over your behavior, and to an extent, your finances. You can learn to be pleasant and enjoy the company of family and neighbors in your new home. Your other choice is to continue as you have and find yourself alone in your remaining years. You must live within your means--one thousand pounds per year--for you will receive no help from us. If you cannot live on the income allowed you, you shall need to seek employment to support yourself."

"My husband speaks the truth. If you can improve, we will allow you more and more into our company. However, if you continue to complain and make demands, you will find yourself isolated and lonely. We will visit you every few days while you are recovering. The quality of our reception will determine when or if you shall receive your first invitation to the main house. Also, Mr. Collins will not be attending to you.

"Indeed, you should not count on his aid," said Andrew with a chuckle. "His interruption of the wedding brought him to the attention of my godfather, the bishop. Because Mr. Collins lacked the wisdom to stand up to you and did your bidding instead of attending to parish duties, he is now under the watchful eye of the church. Mr. Collins must prove himself worthy of the position he holds or risk losing it." Lady Catherine's eyes widened at this pronouncement. The bishop had never been fond of her and would take great delight in seeing her brought low.

Her eyes snapping with anger, her tone curt, Lady Catherine said, "I understand your wishes. Please leave me now, as I am tired and need to rest." The older woman turned onto her side, giving her back to the others. Lord Matlock looked at his son and new daughter and shook his head. The group let themselves from the room and down the stairs to the drawing room. "I will be interested to learn from the two of you what decision she makes. I cannot decide if she turned her back as evidence of her displeasure and disagreement, or if she did not wish us to see her accept defeat," said the earl. Andrew and Anne merely shrugged, also unsure of her meaning. "Shall we return to the others?"

The party from the dower house entered the red drawing room just as the tea tray arrived. Lady Matlock looked at her husband. "How did it go with Catherine?"

"She did not have much to say, nor did she argue with us. We cannot decide if she is accepting defeat or plotting her future actions."

"Either way," said Andrew, "I believe all of you should return to your homes. Anne and I greatly appreciate all your recent assistance. We realize your good counsel and support is but a letter away. Shall we plan to meet in London for the Little Season?"

"I think it would be a good idea for both Anne and Elizabeth to get a little exposure to the ton during that time," said Lady Matlock.

"Then perhaps you would also join us for Christmas at Pemberley," said Elizabeth. "I hope we will invite my family as well. You met my father and Jane, and they are the best of them. Unfortunately, my mother and younger sisters are excitable, loud, and flighty, so if you do not wish to come, I would certainly understand."

"We would love to join you," said the countess. "Perhaps the exposure to proper society will provide your mother and sisters with a better understanding of acceptable behavior."

Elizabeth's expression of worry and hopefulness broke Darcy's heart. "I believe you could be right, Aunt. The way our family pulled together when things became difficult impressed your father, Elizabeth. He expressed his plans to take the family in hand. I am sure he will have made progress by the time Christmas rolls around."

"Indeed, Elizabeth, you need not worry. We would not think less of you for your family's behavior. Besides, all families contain someone who can cause embarrassment. After all, did we not just contend with Lady Catherine?" Lady Matlock's words made everyone laugh, breaking the tension and easing Elizabeth's worry.

19. Surprising Investigation Results

The butler appeared in the doorway, interrupting their conversation, to announce, "Lord Carstairs is here to see Mr. Fitzwilliam and Mr. Darcy."

"Show him to the study, Jackson. We will join him directly," said Andrew.

He and Darcy stood to depart, but Darcy heard Elizabeth clear her throat. When he turned, he saw her raised brow and knew she wished to participate in this discussion.

"Elizabeth, Anne, I believe you know the constable and Lord Carstairs intended to investigate whether any locals assisted Wickham in preparing for the attempted kidnapping. I can only assume he has some information for us. Do you wish to participate?"

"I should like to hear what he says, William," replied Elizabeth.

Andrew turned to Anne. "Do you wish to join us?"

"Why do you not request Lord Carstairs join us here?" said Anne. "We need not keep the information from your parents."

Darcy returned to his seat beside Elizabeth, while Andrew stepped into the hallway, directing Jackson to bring their visitor to the drawing room.

Andrew introduced the magistrate to his parents and alerted him to the weddings that had taken place in London.

"My congratulations to you, Mr. and Mrs. Fitzwilliam, and you, Mr. and Mrs. Darcy."

Andrew said, "Have you learned anything regarding the hold-up, Lord Carstairs?"

"I did, but I do not think you will be happy when you hear what I discovered."

"What did you find?" inquired Darcy.

"In our investigation, we discovered a young lady sent letters to Mr. Wickham."

"How did you learn this?" asked Darcy.

"The innkeeper thought it odd the parson's sister was coming in unattended, and even more so sent letters to a militiaman. It was only respect for Mrs. Collins that kept him silent on the matter."

"I always thought Maria was more intelligent than Lydia. I know she was much better chaperoned." *When did Wickham have enough time to encourage Maria to go against what her parents taught?* wondered Elizabeth. "Charlotte will be quite distressed to learn this."

"I am afraid there is more to cause concern for Mrs. Collins," added Lord Carstairs.

"What do you mean, sir?" questioned Darcy.

"We discovered on the day you brought Miss Bennet, excuse me, Mrs. Darcy, from the parsonage to Rosings, an angry Mr. Collins turned up in the pub mid-afternoon. Later in the day, Mr. Wickham joined the gentleman. Mr. Collins did not appear to recognize him at first, but he permitted the newcomer to sit with him. Mr. Collins ordered cider when he first arrived.

However, after that, Mr. Wickham took over ordering ale for the two of them. He then had to practically carry the parson home."

"Do you mean to say my cousin assisted in the attempted kidnapping? I knew of his anger toward me, but cannot understand him putting Miss de Bourgh at risk."

"As near as I can tell, Wickham encouraged Collins to express his feelings about you, offering sympathy and support. Wickham offered to separate you from Darcy and asked when you planned to depart, from what those in the tavern overheard. I suspect Mr. Collins was so inebriated, he unintentionally provided information Mr. Wickham used to formulate his plans."

"This will devastate Charlotte. Both her sister and her husband unwittingly played a part in attempting to kidnap Miss de Bourgh," said Elizabeth. "William, I must be the one to explain things to Charlotte. What do you plan to do about Mr. Collins?"

"I suggest we invite them both. You may deal with Charlotte, and Andrew and I will handle Mr. Collins in the study. Is that acceptable to you?" Darcy turned to look at his cousin. Andrew nodded.

"How much time do you think you will need to speak with Charlotte?" asked Anne. "I will allow you some time with her and then bring in tea for us to share. I would like to become better acquainted with her."

"I believe you will truly enjoy her company. Charlotte is witty, level-headed, kind, and practical."

The note sent, Lord and Lady Matlock decided to stroll in the gardens while the others handled matters. The gentlemen departed for the study and Elizabeth watched from the parlor window for Charlotte's arrival. When the Collinses arrived, Jackson led Charlotte to the parlor, where Elizabeth awaited her. Her husband looked at Charlotte in surprise when directed to join the gentlemen in Mr. Fitzwilliam's study.

Elizabeth stood to meet her friend. "Charlotte, I am delighted to have another opportunity to visit with you."

"And, I you, Eliza, though it surprised us to get such a *summons* from Rosings."

"I am sorry for the abruptness of the request, Charlotte, but there is some crucial information of which I must make you aware."

"This sounds serious. Why do you not just tell me what is wrong?"

"Charlotte, you are aware someone attempted to hold up our carriage on the way to London." Seeing her friend's nod, Elizabeth continued. "Lord Carstairs and the constable investigated to see if any of the locals assisted in the situation."

"I am glad he investigated further. Do you know what the magistrate discovered?"

" His findings are the reason we asked you and Mr. Collins to pay us a visit." Charlotte's confusion evident, Elizabeth relayed the news they had learned from Lord Carstairs about Maria Lucas.

Charlotte slumped back into her seat. "I cannot believe my sister would do such a thing. We often spoke of proper behavior with a gentleman. Why would Maria go against everything she knows about propriety?"

"Mr. Wickham was a charming scoundrel and a practiced seducer. I would imagine he promised to marry her. It would not be inappropriate to write to her betrothed."

"But there was no betrothal. Wickham never approached Father."

"True. However, the cad probably convinced Maria he would do so upon her return, and why they should not write in the meantime."

"You are most likely right. I never did understand what you and others saw as far as Mr. Wickham's so-called charms."

"I am ashamed I could not see through his lies. Until I so misjudged William and Mr. Wickham, I thought myself a good judge of character. I learned a valuable lesson, but we are getting off-topic. I do not doubt you will be able to explain the situation to Maria and set her on the correct path. Regrettably, your sister's involvement is not the only thing I must discuss with you." Charlotte looked as if she were waiting for the other shoe to fall, so Elizabeth quickly continued. "On the day after I moved to Rosings, did you notice anything unusual about Mr. Collins?"

Charlotte cast a wondering look at Elizabeth. "How could you have known that?"

"Known what?"

"Mr. Collins was extremely hungover the day after you left."

"Are you aware of what he did after my departure?"

"Having no sympathy for his behavior toward you, I chose to ignore him and returned to my parlor after you left. He stomped about the house for a while, almost shouting unkind things about you. I heard him cross to his study, and then a short time later, the door slammed as he left the house. I can only guess he spent the afternoon and evening at the pub, as he did not return until after I retired for the evening."

"You are correct, but I am not sure he was to blame for his condition. From what Lord Carstairs learned, Mr. Wickham approached my cousin at the inn and spent the evening conversing with him. The innkeeper said Wickham did the ordering and helped Mr. Collins upon departure."

"How will I ever face Mr. and Mrs. Fitzwilliam again? Not only my sister, but my husband, provided information that led to a hold-up and attempted kidnapping."

"There is no need for concern," said Anne, entering the room as though on cue. "You did nothing wrong. Your sister is an innocent young girl manipulated by a master of the art. Your husband is a fool--except for having the good sense to marry you--who let his emotions run away with the little sense he possesses. You are not responsible for either of their behavior. My husband and Mr. Darcy will take care of Mr. Collins, so I would prefer we discuss a more interesting topic."

"I thank you for your kindness, Mrs. Fitzwilliam. Few would be as thoughtful under the circumstances as you are being."

"I am sorry we have not had much opportunity to get to know each other since you arrived at the parsonage. Lizzy tells me you are a wonderful friend, and I could use a few good friends."

"Having observed how your mother dominated your life, I imagine friendship is not something you have often experienced."

"You would be correct. Lizzy is the first real friend I have ever had, and now we are cousins through marriage. I could not be happier!" Elizabeth responded to Anne's statement with a smile and a squeeze of her hand before changing the topic. The ladies enjoyed tea for the next three-quarters of an hour.

Meanwhile, in the study, Mr. Collins was not enjoying the experience as much as his wife. When he entered the room, the sight that met his eyes was completely unexpected. Behind the desk sat Mr. Fitzwilliam and Mr. Darcy, both wearing impressive scowls. Having done as they asked after the wedding, Mr. Collins could think of no reason for their expressions.

With his most unctuous smile, the parson said, "Mr. Fitzwilliam, Mr. Darcy, how can I be of service to you gentlemen today?"

"You can provide us with some information." Mr. Darcy's cold voice startled the man.

"Of course, sir, it is a pleasure to be of aid to you."

"Are you acquainted with a man by the name of George Wickham?" asked Andrew.

The gentleman before them looked confused and did not immediately answer.

When he looked as if he would deny the acquaintance, Darcy encouraged, "Think hard, Mr. Collins."

Due to the commanding tone, Mr. Collins screwed up his face and continued searching his memories. At last, he recalled meeting the gentleman on a walk into Meryton, early in his visit with the Bennets last fall. His face cleared as he remembered that the gentlemen from Netherfield were there briefly. "Yes, as I recall, we met last fall in Hertfordshire, which you should remember, Mr. Darcy."

"Nothing more recent?" asked Fitzwilliam.

The parson repeated his thought process, facial expressions and all. A fuzzy memory flashed in his mind--a man calling his name at the inn some time back. Collins had tried to ignore the man, but Wickham had forced his presence on the parson and encouraged him to let loose his anger. How the evening ended, Collins could not say, for everything had gone black at some point. "Though the memory is somewhat hazy, I remember Mr. Wickham reintroducing himself to me some weeks back when he passed through the area to visit family in Ramsgate. He said he recalled our earlier introduction."

Darcy nodded curtly, while Andrew asked, "And what did you discuss?" Andrew raised his brow and stared at the man while he thought.

"I remember it was a difficult day for me," said Mr. Collins with unusual brevity

"And?" said Mr. Darcy.

"I am afraid I do not recall the discussion, so it cannot have been important," came the sheepish reply.

"It was important. You provided personal information to Wickham when you told him about our travel plans," said Andrew.

"I did?" Mr. Collins could not imagine where this conversation was leading.

"Yes, and did you learn that an attempt to hold up my carriage occurred when we departed Rosings?"

"I did not, Mr. Darcy. What a dreadful experience. I hope no one sustained harm or injury."

"Those of us in the carriage suffered no harm, but a servant was shot, and Wickham died. As you gave Wickham the information about our travel, you are partly responsible for what occurred."

The parson's face drained of all color.

Andrew continued when Darcy stopped speaking. "Because Wickham did not succeed in his desire to kidnap my wife and Mrs. Darcy and hold them for ransom, we decided not to prosecute you. However, should something like this ever occur again, you will not be so lucky. Mrs. Fitzwilliam and I expect proper behavior from you going forward. We will not tolerate the fawning, gossiping, and interference my aunt demanded. You are to devote yourself to the needs of your parish, reporting only to us when there are problems with which you need our assistance. We expect well-thought-out sermons on topics to uplift and inspire. Lady Catherine chose your topics to force her will and beliefs on the neighborhood. I doubt seriously that our Lord or the church appreciated her interference. I know the parishioners did not. You lack common sense, Mr. Collins, but you were most fortunate in marrying a woman with uncommon sense and practicality. I strongly suggest you turn to your wife whenever you are uncertain about how to act or about your sermon topic. Her connection to the members of your parish will allow her to guide you correctly. If you are lucky, you may someday develop the sense your wife possesses."

Looking affronted at the suggestion to take advice from his lowly wife, Collins blurted, "How can talking to a country girl who was not even born a gentlewoman be of benefit to a man who attended university?"

"Nor were you born a gentleman, Mr. Collins," said Darcy, his tone cold, "which is apparent since you just insulted the lady who is your wife." Mr. Collins appeared abashed at the comment, but he could not hide his pout at what he perceived as an insult. "With the way she assists your parishioners and manages your home, Mrs. Collins has proven her abilities. You should thank God every day such a woman accepted you." Darcy could scarcely conceal his disdain for the man.

"Furthermore, our godfather, the bishop, told us of your time at school," said Andrew. "It appears you barely managed to qualify for a position in the church. Yet, Mrs. Darcy told us that Mrs. Collins was an integral part of making her father's business a success before his knighthood."

"Remember, Mr. Collins, both the church and Mr. and Mrs. Fitzwilliam will be watching you to determine whether you keep your post. If you lose your position, what will you do? Your actions toward Mrs. Darcy ensure Mr. Bennet will not wish to assist you before his passing. Mrs. Collins's family cannot provide for you. How will you live? How will you support your wife? I advise you to take Mr. Fitzwilliam's words as more than a suggestion if you wish to have a successful future."

Looking chagrined, Mr. Collins said, "I understand and will do as you wish."

The gentlemen dismissed Mr. Collins, advising him to return to his home. "I will arrange Mrs. Collins's return to the parsonage when she finishes her visit," said Darcy.

They walked the gentleman to the door and then joined the ladies, who had almost finished their tea. While Darcy requested Anne's phaeton to return Mrs. Collins to her home, Andrew made sure to inform her of their discussion with her husband. "I believe he understands the precariousness of his situation. We do not necessarily wish to make a change and hope he grows from this experience. Please be sure to inform us of any problems, notably should his temper get the better of him."

"There are no words to express my appreciation for your kindness under the circumstances, Mr. and Mrs. Fitzwilliam and Mr. and Mrs. Darcy. I will endeavor with all subtlety to guide my husband toward the improvements you desire."

When Darcy informed them the carriage was ready, the ladies accompanied Charlotte to the door. Elizabeth hugged her friend and wished her well, ensuring her they would visit whenever the Darcys were at Rosings. Anne offered both her hands to Charlotte, giving them a little squeeze. "I hope you will visit me often, and be sure to let me know of anything you might need."

"I will, Mrs. Fitzwilliam. Good-bye, Lizzy. I shall miss you but wish you and Mr. Darcy all the best.

Lord and Lady Matlock rejoined the group as they reviewed the afternoon.

"Are you sure there is nothing else we can assist you with before we depart?"

"Absolutely not! I suggest," said Anne, "we relax and enjoy your last day here. We will have an exceptional dinner, celebrate family, and make plans for our reunion in October."

20. Returning to Hertfordshire

Upon returning to London from Rosings, the newlyweds informed Georgiana of what had occurred in Kent. Then they spent time together as a family. The Darcys visited the British Museum at Montagu House, which Elizabeth found enthralling. The majority of the ton had left for their homes in the country, but there were still a few events to enjoy. Darcy happily danced the night away with his lovely bride at a ball thrown by one of the earls who had attended the wedding and wedding breakfast. Both were aware of the many whispers they incited by flouting convention and dancing almost exclusively with each other. When the final pieces of her trousseau arrived, the three Darcys departed for Hertfordshire.

It was two weeks before the wedding of Bingley and Jane. The Darcys would reside at Netherfield before the event. Learning from Bingley that the Hursts, Miss Bingley and his aunt would also be in residence, Darcy and Elizabeth wondered how Miss Bingley would act upon their arrival. However, neither expected the greeting they received.

As expected, Bingley greeted them on the porch, but Jane--and not Miss Bingley--stood beside him. "Darcy, Mrs. Darcy, Miss Darcy, welcome to Netherfield. We are delighted you could join us for this wonderful occasion." Elizabeth and Jane rushed to hug one another before Jane also hugged Georgiana and presented her hand to William in greeting. They entered the house and Mrs. Dawson, the housekeeper, showed them to their rooms. With no sight of Miss Bingley, they were not sure whether to be relieved or slighted. After refreshing themselves, the Darcys returned downstairs to the green drawing room, where they found the rest of the family gathered. Miss Bingley greeted them pleasantly, then turned back to her conversation with Mrs. Hurst and her aunt. Darcy and Elizabeth exchanged a look and seated themselves near Jane and Bingley to discuss the plans for the wedding. Throughout the evening, Miss Bingley remained polite and distant, but neither Darcy nor Elizabeth could detect any anger or insincerity in her tone or attitude.

The next day, Elizabeth and Darcy visited Longbourn for the first time since their wedding. Elizabeth took a deep breath before they entered the parlor, as she dreaded the dressing down she would receive from her mother for being excluded from the wedding. Darcy, who sat holding her hand, could feel her action and guess at her concern. "Fear not, my love, I will not allow your mother to berate you. I shall take the blame for our circumstances and be sure she understands you did not have much control over the situation."

When they entered the room, Mr. and Mrs. Bennet, Jane, Mary, and Kitty were present. The ladies engaged in quiet conversation. Mr. Bennet, the first to note their arrival, rose to greet them.

His actions drew the attention of the others in the room.

Mrs. Bennet rose and rushed to her daughter. In a polite and well-modulated tone of voice, she greeted the newcomers. "Lizzy, Mr. Darcy, congratulations on your marriage. I hope you are both happy?" She leaned in, hugged Elizabeth, then pulled back, looked at her, and studied her daughter's face as she waited for Elizabeth to answer.

Surprised by her mother's expression, Elizabeth did not hesitate to reply. "We are extremely happy, Mama." She broke the gaze with her mother to smile at her dear husband.

Darcy grasped Elizabeth's hand and brought it to his lips. "Indeed, we are incredibly happy," he agreed, not releasing his wife's hand.

Mary and Kitty both stepped forward to offer their congratulations as well.

"Congratulations, Lizzy, sir. I wish you both much happiness." Elizabeth accepted her sister's words and waited for the usual sermon quote she expected to follow, but Mary said nothing more.

Kitty next extended her good wishes. Elizabeth and Darcy again offered their thanks.

Elizabeth asked, "Where is Lydia?"

A glimpse of the excitable Kitty appeared when she replied to Elizabeth's question. "Papa confined her to the schoolroom because she called you something unflattering when she learned you married the man who had treated Mr. Wickham so poorly."

"Mr. Darcy never treated Mr. Wickham poorly," stated Elizabeth indignantly. "He told us just enough truth to sound believable, but he left out the most important points. Mr. Wickham refused the living and demanded money instead. Mr. Darcy paid him three thousand pounds in lieu of the living, and Mr. Wickham signed away all future rights to the bequest. The elder Mr. Darcy also gave him one thousand pounds in his will. Then Mr. Wickham went through all four thousand pounds in less than two years. He returned and asked Mr. Darcy for the living. Of course, William denied the request."

"Well, I should hope, so," declared Mrs. Bennet. "What a dreadful young man he turned out to be. He disappeared from the militia without permission and left a string of debts with the local merchants." Mrs. Bennet leaned closer and lowered her voice. "Gossip says he left one or two of the village girls in a bad way. Everyone wonders what became of him."

Elizabeth and Darcy shared a glance. Elizabeth raised her brow and nodded to her husband, so after they seated themselves, Darcy began to explain. "Mr. Wickham, whom I have known since childhood, appeared in the neighborhood of my aunt's home. Her staff often detected him skulking around the estate, and so, due to past experience, my cousin and I took extra precautions with our travel plans from Rosings to London." Darcy continued to tell them of the hold-up and attempted kidnapping. "Wickham will never hurt anyone again, as he died during the event."

"Did he really try to kidnap you, Lizzy?" asked Kitty, wide-eyed.

"It may have been his intention, but the gentlemen's well-thought-out strategy to protect both Miss de Bourgh and myself thwarted him."

"Lydia will never believe what you say. I hope she will not speak as cruelly as she did when she learned of your marriage," said Kitty, doubt coloring her voice.

"I am sure I can handle anything Lydia might wish to say to me."

Changing the subject, Mrs. Bennet said, "I wanted to allow you a few days to rest before hosting the celebration of your wedding. As a result, we will hold a large dinner party on Friday evening. I do hope you brought some new gowns reflecting your increased status. I wish for all the neighbors to see how fine your life will be as Mrs. Darcy."

Elizabeth, who up to that point had been well pleased with her mother's calm behavior, shook her head at the return of her former ways. "You need not worry, Mama. The modiste completed my trousseau before we departed London. I shall wear one of my new gowns if it makes you happy."

"Might we wear the new dresses made for Jane's wedding to this party, too, Mama?" implored Kitty.

"No, you must save those for the wedding," responded her mother to her crestfallen daughter.

"Why do we not go into Meryton today, and I will purchase things for you to remake a gown before the party," said Elizabeth.

"Really?" cried Kitty. Elizabeth noted with surprise that even Mary's countenance brightened at the suggestion.

"William, do you wish to accompany us?"

Before her husband could reply, Kitty interrupted, saying, "What about Lydia?"

Elizabeth looked at her father. "What is your opinion, Papa, under the current circumstances?"

After a moment's thought, he said, "I believe I should explain to her about Mr. Wickham. Her words will determine whether or not she can attend. Do you wish to accompany me?"

"It might be for the best, Papa. Learning that rewards from her older sisters will be predicated on appropriate behavior is a lesson she needs. It might be the most effective lesson for her. I shall remain in the hallway out of sight while you speak to her. Depending on her reply, I will either invite her to go or explain what is expected should she wish to receive gifts in the future."

Darcy looked dubiously at his wife as she turned to depart. He did not doubt Elizabeth's ability to handle her sister but hated her exposure to Lydia's unkindness. "I shall be ready to accompany you when you return," Darcy said in a quiet tone, giving her hand a reassuring squeeze as she walked past him.

Elizabeth followed her father up the stairs. "I am delighted to see you so happy, my dear Lizzy. My opinion of Mr. Darcy improved when he wrote about rescuing you from my cousin. It continues to grow as I behold the care and concern with which he treats you."

"He truly is the best of men, Papa. Even with all the problems Mr. Wickham caused the Darcy family, William and his cousin gave him a chance to surrender and face transportation rather than hanging. Evil to the end, he pretended to agree, to try to lull the others into relaxing their caution. Then he attempted to shoot William. Had the Darcy coachman not shot Wickham's hand, causing the shot to go wide, William might be dead. I can find no sympathy for the evil man. He made the choices that led to his demise."

Before her father knocked, Elizabeth positioned herself on the far side of Lydia's door, where Lydia would not see her.

"Go away!" came her youngest sister's sullen voice.

"Open the door, Lydia. I wish to speak with you."

Even with the firmness of her father's tone, Lydia did not promptly comply. "Am I to be released from my prison?" she demanded in a petulant whine.

"Based on your attitude, I would say no, but I must discuss something with you."

Lydia stepped back from the door and her father entered, pushing the door almost closed behind him. The girl again lay sprawled on the bed, flipping desultorily through the pages of an old fashion magazine.

Mr. Bennet took a seat on the edge of the bed across from Lydia's. "Please put down the magazine and sit up. I require your attention. I recently discovered that Mr. Wickham participated in an attempted hold-up of a carriage traveling from somewhere in Kent to London."

"Mr. Wickham would never do something so scandalous unless for a lark."

"Holding up a carriage is not a lark, young lady. Highway robbery is a crime, especially when guns are involved. He admitted to planning to kidnap the two young ladies inside."

"Why would you tell such a lie about him? He would never do something so underhanded, Mr. Wickham is a charming gentleman."

"Mr. Wickham is not a gentleman but the son of a servant."

"What does it matter if his father was a servant? Mr. Darcy's father sent him to university and gave him the living so George could live the life of a gentleman."

"Mr. Wickham turned down the living for a sum of money and then gambled away four thousand pounds in less than two years."

Lydia's eyes grew wide in shock at such a large sum. Then a stubborn, mutinous expression returned. "Who told you such lies, and how could you believe them? Mr. Wickham was so kind to our family."

"Simply because someone presents himself as kind and charming does not make them a good person," said Mr. Bennet.

"I know Lizzy arrived. Did she tell you these ridiculous lies? She is just jealous because Wickham likes me better than her."

"It was Elizabeth and her friend, Miss de Bourgh, whom he attempted to kidnap."

"I do not believe you."

"Believe what you will, but in front of several witnesses, he claimed he would hold Miss de Bourgh for ransom so Darcy would finally give him that to which he believed himself entitled. He also stated that he planned to ruin your sister to spite Mr. Darcy. He wanted Darcy to be miserable, pining for Elizabeth for the rest of his life."

"Mr. Darcy deserves to be miserable after cheating Mr. Wickham."

"No cheating was involved, Lydia. Mr. Darcy possesses papers signed by Mr. Wickham and witnessed by his solicitor and his cousin, Colonel Andrew Fitzwilliam, of the regulars. Wickham accepted three thousand pounds in lieu of the living. Then, as I already stated, he gambled away the money in less than two years. However, we are getting off-topic. Mr. Wickham's actions resulted in his death, Lydia. He pretended to surrender but then attempted to kill Mr. Darcy. The coachman and Mr. Darcy's cousin had no choice but to shoot Wickham to protect Mr. Darcy."

"They murdered my Wickham," screamed Lydia. She clutched her hands to her breast and began to wail. "Oh, my poor Wickham. He promised to marry me when he returned from his leave. He said he must go to collect an inheritance he received." She flopped back on the bed and threw one arm across her eyes as she wailed in a loud voice, "Oh my poor Wickham," over and over. "It is bad enough Lizzy married before me, but now the man I love is dead!"

Her father looked at her in disgust. "Stop that noise this instant! The man did not leave. The reprobate abandoned his post like a coward. If he had asked me for your hand in marriage--which he did not--I would have refused him, as you are totally unprepared to be a wife."

"He did ask me to marry him."

"And just how did you expect a lieutenant in the militia--one who left a mountain of debts behind him--to support you? If it is not already certain you are one of the silliest girls in the country, your current behavior proves you are far too young and insensible to be out in society, much less to marry. You shall be returning to the schoolroom. You will have lessons, and you will not leave the house without proper supervision-- which does not mean Kitty or even Mary." Mr. Bennet paused a moment, as a horrifying thought occurred to him. "If you thought yourself engaged, did you give your virtue to this scoundrel?"

The wailing stopped, but Lydia made no answer.

"You will answer me, now, girl!" bellowed Mr. Bennet.

Lydia, having never before experienced her father's rage, grumbled, "I did not mean to, but his kisses were so sweet, and since he asked me to marry him, it did not seem to matter."

"How could you, an underage girl, be engaged without your father's consent? Were you going to compound your bad behavior by eloping?"

Frightened at his growing anger, she murmured, "Yes, Papa. An elopement would be ever so romantic."

"I now see what my lenience has done. You have ruined your family and the chances of your unmarried sisters as well, unless I can find a way out of this mess. Some changes will be made from this day forward. You will no longer be allowed to share a room with Kitty. Your belongings will be moved into Mary's room, and--"

"But Mary's room is the smallest one," whined Lydia. At the expression on her father's face, she shrank back, closing her mouth.

"Kitty shall retain this room and Mary can share with Jane until her marriage. You will not leave this room until we know if you are with child or not."

"How could I be with child when I am not married?" Lydia spoke like the bewildered juvenile she was.

"Becoming with child is the risk of your behavior. That is why young women require chaperones and are not left alone with a gentleman before they are married." Thinking a moment, he asked, "How did you manage to be alone with Wickham? Never mind. I do not wish to know. You will remain alone in this room until we discover if you are with child. If so, I will send you away until after the baby is born. We will be lucky ever to find someone willing to marry a despoiled brat, even if we are successful in keeping the scandal at bay." Mr. Bennet rubbed his hand over his face as the weight of the world and his family's fate settled on his shoulders. "Do not leave this room. I will send the servants up to make the necessary changes. You are to speak of this to no one--ever!"

"Yes, Papa," answered Lydia with surprising meekness.

Mr. Bennet turned on his heel and marched from the room, pulling the door closed behind him before slumping against the nearby wall. Elizabeth stood silently, looking at her father, an expression of horror and disgust on her face.

At the sound of raised voices--though the words were not clear--William came upstairs to offer his support to Elizabeth. Catching the end of Mr. Bennet's speech, Darcy offered Mr. Bennet his arm and led him downstairs to his study. Elizabeth followed.

Once Bennet was seated in the chair behind his desk, Darcy poured him a large glass of brandy and took a seat beside Elizabeth, facing his father-in-law. After a large gulp of the amber liquid, Mr. Bennet said, "I am sorry I did not listen to you, Lizzy. You warned me she would ruin our family, and she has. You were always the most intelligent of my daughters. I should have acted on your fears. Now there is nothing to be done but suffer the consequences. There is no family to whom we can send her if she should be expecting. The Gardiners are our only relations not residing in Meryton. I could not ask them to take in Lydia with daughters as young as theirs."

"I know of a few charities that provide homes for unwed mothers. Most of the women they care for are not in those circumstances by choice, so I am not sure they would accept someone like Lydia." Darcy thought for a moment. "I could hire someone to stay with her at my estate in Scotland. You could put out the story that she is sick and must go to the seaside to recover. Elizabeth and I could take her directly to my estate before going to Pemberley."

"Her companion will need a commanding presence and a thick skin to survive living with Lydia. One who can withstand all her whining and wheedling," said Elizabeth.

"I believe I know just the person, and she is very loyal to the family. If my cousin, Anne, can spare her for a few months, I believe her companion, Mrs. Jenkinson, would admirably fill the post. After all, she stood up to Lady Catherine all these years."

"True, William, but she suffered those things because she loves Anne. Even though she is married, Anne will not wish to lose her companion. I am sure there are ways Mrs. Jenkinson can assist as Mrs. Fitzwilliam takes on her new role. Lydia would try the patience of a saint. She needs someone who is unmovable in teaching her right from wrong. If Lydia learns nothing from this experience, there is no guarantee she will not repeat her bad behavior. I would not wish to burden Mrs. Jenkinson with so much."

"Then allow me to hire someone for this situation," offered Darcy.

"The problem is not yours to resolve, Mr. Darcy. My lack of supervision created this problem. I must be the one to find a solution."

"I am partially responsible for what Wickham did, as I did not refute his lies or tell the citizens of Meryton about his habits. Why not allow me to help find a place for Lydia should the worst occur? If you feel your other daughters, or perhaps even your wife, would benefit from additional training, you could hire a companion to live here and assist them or allow me to find a school for the girls."

Mr. Bennet looked at Darcy for several minutes before turning to look at his second eldest daughter. "What do you think, Lizzy?"

"I believe William's suggestion is a good one, Papa. Perhaps his Scottish housekeeper would know of someone local who is suitable to assist Lydia during this time. Sending her away would keep the scandal far from the ton and better help us contain the situation. We could write to an agency in London for a companion for Kitty and Mary. Also, I suggest they take their lessons in the same room as Mama. That would allow Mother to learn a better way to behave without the embarrassment of being told she lacks in some ways."

Mr. Bennet considered the discussion as he sipped the remainder of his brandy. He stood and crossed to the window, standing with his back to them as he continued contemplating the situation. "How do we explain to the others why Lydia is going away?"

"I believe you must trust them with the truth and the consequences that will occur should anyone else discover her situation," said Darcy.

"William is correct, Papa. Kitty follows Lydia in everything. Can we be sure she is not in a similar condition?" Her father's face paled as he gripped the window frame tighter. "Allow me to bring in the others and we will help you through this," said Elizabeth, her voice filled with compassion. However, her husband easily discerned her anger with her sister.

"Wait, Lizzy," said Mr. Bennet. "Take your sisters for the shopping that you promised them. I need time to think about what to say. We can discuss this when you return."

"All right, Papa."

"Just send in Mrs. Hill before you depart."

As Lizzy had left the door open, the housekeeper appeared in the opening. "You wished to see me, sir?"

"Mrs. Hill, Lydia is to remain separated from the family for a while longer. I think sharing a room with Kitty is not enough of a punishment. Please pack Mary's belongings and move them into Jane's room. Then Lydia's things must be moved into Mary's old room. However, please remove all party gowns and all but the plainest of her day dresses. Also, remove anything that makes my daughter look older than she is. Take the maids to help you, if needed. No one is to speak to

Lydia. She will begin taking all her meals in the schoolroom, starting today."

"Yes, Mr. Bennet. I will take care of it right away." The housekeeper left the room to attend to her master's requests, closing the door behind her. *It is about time someone took the spoiled brat in hand before she ruins her family.*

Mr. Bennet put his elbows on the desk and lowered his head to his hands. Losing himself in the pleasure of his books had caused him to fail his family, with catastrophic results. He sat so lost in thought that Mr. Bennet did not notice the noisy departure of his daughters and new son.

An hour and a half later, the sound of the returning shoppers did reach Mr. Bennet's ears. Taking a deep breath and a final sip of the brandy he had nursed throughout the afternoon, he squared his shoulder and rang for the housekeeper. When she appeared, he said, "Mrs. Hill, I must discuss a few things with my family. Please ask them to join me." As she turned, he added, "Oh, and if Mr. Bingley is visiting, please ask his forgiveness, and if he would mind waiting for Jane until we are through."

"Yes, Mr. Bennet."

When the housekeeper stepped to the door of the parlor, she spoke to the family. "Mr. Bennet wishes to speak with all of you in his study." Mrs. Bennet, Mary, and Kitty grew wide-eyed at her statement. Rarely were they permitted in Mr. Bennet's study.

While waiting for his wife and daughters to arrive, Mr. Bennet poured himself a second glass of brandy. Presently, Mr. Hill arranged the chairs before the desk closer to the settee. Then, as instructed, he poured a drink for Mr. Darcy, a glass of wine for Mrs. Bennet and the two eldest, and watered wine for Mary and Kitty. As everyone took a seat, Mr. Hill distributed the beverages before departing the study, closing the door firmly behind him.

"Is Lydia to join us, Mr. Bennet?" asked Mrs. Bennet.

"No, my dear wife. What we are about to discuss must not leave this room." The eyes of the residents of Longbourn widened. "Earlier today, I learned something from Lydia that has the potential to destroy our family."

"Whatever do you mean?" asked Mrs. Bennet as she began fluttering her handkerchief.

Ignoring his wife, the patriarch spoke to his second youngest daughter. "Kitty, when you and Lydia ventured into Meryton, did she disappear on occasion?"

Kitty thought for a moment. "Now that I think back, there were times when she seemed to wander off. When she returned, she blamed me for leaving her," Kitty finished in a huff.

"I require you to remain quiet and speak softly at the news I am about to reveal. While I explained to Lydia about Mr. Wickham's death, she informed me of a situation. This news, should it become common knowledge, will ruin our family, removing any chance that you--Mary and Kitty--might marry well, if at all. The incident may even jeopardize Jane's marriage."

Mrs. Bennet's handkerchief fluttered even faster as she begged, "Do not keep us in suspense. What has happened to my poor Lydia?"

"Your youngest daughter, believing herself secretly engaged to Mr. Wickham, allowed him the privileges of a husband and may be with child."

Mrs. Bennet, shocked into speechlessness, said not a word but fainted dead away. Lizzy, who had the forethought to get her mother's smelling salts from the housekeeper before entering the room, rushed to her mother's side and waved them under her nose.

Mrs. Bennet returned to consciousness with a wail. "Whatever shall we do?" Elizabeth clapped her hand on her mother's mouth to quiet her and put a finger to her lips before removing her hand. "Whatever shall we do, Mr. Bennet?" asked his wife in a voice barely above a whisper.

"I will tell you of my decision, and the plans Darcy and I made, in just a moment. First, I must ask our next-to-youngest a question." Every eye in the room turned to study Kitty. "Your sister snuck away to meet with Mr. Wickham, which left you unchaperoned, as well. You must answer honestly, Kitty. Is there any chance you might be in the same condition as your sister?"

"Of course not, Papa. Such behavior is very wrong. I would never allow a gentleman to treat me in such a manner until after our wedding."

"Thank the Lord for small favors," said Mr. Bennet. "Now, here is the plan to deal with this situation." Mr. Bennet outlined what they had discussed. "While you were shopping, I asked Mrs. Hill to pack Mary's items for the move. Lydia's as well."

Lizzy turned to her next-to-youngest sister, speaking scarcely above a whisper. "It is nearly two months since Mr. Wickham left Meryton. Do you know if Lydia has experienced her monthly courses?"

Keeping her voice equally low, Kitty said, "I am not sure, Lizzy. Lydia's courses are sometimes irregular."

"Well, then, we should not have long to wait before we know the truth--perhaps even by the time of the wedding. Has Lydia been sick in the morning or unusually sleepy?"

Kitty shook her head in reply.

The gentlemen buried their faces in their glasses to hide their mortification at the whispered conversation they overheard. However, after a large swallow of his brandy, Mr. Bennet spoke again. "I cannot stress enough to all of you-- particularly you, Mrs. Bennet, Mary, and Kitty-- that what we discussed here can never be spoken of again. Not to or amongst the family, including the Gardiners and particularly not Mrs. Philips. If anyone discovers Lydia's circumstances, our neighbors will shun us. With all of the upcoming events, we will excuse Lydia's absence by saying she is unwell. If the worst comes to pass, we will send her away until the baby is born. If not, she will one day rejoin society, but not for some time, as she obviously has a great deal to learn before she can be trusted to behave as a proper young lady should. For too long, I left you to your own devices. I will hire a companion to teach you girls all you are lacking. You will learn to be proper young ladies, or you too shall withdraw from society. Mrs. Bennet, I expect you to sit with the girls while they are learning to reinforce the companion's teachings. And, Jane, you are free to discuss this with Mr. Bingley if you think that is for the best. I would only caution you to be assured of your privacy when you discuss the matter. I do not doubt Miss Bingley would speak of this situation merely to separate you from her brother."

Jane replied, "I owe Charles the opportunity to withdraw because of this, Father, but I will be certain we are somewhere no one can overhear us. I give you my word."

Miss Bennet's expression clearly showed unease, so Darcy offered her words of comfort. "Jane, Charles is aware of much of Wickham's background. I do not believe you need to worry about his response."

"I thank you for that, Mr. Darcy. I do not think he will wish to call off our wedding, but I dislike having to reveal the extent of my youngest sister's ill manners. Her behavior often causes embarrassment, but I never thought her capable of such action."

"You must not lay all the blame on Miss Lydia. Wickham was a practiced seducer. I have found homes for some of his illegitimate offspring. He prefers young women, as they are more likely to fall for his dubious charms."

"What will happen if Lydia is not, uh, um . . ." Kitty's question trailed off as she could not bring herself to say the words out loud.

"At this point, she will be kept in the schoolroom until she is at least eight and ten-- longer if necessary. There will probably be other consequences, but I do not yet know what they will be."

Elizabeth, who had thought much on the matter since overhearing her sister's words earlier in the day, said, "I have a suggestion, Papa. Lydia thinks being married to a man in a red coat would be one continuous ball and party. Why not teach her what her life would actually be like in such a situation?"

"What are you thinking, Lizzy?"

She went on to outline her plan. In her sisters, she could see pleasure, for Lydia always dominated their shared maid and managed to avoid doing chores or assisting with household matters of any kind.

Though Mrs. Bennet looked doubtful, her husband thought otherwise. "What an excellent idea, Lizzy. Perhaps removing the glamour of her dreams is the perfect solution to the problem. Now I want to remind all of you again that we are never to discuss this once we leave this room, except for Jane's conversation with her betrothed."

"Yes, Papa," replied his three unmarried daughters.

"You are quite right, Mr. Bennet," said his wife.

Elizabeth leaned over and whispered a question to her husband, who nodded his agreement.

"Mary, Kitty, if you will work hard to learn what your companion teaches you, William and I will allow each of you a season when we believe you are ready for such an experience."

"That is very kind of you both," said Mary.

"Do you mean it, Lizzy? A London season is something I never thought to enjoy."

Kitty's excitement grew, causing Lizzy to remind her, "The behavior that is acceptable here in Meryton is not acceptable in London. You must learn all you can--particularly controlling your exuberance. Mr. Darcy's sister, Georgiana, whom you will meet soon, is an excellent example of what a young lady should be. She is a bit shy--so try not to overwhelm her--but you can learn much by observing her behavior. Mary, Georgiana is quite accomplished on the pianoforte, so you have much to discuss. Kitty, though you do not often spend time on it, I know you like to draw. Georgiana is a talented artist as well. I believe you will enjoy her company very much."

"Are there any questions before we leave the room?" asked Mr. Bennet.

Everyone looked at everyone else, but in the end, there was nothing but shaken heads and quiet. The group dispersed just as Mr. Bingley arrived. Mrs. Bennet invited him to stay for supper, which he accepted just before Jane suggested they walk in the garden.

21. Lessons for Lydia

The few days between the discovery of Lydia's behavior and the dinner in celebration of the Darcys's marriage passed in the blink of an eye. With the changes in conduct of her mother and sisters, Elizabeth found it to be a surprisingly pleasant time in her family home. The only unpleasantness occurred the morning after they learned of their youngest sister's possible situation. Elizabeth and her sisters gathered in Jane's room as they updated the gowns they would wear to the party for Elizabeth and Darcy. Though not as loud as in times past, the sisters enjoyed one another's company, with much laughter and conversation as they worked on updating their gowns.

In the small room next to Jane's, previously occupied by Mary, Lydia managed to learn of the gifts Elizabeth had purchased for her sisters. Consequently, she marched from her room, threw open the door to Jane's chamber without the politeness of knocking and asking for admittance, and demanded her gift. Jane looked at her sister with disappointment, Mary with disapproval, Kitty with trepidation, and Elizabeth with disdain.

Calmly, Elizabeth said, "You are not supposed to leave your room, Lydia. You should return there before Papa discovers your disobedience."

"No! I want a present, too." She stood in the doorway, a pout on her face, her arms folded across her chest.

"I offered to purchase some trim so my sisters might update their dresses for the dinner on Friday. As you will not be attending, you did not need anything. Also, as you are in trouble for speaking unkindly of myself and my husband, why do you think you should receive a gift from me?"

"The reason I am being punished and cannot attend is all your fault. Why did you marry that horrible Mr. Darcy? Everything bad that happened to my Wickham was all his fault, and now I have lost my betrothed."

"There was no betrothal, as Mr. Wickham did not obtain Papa's permission, and you should be grateful you will not be marrying such a man. A life with Mr. Wickham would have been one of poverty, infidelity, and unending misery. The man may have been charming, but only to cover his many failings. He was a gambler, cheat, debtor, and womanizer."

"You are just jealous he wanted me, not you!"

"Why should I be jealous that a man with no honor did not desire me? Much to my shame, my injured vanity led me to believe his lies when he first arrived in Meryton--lies he told only to put himself in a good light, and Mr. Darcy in a bad one. Unfortunately, I learned his true nature first hand, as he attempted to kidnap Miss de Bourgh and me when he held up Mr. Darcy's carriage. Wickham intended to hold us for ransom. His sense of entitlement was one of Mr. Wickham's greatest flaws. The man expected to receive the good things in life without having to work for them. If he was unwilling to work, how would he have supported you and a family?"

"Shut up, Lizzy. Your words are nothing but lies."

"Lydia," admonished Jane with unaccustomed firmness, "you should not speak so to anyone, much less someone older than you." Her younger sister just rolled her eyes.

"You are the only liar," Elizabeth said. "You are lying to yourself if you believe he intended to marry you. Are you aware Mr. Wickham ran out on over seven hundred pounds of debt in Meryton? William tells me it would take his entire salary for the next eight years to repay. Mr. Wickham also left two of the shopkeepers' daughters with child--ones he also seduced with promises of marriage."

"My dear Wickham told me how those other girls threw themselves at him. He said such incidences happened often. They are to blame for their condition, not my Wickham."

"So you are fine with your husband accepting the attentions of any woman who throws herself at him, despite the vows he would make to you if married?"

"He cannot help it if the women want him. That is the nature of men."

Elizabeth laughed. "What do you know of the nature of men? You are not yet six and ten. Only men of low morals accept the behavior of such forward women. The actual marriage vows you are so anxious to take ask a husband if he will ' *...forsaking all other, keep thee only unto her, so long as you both shall live'* (5) Does that sound

285

like the Lord finds such behavior acceptable, as just the nature of men, as you say? William made a solemn promise before God and a room full of family and friends to be faithful to me. You often remarked on how Miss Bingley, who is not unattractive and is well-dowered, throws herself at William and has for several years. However, he managed to resist her every attempt at capturing his attention or compromising him into marriage."

"Only a snob like Miss Bingley would want such a cold, unfeeling man as Mr. Darcy."

"Unless you wish to receive a smack in the mouth, you will never again say anything unflattering about my husband. Mr. Darcy is without question the very best man I have ever known."

"You never liked him! You married him only for his money!"

This time Elizabeth did, indeed, smack Lydia's face. "You have the audacity to bad-mouth my husband and myself and demand gifts at the same time. While Mama may have spoiled you and indulged your every whim, I never approved of her decision, and I shall certainly not support such greedy behavior. Your selfish actions and careless disdain for the feelings of others might ruin our family. You will not share in the privileges my new position in life can offer my other sisters until you prove yourself worthy of them--especially if you continue in this manner."

As the sister's argument continued, Lydia's voice grew in volume. Darcy and Mr. Bennet, enjoying a chess game in the study, immediately discovered the problem.

Darcy listened to the ridiculous words sprouted by the bratty youngest Bennet daughter.

However, he was proud of how his wife retained her calm and handled the situation.

Mr. Bennet allowed the encounter to continue only long enough to discover whether Lydia would learn anything. When Elizabeth smacked her, he knew he had to intercede.

"Return to your room this instant, Lydia. How dare you leave it after our discussion yesterday?" said her father with a glare.

Many of those who attended the celebration of the Darcys's marriage claimed the event to be the finest ever seen in the neighborhood, which left Mrs. Bennet beaming with pleasure. Darcy made a better impression on everyone, due almost entirely to the besotted smile he wore for one of their own. He also learned about many of Lizzy's childhood adventures.

With the Darcys's wedding celebration behind them, Mrs. Bennet and all but her youngest daughter turned their attention to the final preparations for Jane's wedding to Mr. Charles Bingley. As expected, at learning the information of Wickham's treachery, Bingley forgot himself so far as to curse the gentleman's name, then found it necessary to apologize to Jane for his language.

Two nights before the wedding, a ball for the engaged couple took place at Netherfield. Many of Bingley's family came from Yorkshire, as did several friends from his university days and town. Lord and Lady Matlock arrived with Andrew and Anne.

While the Matlocks rested, the three couples sat in the library on the afternoon of the ball, catching up with one another, delighted to be together again. Anne shared with the others the progress on the updates at Rosings and her mother's behavior.

"Daily, letters arrive from the dower house filled with complaints," said Anne.

"We found it necessary to discontinue visiting because Lady Catherine berates Anne at every turn. I did not wish her to suffer such behavior, so I ensured my aunt understood that her lies are what caused her expulsion from the house. Had she willingly stepped down, Anne and I would have allowed her to live with us. The choices she made put her into her current position."

"I am sorry she is causing so much trouble for you both. If the situation becomes unbearable, you are welcome to visit us at Pemberley," said Darcy with a laugh.

"Indeed, we would love for you to join us," seconded Elizabeth.

"I am sure we would enjoy it, but I am afraid of what Mother might do in our absence."

Changing the subject, Andrew grinned at his cousin but spoke to his host. "Bingley, I must ask you, is Miss Bingley well? She seems much changed since her time in town."

"Believe it or not, after her scene at Darcy House the night of the family dinner, Louisa and Hurst managed to point out to her the many ways she was at fault in what occurred. The honest expression of their disgust at her behavior started the change. However, I believe Hurst's repetition of several comments Darcy made about Caroline's behavior finally brought her to accept her situation. She left for the north the next day. According to my aunt, Caroline sequestered herself away in her room for nigh on a week. When my sister arrived with my aunt for the wedding, it was with much-subdued behavior. She speaks of finding a husband next season if the gossip of her is no longer a topic of discussion."

"I hope she will be successful," said Elizabeth, "for her sake and yours and Jane's." Changing the subject, she continued, "William and I spoke to Charles and Jane about our plans for October, and they look forward to joining us."

"Indeed, we do," answered Bingley. The party soon separated to prepare for the ball, while Charles walked Jane to the door. His carriage would return her to Longbourn to make her preparations.

The engagement ball was a joyous occasion. The Bennet family arrived first so Jane and her parents could participate in the receiving line. Mary made her way to Elizabeth upon entering the ballroom and quickly reported to Elizabeth the fuss Lydia had made at being excluded. "Father even threatened to turn her over his knee if she did not stop her complaining. I feel certain such an action cannot be far away. Lydia still refuses to believe Mr. Wickham did anything wrong and will not apologize for speaking so of you and Mr. Darcy."

"I am glad we are departing soon. I do not know how much more of Lydia's ridiculous behavior I can tolerate without losing all patience with her."

Elizabeth and William stood with her sisters and Georgiana as they waited for the dancing to begin. As expected, Mary, Kitty, and Georgiana delighted in their new acquaintance. The three were often found with their heads together in quiet conversation, frequently punctuated with girlish laughter. Darcy enjoyed seeing Georgiana become more outgoing, and to see Elizabeth's sisters working hard to emulate Georgiana's refined manners. Anne and Andrew soon joined them, as did the Matlocks.

The musicians began tuning their instruments as Jane and Bingley joined the small family group at the side of the ballroom. Upon arriving, Bingley said, "Jane and I would like you and Lizzy, and Anne and Andrew, to take the places just below us in the set. Everyone knows you are newly married, so we can make this a celebration of all of us."

The three young couples lined up as planned, with Lord and Lady Matlock, the highest-ranking members of the peerage, next in line. Following them, other members of both the bride's and groom's families took their places. After Elizabeth convinced Darcy to allow Georgiana to observe the dancing and stay for supper, Kitty also agreed to retire at the meal's conclusion.

The change in Mr. Darcy's behavior continued to be a topic of conversation among many residents. Tonight they discovered further changes in the aloof gentleman's behavior. Though still somewhat reserved, he spoke kindly with everyone who approached. He also danced a great deal with his new sisters, Bingley's sisters, and a few of the young ladies of the neighborhood. However, he still spent the majority of his time with his new wife. Many of the ladies present-- young and old--wished to discover what it would be like to enjoy the kind of relationship they observed between the newlywed Darcys.

The day before the wedding, the Bennet family received some news that let the whole house, and those at Netherfield who were aware of the situation, breathe easier. Lydia's courses began that morning. Marching to her father's study, she knocked and entered at his call. "There is proof this morning that I did nothing wrong. I wish to attend Jane's wedding."

"You say there is proof you will not suffer the consequences of your actions?"

"Yes, Papa."

"Can one of your sisters confirm this?"

"Mrs. Hill can, as she brought me the cloths I would need." Lydia's face was bright red to be discussing such a thing with her father.

"What a relief, but it is not proof you did nothing wrong. Giving yourself to a man who is not your lawfully wedded husband is one of the worst things a young woman can do. As we waited to learn of your condition, did you consider what your life would be like if you conceived a child? You are little more than a child yourself."

"I am not a child. I am out in society, which makes me a proper young woman."

"You *were* out in society. As I said, your behavior proved you are too young to be out, so

291

you will stay in the schoolroom until you are at least eight and ten--longer if you do not learn how to behave in society by then!"

"That is not fair, Papa!"

"Did you consider fairness when you put the reputation and social acceptance of our family and your unmarried sisters in jeopardy for a few moments of sinful behavior? Now, since you left your room without permission *again*, you will sit down as I explain your punishment."

"Punishment," she began to whine. However, at the look of anger on her father's face, she quieted.

"You are a spoiled, selfish, uneducated child, and that will change. You will return to the schoolroom, where a governess will oversee your education and where you will take your meals until I am satisfied that your behavior has improved enough to dine with the family. As you are not out, you will also need no allowance. Again, it shall be returned to you only when your behavior proves that such a privilege is warranted."

"Additionally, as you are so enamored of marrying a man in a red coat, I believe you should prepare yourself for such a life. You will begin assisting the maid with the dusting, cleaning, and laundry. You will also learn to cook and do dishes, as your husband's pay will not cover the employment of servants. You will not have the assistance of a lady's maid and will be responsible for getting your bath water, dressing, and doing your hair--everything the lady's maid used to do. You will learn how to make your clothes and do the mending. Eventually, when I can trust your behavior enough, you will accompany your sisters when they visit the tenants and will supervise the children while they speak with the mistress of the house. Talking loudly or on inappropriate topics, as well as flirting, pouting, and whining, will not be tolerated. You are the one who is the least considerate of others in this house--family and servants alike--even though they make your life comfortable. Perhaps you will learn to appreciate all you have and all others do for you when you find out how hard the work is. You will be doing much more reading, and fashion magazines do not count."

Throughout her father's recitation, Lydia's eyes continued to widen. Shocked that she would be treated like a servant in her own home, she opened her mouth to complain but closed it again quickly when she recalled the words he had just uttered.

22. First Look at Pemberley

A beautiful sunrise greeted the Darcys on the morning of the wedding of Jane Bennet and Charles Bingley. Rising at their usual early hour, they took a brief walk in the gardens, enjoying some quiet time together before the bustle of the day. Upon returning to their room, they cuddled until the noises of the waking house reached their ears. As they would attend the bride and groom, both of them had a busy morning. Lizzy dressed in a simple day gown and gathered the items she would need for the wedding. The Darcy carriage delivered her to Longbourn, where she would help Jane prepare for her special day.

After breaking their fast in Bingley's chambers, the gentlemen set about dressing before heading to the church. While they waited in the clergyman's office to take their places, Darcy chuckled as he watched his usually happy friend display a decided case of pre-wedding nerves.

"You are uncommonly nervous, Charles. You fell for Miss Bennet the moment you laid eyes on her, and despite the difficulties along the way, you achieved your heart's desire when she accepted your hand. What is causing your nervousness?"

Bingley continued to pace in the small space. "I am not nervous. I just want the ceremony to be over. Then I will know nothing will ever come between us again."

"You are worrying about nothing. How could things be any better?"

The Darcy carriage dropped Lizzy at Longbourn and would remain to take the bride, her father, and Mrs. Darcy to the church. Elizabeth arrived earlier than needed, as the two sisters desired some time alone before Jane, too, became a married woman. Mrs. Hill admitted Elizabeth and sent her up to Jane's room while going to fetch a breakfast tray for them.

She knocked on Jane's door, slipping inside at her quiet call. Jane sat against the headboard, undoing her braid.

"Good morning. How is the bride?"

"A little nervous, but mostly excited."

"That is just what I expected." Lizzy slipped off her shoes and copied Jane's position on the bed. Mary had spent the night in Kitty's room to allow Jane to rest more comfortably.

They laughed about the horrifying explanation Mrs. Bennet had given the previous evening about what occurs in the marriage bed. Jane felt relief to have heard this from Mrs. Gardiner upon Elizabeth's marriage. Elizabeth, however, struggled not to laugh at the ridiculous things her mother said.

"Please tell me you did not experience nightmares about mother's speech," said Elizabeth with a giggle.

"Fortunately not, but I would not be averse to hearing some reassuring words from you."

Elizabeth leaned close and began to whisper with her sister. Fifteen minutes later, Mrs. Hill arrived with a breakfast tray for the two of them. They heard the servants carrying water to the bathing room at the end of the hall.

Jane and Elizabeth shared memories over their meal. When Jane left to bathe, Elizabeth began laying out her things for the wedding. She placed a small box tied with a blue ribbon on the dressing table for her sister. When Jane returned, she picked up the box and moved to the window seat, where Elizabeth waited. The bright sun and warm breeze coming through the window would help her hair to dry faster than usual. "What is this, Lizzy?"

"Just a small gift for my favorite sister and the bride-to-be."

Jane removed the ribbon and opened the box to reveal two beautiful hair combs. There were sapphires and small diamonds in the floral pattern of the filigreed silverwork. "Lizzy, they are beautiful, but this is much too expensive a gift!"

"Actually, they barely made a dent in my monthly pin money. I wanted something beautiful to be decorating your hair during the wedding breakfast, as you will not wear your bonnet in the house. As much as I appreciate the changes in Miss Bingley, I cannot allow her to outshine the bride. I thought you needed some jewelry of your own for the day."

"They match perfectly with the set of sapphires Charles bought for me."

Elizabeth smiled but did not tell Jane she had helped Bingley with the choice, which had inspired her purchase.

The peace of their morning did not last much longer, as Mrs. Bennet burst into the room. She began to fuss over Jane and the need to prepare so they would not be late to the church. While the maid started styling Jane's hair, Elizabeth slipped into her gown for the wedding. Then, when Mary and Kitty finished dressing, they joined their sisters and watched as Jane's new lady's maid put the finishing touches on her hair. Her next three younger sisters helped Jane carefully slip her wedding gown over her head so as not to disturb her *coiffure*.

When Mr. Bennet knocked on the door, the three younger girls headed downstairs to join the rest of the family. Elizabeth calmed Mrs. Bennet and urged her and the girls to depart in the carriage, assuring them that Jane and their father would be down momentarily. The Gardiners assisted in getting everyone out of the house, and soon the two vehicles were moving away from the manor. Darcy's coachman pulled up to the main entrance of the house, and a footman stepped down and placed the steps before the door.

When everyone had departed, Elizabeth went to the stillroom to retrieve the bouquets she and Jane would carry. When she returned to the hall, Mr. Bennet and Jane descended the stairs. She followed them out of the house. The footman assisted Jane into the carriage. Elizabeth passed Jane her flowers, then took the footman's offered hand and sat beside the bride. Mr. Bennet seated himself across from his two eldest daughters. As the carriage pulled forward, he stared at Jane and Elizabeth, his eyes shining with tears. "I could not be prouder than I am of the two of you. You were always the best of my daughters. I am delighted both of you found men worthy of you and I do not doubt you will be extremely happy in your marriages. Jane, if I might offer you a piece of advice? You may soon find you wish for a bit more distance between Longbourn and your home. You are not to feel guilty if that occurs. You and your husband deserve some peace and happiness. I am not sure you will get much privacy with your mother's constant presence in your home. I suggest you consider not renewing the lease on Netherfield when it expires."

"Oh, Papa, you had better not let Mama hear you say such a thing. However, Charles and I have already discussed the possibility based on all the many comments and hints from Mama, who offered to help me redecorate and plan my first entertainment." All three of them burst into laughter.

The Darcy carriage stopped in front of the church and the footman assisted the ladies down. They stepped into the narthex, where Elizabeth straightened Jane's gown and brushed a wrinkle or two from the sky blue silk, which matched her eyes. Belgian lace trimmed the neckline and sleeves and provided a double flounce at the bottom of the gown. White silk roses matched her bouquet and the same lace as her gown adorned her wedding bonnet.

Elizabeth followed her father and sister down the aisle and smiled when Bingley caught his first glimpse of Jane. His eyes widened and his jaw dropped. She saw William put a hand on his arm as Bingley looked like he would move forward to greet Jane. Then Elizabeth caught her husband's eye, and they shared a tender glance.

The service passed much like any other. Darcy and Elizabeth maintained eye contact and, if one looked closely, also appeared to repeat the vows. After signing the registry, the bride and groom started down the aisle. Darcy held his wife back, allowing all the guests to exit the church. Then, tucking her hand in his arm, he covered it with his other hand and moved to stand where Jane and Charles had so recently stood.

"I hope you do not regret that we did not marry from your home church with your sister."

"I am happy to be here with them, but I would not change anything about our wedding. The location did not matter near so much as the gentleman standing next to me. I would not trade the last month together for anything."

Darcy leaned down and brushed his lips against Elizabeth's. "Shall we go?"

"I believe we must if we do not wish to incur Mama's wrath for being late."

They moved down the aisle and out the door. Georgiana was waiting in the Darcy carriage. Darcy handed up his wife and then himself. When they arrived at Longbourn, the carriage deposited them at the front door and returned to Netherfield to load the family's luggage for the trip to Pemberley.

The wedding breakfast proceeded smoothly, again, garnering praise for Mrs. Bennet. When the time for the bride and groom to depart arrived, heartfelt farewells took place. Bingley and Jane would spend a week at Boston Spa in West Yorkshire before going on to Scarborough to meet the remainder of his family. They planned to stop at Pemberley for a few days before returning to Netherfield Park.

The departure of Jane and Charles was significant for Elizabeth, as well. It marked the beginning of her journey to her new home. From the stories told to her by both William and Georgiana, Pemberley achieved perfection status. Containing her excitement to see the estate and grounds was difficult. Georgiana would travel north with the Matlocks and stay with them for a month before joining her brother and sister.

The three-day journey to Pemberley was a new adventure for Elizabeth. She enjoyed the constantly changing scenery that passed her window as they traveled north. They had the best suites in the best inns along the way. The further north they went, the more respect William received from the innkeepers. It pointed out to her the importance of the Darcy name.

Elizabeth's excitement mounted as they began their last day of travel. The landscape started to change, dramatically increasing her enjoyment of the journey. At mid-afternoon on the third day of their travels, the Darcy carriage stopped at the top of a steep rise. Looking out her window, Elizabeth did not see any sign of a manor house. When she turned back, Darcy was standing outside the carriage, his hand extended in her direction. She took the offered hand and stepped down, Angus at her heels. Darcy wrapped her arm around his and led her up a small incline. Climbing the slight rise, Elizabeth saw her new home for the first time. There in the valley below her, beyond a clear lake mirroring its glory, stood

Pemberley. Built of white limestone quarried from the nearby white peak area, the manor appeared to glow in the sunlight, and the numerous large windows shone with reflected light.

"This is our home?" Elizabeth's voice held a note of worshipful awe.

"Yes." Darcy studied her face as he continued, "What do you think of Pemberley?"

"I have never seen a more magnificent sight. The building glows as if made of polished marble and is set off beautifully by the dark rise of the deep green trees at the rear. The manicured lawn and the lake are beautiful, but there is an untamed natural beauty at the same time. Not even paradise could be more beautiful than this spot of Derbyshire."

Darcy's face beamed with pleasure at her description of his family home--their home. "Shall we continue and see the inside of our home?"

"I would love to!"

And so Darcy and Elizabeth rode toward their future and a life filled with family, friends, and enduring love.

THE END

For the first time when writing a book, I did not feel like the story needed an epilogue. However, most of you replied to my survey that you liked epilogues. Therefore, I will leave it up to you, the reader, as to whether you wish to know more. If so, turn the page for the epilogue.

EPILOGUE

Within two months of arriving at Pemberley, Elizabeth gave her husband the news that they would soon be parents. Six months later, she gave birth to the first of four children: a son named Bennet William Andrew Darcy. Following Bennet were Stephen Charles, Margaret Anne, and Juliana Jane. The four Darcy siblings, with their parents as an example, all married for love. They gave their parents twenty-three grandchildren and several great-grandchildren before the deaths of William and Elizabeth.

The family did gather for Christmas that first year of the Darcys's marriage. Mary, Kitty, and even Mrs. Bennet had significantly improved. It was during this visit that Mary came to the attention of the vicar of Kympton, Evan Prescott. The fourth son of an earl, Evan had held the position for three years. Upon meeting Mary Bennet, he fell in love. Mary remained at Pemberley after the holiday, and the couple married six months later. They became the parents of four girls. During this first visit, Lydia, who had rebelled against all the governess tried to teach her, found herself relegated to the nursery with the Gardiner children.

Mr. Bennet's advice to Jane on her wedding day turned out to be correct. When their lease expired in November, five months after the wedding, the couple journeyed to Pemberley ahead of the family to begin looking for an estate within a day's drive of William and Elizabeth. They found precisely what they desired in Bellwood, about fifteen miles south of Pemberley. The Bingleys moved into their new home in March of 1812. Jane gave birth to their first child, a girl, four months after settling at Bellwood. She and Bingley went on to have six more children: two boys and four girls.

Because of the confidence she gained as Elizabeth Darcy's younger sister, Georgiana Darcy and Kitty Bennet came out in 1813. The beautiful, witty, confident young women took the ton by storm. Kitty married Giles Hayward, Viscount Beaumont. Georgiana made an even better match, marrying Christopher Burton-Smythe, the eldest son of the Duke of Ashburton.

Mrs. Bennet, who sat in on all the lessons with Mary, Kitty, and their companion, steadily improved. She learned to control her loud speaking and flighty behavior. With these improvements, Mr. Bennet became more patient, explaining things to his wife rather than laughing at her. He also took a greater interest in his estate but made sure to tie up the funds in such a way that, at his death, they would go to his wife, children, and grandchildren, rather than to Mr. Collins. With Mrs. Bennet's improved behavior and the enhanced relationship between her and Mr. Bennet, the couple desired to travel more. Darcy helped Mr. Bennet hire an excellent steward who continued to increase the estate's income.

Consequently, Mr. and Mrs. Bennet spent three months in Derbyshire annually--one each with Jane, Elizabeth, and Mary. Kitty's home in Oxfordshire was the closest to Longbourn. Occasionally, they ventured to London, where they stayed with the Gardiners, for the shopping and culture.

Unfortunately, despite the excellent behaviors all around her, Lydia stubbornly clung to her bad behavior rather than consider the fact that she might be wrong. She remained in the schoolroom at Longbourn until her twenty-first birthday. Mr. Darcy helped her father arrange a marriage to a man in the regulars. Lydia joined him in a posting to Upper Canada and never contacted her family again.

Andrew and Anne Fitzwilliam did, indeed, make a success of Rosings, increasing its annual income to eight thousand pounds per annum. They also had three children: a boy, Lewis Duncan deBourgh Fitzwilliam, and two daughters, Juliana and Cecilia.

Under the tutelage of his wife, Mr. Collins slowly improved. He gained in common sense, learned to speak plainly and succinctly, and lost that subservient sycophancy that everyone deplored.

Caroline Bingley continued to improve. Gossip kept her from London until the Little Season in the winter of 1812. While residing with her aunt, she met a landowner, Graham Coleville, whose income was on par with her brother's. Graham also decided to spend the Little Season in London, where he squired Caroline to many events. He proposed on New Year's Day, and they married in early February. Caroline loved her husband, and together they had four children, all of whom were kind, polite, and down to earth. As Graham's estate was also in the north of England, they were frequently in company with both the Bingleys and the Darcys, with whom they developed a respectful friendship.

Shortly after Caroline left their home, the Hursts discovered they would soon be parents. With a significant source of stress removed from his home, Oliver Hurst stopped drinking. He was ecstatic to become a father to his first son, which also helped him return to a more youthful figure. They went on to have two more children: a boy and a girl.

On the whole, the families were happy and content with their lot in life. The friendships grew, and they supported one another during the difficult times that life brought their way.

ENDNOTES

(1) Ightham Mote -
https://www.nationaltrust.org.uk/ightham-mote

(2) The Holy Bible, Matthew 7:3-5, King James
Version (KJV)

(3) Lullingstone Roman Villa -
https://www.english-
heritage.org.uk/visit/places/lullingstone-roman-
villa/

(4) Church of England Marriage Ceremony from
the 1662 version of the Book of Common Prayer -
http://justus.anglican.org/resources/bcp/1662/m
arriage.pdf

(5) Church of England Marriage Ceremony from
the 1662 version of the Book of Common Prayer -
http://justus.anglican.org/resources/bcp/1662/m
arriage.pdf

ABOUT THE AUTHOR

Linda C. Thompson has had a life-long love affair with Pride and Prejudice in particular, and the Regency Era in general. She cannot get enough of the love story between Fitzwilliam Darcy and Elizabeth Bennet. This love affair has led her to author nine books, which reimagine the love story between Darcy and Elizabeth.

Linda's husband of 32 years is the Elizabeth in their relationship. Linda is the shy, formal one and uses her writing as an outlet for her romantic nature.

Hearing from fans is one of her biggest joys. You can keep in touch with the author in the following ways:

Email: lindathompson.author@gmail.com
Facebook: Linda Thompson Books page
Instagram: Lindasusancooperthompson
Twitter: @LindyT07
Website: lindacthompsonbooks.com

OTHER BOOKS BY LINDA C. THOMPSON

HER UNFORGETTABLE LAUGH
Her Unforgettable Laugh Series, Book 1
A Pride and Prejudice Variation

Dark curls and an unforgettably sweet laugh are all he knows of his sister's rescuer. Later, a second glimpse shows her to be lovely, and he hears her melodious laugh again. Darcy wonders what it would be like to meet this remarkable—and remarkably lovely—young woman. Would the spirit that compelled her to assist a stranger bring some joy into his lonely life? Would they ever meet? Or will he always be left wondering?

Little does Fitzwilliam Darcy know that his trip to Hertfordshire will bring him face to face with the lovely young woman whose unforgettable laugh has haunted his dreams for the last several years. Will she be anything like the woman he has built up in his dreams? Will he be able to avoid Miss Bingley long enough to discover more about this mysterious young woman?

Laughter Through Trials
Her Unforgettable Laugh Series, Book 2
A Pride and Prejudice Variation

Dark curls and an unforgettably sweet laugh . . .

In Book 1 of the Her Unforgettable Laugh series, a trip to Hertfordshire brought Fitzwilliam Darcy face to face with the woman who had haunted his dreams for five years. Their chance meeting led to a courtship, despite the efforts of those who wished to separate them. Now Elizabeth Bennet is traveling to London, where she will be introduced to Darcy's family and the ton. How will Elizabeth be received? Will their love flourish and grow? Or will new trials overwhelm them?

THE LAUGHTER OF LOVE
Her Unforgettable Laugh Series, Book 3
A Pride and Prejudice Variation

Dark curls and an unforgettably sweet laugh . . .

In Book 2 of the Her Unforgettable Laugh series, Darcy and Elizabeth celebrated their courtship as Elizabeth was introduced to the Fitzwilliam family and London society. Their sojourn in town presented a few difficulties. However, the strength of their love allowed them to face their challenges and outwit their enemies.

Now Darcy and Elizabeth are returning to Hertfordshire for their wedding. Elizabeth worries about the one trial they have yet to face: Mrs. Bennet. Her mother refuses to prepare the simple, elegant affair the couple wishes for their wedding day. Will it be the day of their dreams ... or a disaster?

Ultimately, the wedding turns out and Darcy and Elizabeth are excited to begin their life together. The bright future before them fills their hearts with joy. Both know that they will face periods of contentment and heartache; however, united, they will confront whatever comes their way. Will those whom they have previously encountered allow them to enjoy their happiness? Or must they overcome more misfortune?

THE COMPANION'S SECRET
A Pride and Prejudice Variation

"You must marry her," the stern voice said. "I need to gain control of her inheritance before she reaches her next birthday. It need not be a long marriage, but marry her you must."

Alone in the world, Elizabeth Bennet has had to rely upon herself. She knows that escape is the only way to ensure her safety. With the help of Longbourn's faithful servants, Elizabeth disappears from her home and the odious heir. She is determined to find a way to support herself and remain hidden until after her birthday.

Fortune smiles on Elizabeth when a series of events offers her the role of companion to Georgiana Darcy. Despite her position, Elizabeth finds herself attracted to her new employer. Can he ever see her as more than his sister's companion? Sometimes, Elizabeth thinks that Mr. Darcy cares for her, too. Yet will his attraction—if that is, indeed, what he feels—survive when he learns the truth about her?

Hidden away at Pemberley, will Elizabeth be able to safely conceal herself until she comes of age? What surprises does the future hold in store for her?

A MATTER OF TIMING
A Pride and Prejudice Variation

They say that timing is everything . . .

Their chance meeting at Pemberley helps Elizabeth Bennet realize her true feelings for Mr. Darcy. That same meeting gives him the opportunity to show Elizabeth that he has taken her criticism to heart and made improvements to his behavior. Will this new start finally lead to their happily ever after?

How might the relationship between Elizabeth and Darcy have been different if they had become betrothed before Elizabeth learned of Lydia's elopement? Would they have traveled to London together? Would Elizabeth have helped with her sister's recovery? Would Lydia and Wickham still have married? Or would Elizabeth have found another way to save her youngest sister?

A Matter of Timing answers all these questions and more.

AN ACCIDENT AT PEMBERLEY
A Pride and Prejudice Variation

In the time before Mr. Bingley takes up residence at Netherfield Park, Elizabeth travels into Derbyshire with her Aunt and Uncle Gardiner. One day, as her friends and relations visit with some of Mrs. Gardiner's childhood friends, Elizabeth explores the small village. Without realizing it, she strays farther and farther from the village, unconsciously walking in the direction of Pemberley, the estate that the group had visited two days prior.

Lost in her thoughts and the beauty of the Derbyshire countryside, Elizabeth fails to notice the storm clouds building above her. At the first flash of lightning and peal of thunder, she seeks shelter from the storm, Rushing for a dense tree line where she might avoid the impending rain, Elizabeth Bennet meets with a dreadful accident.

Returning from business in London, Fitzwilliam Darcy races across the grounds of Pemberley, trying to outrun the storm. After coming across a beautiful young woman who has been injured, he takes her home so that his staff can care for her. Darcy hopes her presence will help lift his mother's melancholy.

When Elizabeth regains consciousness, she has no memory of her name or her past. During the many weeks of her recovery, Elizabeth grows close to Mr. Darcy and his mother, Lady Anne. When Elizabeth recovers enough to leave the estate, the Darcys decide that she needs an identity that will protect her from gossip. And so, Miss Elizabeth Chamberlayne, a long-lost Darcy cousin, is born. After receiving two requests, Darcy accepts an invitation to stay with his friend, Mr. Bingley, at Netherfield Park. The ladies will join him.

What will happen when Elizabeth comes face to face with her family? Will she remember them? Or will her memory still be a blank? All the original characters in Jane Austen's *Pride and Prejudice* make an appearance. How will Elizabeth's lack of memory affect her interactions with them?

A TURN IN THEIR DANCE
A Pride and Prejudice Variation

After overhearing Mr. Darcy's cutting remark at the Meryton assembly, Miss Elizabeth Bennet replies with a comment of her own about the sign of a true gentleman. When Darcy hears the statement, he is instantly stricken with remorse. He seeks a quiet place to compose himself and prepare an apology. As Miss Elizabeth moves through the crowd to share the incident with her friend, Charlotte Lucas, she hears an anguished voice from the darkened balcony. Stepping forward to offer assistance, she is surprised at what else she hears.

This event and the turn it makes in the relationship between Darcy and Elizabeth is the premise of this delightful new story. How will an earlier understanding between our dear couple change their interactions with those around them—particularly Miss Bingley, Mr. Wickham, and Mr. Collins?

THE TROUBLESOME MR. COLLINS
A Pride and Prejudice Variation

On the morning of the Netherfield ball, Elizabeth Bennet is surprised when Mr. Darcy appears on Oakham Mount. In the course of their conversation, the two clear up the misunderstandings between them. When Darcy asks for the first dance, Elizabeth regretfully informs him that her cousin, Mr. Collins, has already requested that set. Darcy can tell how little Elizabeth desires to dance with the gentleman and offers to assist in extricating her.

Mr. Collins is quick to believe Mr. Darcy's words concerning Lady Catherine's opinion of the parson's choice of the outspoken Miss Elizabeth. However, upon discovering that Mr. Darcy is himself interested in Elizabeth, Mr. Collins steps in to stop the blossoming romance. When he faces Darcy's wrath for his behavior, the parson calls in reinforcements in the form of his esteemed patroness, Lady Catherine de Bourgh.

The mischief that ensues causes one disruption after another, but nothing can stand in the way of a love destined to be.